SUBMERGED

ALASKAN COURAGE
· BOOK ONE ·

SUBMERGED

DANI PETTREY

BETHANY HOUSE PUBLISHERS
a division of Baker Publishing Group
Minneapolis, Minnesota

© 2012 by Dani Pettrey

Published by Bethany House Publishers
11400 Hampshire Avenue South
Bloomington, Minnesota 55438
www.bethanyhouse.com

Bethany House Publishers is a division of
Baker Publishing Group, Grand Rapids, Michigan

Printed in the United States of America

Library of Congress Cataloging-in-Publication Data
Pettrey, Dani.
    Submerged / Dani Pettrey.
        p.   cm. — (Alaskan courage ; bk. 1)
    ISBN 978-0-7642-0982-6 (pbk.)
    1. Murder—Investigation—Fiction. 2. Alaska—Fiction. I. Title.
PS3616.E89S83 2012
813'.6—dc23   2012000967

Scripture quotations are from the Holy Bible, New International Version®. NIV®. Copyright © 1973, 1978, 1984, 2011 by Biblica, Inc.™ Used by permission of Zondervan. All rights reserved worldwide. www.zondervan.com

This is a work of fiction. Names, characters, incidents, and dialogues are products of the author's imagination and are not to be construed as real. Any resemblance to actual events or persons, living or dead, is entirely coincidental.

Cover design by Koechel Peterson & Associates, Inc., Minneapolis, Minnesota/Gregory Rohm

Author represented by MacGregor Literary, Inc.

12   13   14   15   16   17   18   7   6   5   4   3   2   1

To Michael

For asking me to dance.
It's turned out to be the dance of a lifetime.
I love you.

To Mom

For always believing.
I love you dearly.

Prologue

Never wager unless you control the stakes.
And she'd thought she held such a strong hand.

Agnes Grey forced her head against the rattling seat back, clenched the armrests with such force her nails broke. Perspiration soaked her brow, seeping into her eyes, but she refused to cry. She was too old to cry.

The plane was going down into the water within sight of her home. Home—warm, safe, dry. She'd never see it again.

Her friend Henry Reid strained to look back, his white knuckles bulging on the wheel as he fought to regain control of the spiraling Cessna, but the fiery plane seemed bent on destruction. Panic flashed through his eyes. "Tighten your belts. Put your head between your knees."

His concern was sweet, but it wouldn't change the outcome. Their fate was set.

They were going down—hard and fast. The other passengers' terrified expressions said they knew it too. *Innocents, every one,* Agnes thought, fury on their behalf trumping her own fear. She was the only one on board who knew this catastrophe was no mechanical failure. It was *him.* She knew it as surely as she knew she'd seen her last sunset.

A bitter cry tore from her cracked lips. Any semblance of control on her part had been an illusion.

She'd played her hand, and he'd just called her on it.

If she hadn't been so stinking stubborn, if she'd kept her mouth shut and given him what he wanted . . . But Momma hadn't raised her like that. She'd done the right thing. She only wished she hadn't brought the others down with her.

Managing to crane her neck left, she took in the sight of the loving couple's hands clasped tight, crying as they whispered frantic words to each other.

Agnes's stomach lurched. She'd brought them on this journey, doomed them to a watery tomb.

At least now he'd be satisfied. She'd be gone. They'd be gone. No one was left to . . .

Acid burned up her throat.

Bailey.

1

Off the coast of Tariuk Island, Alaska

Cole McKenna left the chaos at the water's surface for the chaos below. The black water quickly suffocated the floodlights directed down at him from the rescue boats above. Within seconds it was only him, the strobe attached at his waist, and the immense darkness of the sea.

His heart seemed to beat in time with the strobe's rhythmic flash.

Thump. Thump.

It was amazing the things one heard when surrounded by darkness.

Thump. Thump.

Cole checked his depth gauge with his left hand, keeping his right fixed on the lifeline. When diving in depths without any natural light and with no distinguishing landmarks, in an ever-changing current, a few seconds off the line was all it took to get disoriented, and those seconds could mean the difference between life and death.

Thirty feet.

Thirty-five.

"Diver two in the water," Gage instructed over the comm from topside.

He was glad he'd have Landon Grainger at his side tonight. He was going to need all the help he could get.

Sonar had indicated that what remained of Henry Reid's floatplane tottered on the edge of Outerman's Ridge, forty feet beneath the surface. He wished the flight manifest had arrived before deployment so they knew how many passengers had been on board. He hated going in blind.

Forty feet.

He slipped his external light from his utility belt and switched it on. The Cessna glimmered a murky white in its beam.

"I'm going off-line," he alerted topside.

"Be safe, Cole. Diver three is in the water."

Cole swallowed. "Roger that." He shouldn't worry any more about Kayden than Landon. As dive captain, he was responsible for every member on the rescue team. He couldn't allow the fact that Kayden was his sister to affect his decisions. It wouldn't be fair to the rest of the team or to the victims. But a brother's innate protective nature always lingered.

He inhaled, the pressure-demand regulator automatically releasing a puff of oxygenated air into his face mask. The device made him sound like Darth Vader, each breath deliberate and punctuated. His black neoprene dry suit, gloves, and hoses only added to the image.

The glow in the fuselage had disappeared, but the fact the fire had lasted as long as it had bolstered his hope that there was still air trapped in the craft. He prayed their search tonight would end in rescue and not just recovery.

Panning his beam along the vessel, he began his inspection at the tail—torn and jagged—and moved along to the cockpit. His breath hitched at the compressed metal. He prayed Henry had been tossed free before the plane nosedived onto the ridge. At least then there was a chance Ginny would have a body to bury.

"Going off-line," Landon announced a moment before he was at Cole's side.

"Best access is going to be that door," Cole said.

"I agree." Landon pulled the crowbar from the gear bag.

Kayden joined them, her beam of light bouncing off Cole's mask before settling on the fuselage.

"Landon, you're with me," he instructed. "Kayden, watch the currents and how this wreckage is moving. Be ready to help lift to the surface."

"You got it, boss."

Cole wedged the crowbar inside the door's seam and, bracing against the sidewall, heaved back. Heat rippled through his fingers and up his arms with the exertion. Three minutes later, the door hung open on its hinges.

A tangle of wires littered the opening. Cole set to work clearing a pathway.

He checked his dive watch. Five minutes closer to the Golden Hour—the limit for cold-water drowning victims to be revived. Any longer and all hope was lost.

Not tonight. Not on his watch.

He gave Landon the go signal and entered the craft behind him, wedging his body through the opening and to the right.

Landon's auxiliary light reflected through the water ahead. "I've got two. Man and woman. Strapped into their seats, right side."

Cole didn't recognize the couple. In a town Yancey's size, everyone was a neighbor, so he knew most residents of his town by sight. Flying debris had left the woman with a gash on her face, and the man had taken a hard blow to the temple.

He turned the torch on his dive watch. Thirty-five minutes since the crash, another fifteen to get them to the surface, another ten to get them to the hospital . . .

"We take her out first." Cole unclipped the seat harness and cleared the woman from her seat. "Kayden, I need you at the door ready for a lift to the surface."

"Ready, boss."

Cole lifted the woman's legs as Landon lifted her shoulders. He carefully walked backward, measuring the distance to the opening by the steps he took.

"Hold here." He lowered her legs and cautiously wedged himself out of the craft. He leaned back in. "Slowly now." He eased the woman through the doorway. "She's out."

Cole held her upright as Kayden secured her for transport to the surface. Giving pressurized air to an unconscious drowning victim caused more harm than good. A fast lift to the surface and waiting emergency personnel was the best option.

He watched Kayden and the woman disappear into the darkness above, then headed back into the wreckage to rejoin Landon.

"He's almost ready to go," Landon said, kneeling beside the unconscious man. "You want me to lift with him?"

"Yes. As soon as Kayden is back down, you head up with him."

Something bumped into Cole's back, and he panned his torch around. A flash of movement caught his eye. He moved toward the rear of the fuselage and got kicked.

Someone was desperately trying to hug a pocket of air in the raised tail of the craft. "I've got another one—conscious," he alerted Landon.

He stepped on a plane seat, getting as high as he could. A pocket of air, no more than five inches deep, hugged the angled roof of the cabin.

An icy hand hit his face. This time he grabbed and caught it. He lifted his torch and found a pair of terrified eyes staring back at him. "I've got Agnes Grey!" She was standing on the headrest of the last seat, hugging an air pocket barely a hand's width deep. He yanked his pony bottle from his vest, pulled the release to let the air flow, and wrapped her cold hand around it, guiding it to her mouth. He shoved his mask back and tilted his head to move into the air pocket so she could hear him. "Breathe slowly, and stay as still as you can. I'm going to get you out of here."

She nodded in rapid fire as she gulped a deep breath in. Water was lapping against her face, and he wasn't sure how long she could stay upright in the cold water. Her lips were blue, her

12

skin pallid. She'd moved beyond the last of the seats trying to find the air. Getting her to willingly go underwater to get out of the wreckage was going to be a challenge.

"You, two other passengers, and Henry the pilot? That's who I'm looking for? Four people?"

She reluctantly released the air to reply. "Five. Another passenger went forward to try to help Henry." She swallowed hard. "I saw his body floating outside after we crashed."

"Stay right here. I'll be right back. I promise you."

He waited until she nodded, pushed his mask back over his face, and used the seat's headrest to propel himself back toward Landon. "Let's get him outside. Agnes is alert enough—I'm going to try to buddy breathe her out."

Landon nodded. They lifted the man clear of the seats and into the aisle. The plane shifted, toppling Cole forward and causing Landon to lose his balance. The pitch of the fuselage rolled another five degrees. "Move!"

Landon shimmied backward, guiding the man's legs, while Cole supported his shoulders. A torch lit outside of the plane, its beam sliding across the windows. "Kayden's back."

"How's it look?"

Landon disappeared through the door. "Tight, but it's enough." Cole eased the man down as Landon guided him out of the plane. "We're clear."

Cole didn't wait for word they had the man ready to lift; he turned and headed back into the plane for Agnes.

There was no way to safely put her in front, so he'd have to pull her through the wreckage. And he wouldn't be able to communicate with her once they moved out of the air pocket. He hoped she didn't so badly panic he had to knock her out just to get her to safety.

She was submerged now, fully underwater, her eyes closed, clutching the air canister to her chest.

He turned his torchlight on her face.

Her eyes opened, panicked.

He grasped her wrist and nodded as she in turn grasped his. He motioned they were heading down.

The plane shifted again.

He didn't give her time to react to the threat; he pushed them back through the water as quickly as he could, using the seats to judge the distance. She stayed with him, keeping a death grip on his wrist.

An ominous groan reverberated through the fuselage. Water vibrated around them. Cole's gauges swayed with the seat backs.

"Cole." Kayden didn't have to say any more. Her tone said it all.

The ridge wasn't going to hold the plane much longer.

Tugging Agnes, he bolted for the doorway.

Ten feet.

Nine.

Eight.

"Cole, get out of there!"

His heart squeezed at the terror in his sister's voice.

The tail section lurched forward, metal scraping coral with an eerie rasping as the water-filled fuselage teetered on the brink of darkness. This time it didn't stop.

Agnes let go of his wrist and yanked from his hold. Frantically she spun around, her eyes wild in his torchlight.

He reached for her, but she kicked off a seat, trying to propel herself to the opening. With no light and the plane shifting around them, she propelled straight into the AED storage cabinet.

Her body went limp, the air canister floating away.

Cole lunged for her, managing to seize her arm.

With a roar, the right side of the plane broke off, the outside current swirling in.

Struggling against the water's force, he wedged his leg between the seats and used the leverage to pull Agnes back to him.

"I'm coming in."

"Don't you dare, Kayden. Hold position. That's an order!"

He swam down toward the doorway, scraping his air canister on the frame. Keeping Agnes protected as best he could, he scrambled to grab a handhold on the frame.

Another hand met his. *Kayden.*

He wrapped Kayden's hand around Agnes's wrist. "She's unconscious."

"I've got her!"

Cole let his sister pull Agnes through the door, and then slid out of the fuselage behind her.

Kayden got Agnes secure for lift.

"Head up," he instructed.

"You're right behind us." It wasn't a question.

He gave the thumbs-up signal. The search for Henry and the missing passenger would have to wait until after the wreckage settled. He began his ascent, and as the plane faded from view, he saw it slide off the ridge into the darkness. A sick feeling rolled through his stomach. That had been too close for comfort.

Concentric circles spread out in ever-increasing rings above, pinpointing the helicopter's location. At least there was plenty of help above.

He breached the surface to the whirring of rotary blades.

Three paramedics crowded the rescue boat's platform, reaching to help lift Agnes carefully aboard. Cole waited until Agnes and Kayden were clear, then grabbed the ladder.

Ralph Barnes, Yancey's fire chief, leaned over to give him a hand with the heavy tanks.

"Thanks." Cole took a seat on the gunwale and started stripping off the weight of his gear as rain fell around him.

Gage hollered over to him, "The support boat is headed back with the other victims. Landon too. You going to call this?"

Cole nodded. "Get us to shore."

Gage waved off the helicopter and headed to the pilothouse. They would reach shore in less time than it would take to transfer Agnes by air.

Cole watched as the rescue personnel started CPR on Agnes.

With all she'd been through, he wasn't surprised to find her heart had stopped.

"One one-thousand. Two one-thousand. Come on, Agnes."

Kayden sat down beside him. She watched the rescue personnel work. "She's icy cold. That's good. She's got more time," she murmured, more to herself than to him.

Cole squeezed her shoulder. Kayden didn't handle losing people very well—neither of them did. "I hope so." He couldn't do anything for Agnes but hope she could fight for her life one more time. Red lights swirled like beacons from the emergency vehicles on shore, growing closer as the boat neared landfall.

"You should have held position," Cole said quietly.

"And let you go down with the plane? I don't think so."

"Not your call."

"You would have done the same, and we both know it," Kayden replied.

"Probably, but I would rather not find out."

The boat pulled into the dock, and Landon was waiting for them, securing the boat lines as the engine was cut. Cole moved to help the EMTs lift their patient onto a transport board, and then onto land. Through the pouring rain, he watched as they shocked Agnes's heart in the ambulance and moments later started CPR again. They slammed the ambulance doors. The sirens wailed their departure.

Cole wiped at the water snaking in rivulets down his face. He was freezing.

Cole hauled gear over to the town's fire station, where the rescue crew had storage space.

The entire crew was family, with the exception of Landon Grainger—who was as close as family. Cole trusted them all, underwater and above it, to accomplish what rescues could be done, and to cope when there was nothing they could do.

They cleaned and readied the gear for the next call.

Kayden worked beside Cole in silence.

Typical Kayden.

When things hurt she closed ranks, shut everyone else out, but Cole would relentlessly fight his way back in.

Landon shouldered his duffel bag. "I'm heading over to the station to start the report. NTSB will be here in another couple hours."

Cole nodded, not looking forward to the imminent salvage. They would refloat the plane if they could find it again, collect strewn parts, and photograph what they could. The work itself wasn't the hard part—it was knowing lives had been lost that stung. The missing passenger was somewhere on that ridge, and the search for Henry Reid's body would weigh on the entire team, but it had to be done. Ginny Reid deserved no less.

The last to leave, Cole exited the fire station and looked up at the sky. It'd gone from dark to pitch-black. At least the rain had simmered to a slow drizzle, though he doubted the reprieve would last long.

Wind whistled through the empty downtown streets in an eerie cadence. Hunching his shoulders against it, Cole hefted his duffel into his truck. He'd make a quick stop by the hospital to check on Agnes and the two still-unidentified passengers—then swing by the house to talk with Kayden.

Tariuk Island Regional Medical Center sat at the top of the hill overlooking Main Street. Cole left his truck parked in front of the fire station and walked the distance. He passed the sheriff's station on the way and ducked his head in, catching Landon as he was finishing up his report.

Landon lifted his chin in greeting. "I just got off the phone with Ginny Reid."

"How's she doing?"

"Lousy. Sheriff's with her now. I think I'll ride over and see if there's anything I can do."

"Let me know how I can help."

"Will do."

"Any word on the passengers?"

"Ginny said when Henry left for Anchorage this afternoon he was planning to pick up a man named—" Landon lifted his notepad—"Mark Olsen, and Agnes Grey, of course. But when he called her before leaving Anchorage he said two others were added. She didn't even know their names. Henry said they'd settled up when they got to Yancey."

"I'm heading over to check on Agnes. I'll see if there's any word on them."

The disinfectant smell rubbed Cole wrong, always had. The overhead glare of bad lighting and starchy white walls only compounded his discomfort. The hospital held bad memories, and it looked like that record would remain unbroken.

Peggy Wilson leaned against the counter, her brow furrowed as she talked on the phone. "I understand that. The insurance card says he needs preauthorization, but how on earth are you supposed to get preauthorization for an emergency?" She sighed, her face reddening.

She looked up, caught sight of Cole, and covered the receiver with her hand. "I'm sorry. These insurance companies like to drive me insane. What can I do for you?"

"I came to check on Agnes Grey. She was brought in here—"

"An hour ago." Peggy's face fell. "I'm sorry. She didn't make it."

Cole balled his hands at his side. If he'd been faster . . . stronger . . .

"They tried resuscitating her, but it was no use. Her heart just wouldn't beat."

Cole swallowed. "Any word on the couple brought in?"

Peggy bit her bottom lip. "I'm afraid they didn't make it either. They were pronounced DOA."

He closed his eyes as regret bit deep. "I really thought they had a chance." Maybe if he'd taken them out in a different order . . .

Her thick hand clamped on his. "I'm sorry, sugar."

"So am I."

He exited through the automatic doors into the crisp, black night, his heart heavy.

Agnes Grey, gone.

He headed down the quiet street, past darkened shop windows, past the Russian-American Trading Post, where Agnes lived and worked.

Yancey wouldn't be the same without the venerable Lady Grey.

And Bailey? His step faltered as her beautiful face flashed before him. How would she take the news of her beloved aunt's passing?

2

The news sent Bailey Craig back in time. She'd heard what Gus said, heard Agnes was dead, but rather than memories of her beloved aunt, it was memories of why she'd left Yancey that flooded her mind. Twelve years elapsed in an instant, and suddenly she was sixteen again. . . .

The pounding—like little men sledgehammering her skull from the inside out—woke her. *So thirsty.*

She opened her mouth to the horrible feel of cotton suffocating her. She didn't want to open her eyes—didn't want to see, let alone face, the wreckage of what she'd done again.

Not again.

She didn't have to look over to know he was gone. Though she lay on the floor, at least this time she had a pillow beneath her head and something was draped over her—a blanket, her coat? She couldn't be sure.

The place was still. No one else was up yet, or they'd all left the night before.

Where was she? *A party.* But the details were sketchy, as always. She'd come with Kelly and Beth. Had they left her? Disgusted with her drunken antics again?

She rose gingerly on her elbows and opened her eyes, her head swimming with the motion, nausea rolling through her stomach like a thirty-foot wave.

Everything was hazy, dim. She blinked, trying to moisten the contacts dried to her corneas.

Krista's dad's place. That's where she was. He was away for the weekend.

The room was dark, except for the glaring sun forcing its way through a slit in the curtains. The bedroom door was shut. She smiled. Perhaps someone else had done something stupid and she wouldn't be the only one disgraced.

She flipped the bathroom switch, the fluorescent light crackling as it came to life. She recoiled at the image in the mirror. How far she'd fallen. Mascara smudged beneath her bloodshot eyes. The faint impression of the carpet pattern etched in her skin on the right side of her cheek, her hair misshapen and frozen from the overabundance of hairspray.

She'd taken such care to look good, to be appealing and seductive, and now she just looked sick. She splashed cold water on her face, over and over, scrubbing hard, as if it could wash any of the filth away.

Hot tears mixed with the frigid water, and she slumped to the ground, too sick to stand, her heart breaking—shocked there was anything left to break. The cold floor felt good against her hot skin. She curled up in the fetal position. *Not again.*

How did I get here?

She couldn't blame anyone else; she'd brought it on herself. If she could just go back, take that first time back. Not have another drink. Insist they go for food before she got too woozy, insist he take her home. But in her drunken stupor she'd ended up with *the* guy she'd thought she'd wanted, at least for the moment. He was older, more popular—surely it would make her more popular too.

Of course it hadn't lasted past morning, and her course had been set.

There had been so many times she could have turned it around, salvaged her reputation, or at least not made it a thousand times worse, but she always took that next drink, the one to make her feel better, and ended up in the same state so many mornings.

Cole had no idea how bad she felt. How she wanted to run to him, crying, begging his forgiveness . . .

But she knew he wouldn't accept her apology, not after what she'd done. And she couldn't lose face—that would be worse than anything, right?

She was so pathetic.

"Bailey, are you there?" Gus's voice pulled her back to the present.

She blinked hard, wishing away the memories of her youth and the nightmares that accompanied them. "Yeah." She cleared her throat. "Sorry."

"Did you hear what I said?"

Agnes. Dead.

"Yeah." She sank on the edge of the couch, nearly slipping to the floor in the process.

"She left the Trading Post to you. In fact, she left it all to you. We can go over the details when you get to Yancey."

Her throat constricted. "Yancey?"

"Yes. When you arrive home for the funeral."

Home. She'd have to go back. Images of her in high school, curled on that bathroom floor, pounded through her mind.

"How soon can you leave?" he asked.

I can't leave Oregon. Can't go to Alaska. Fear seized her.

"Bailey?"

"Yeah, Gus, I'm here." She swallowed the bile burning up her throat. "I'll make arrangements."

"Agnes took care of the details on this end, didn't want to be a burden to anyone, least of all you. You just have to get here."

"All right."

"It'll be good to see you again."

She nodded, bereft of words, and slipped the phone back in the cradle.

Yancey, Alaska. She'd planned on never setting foot there again. Now she had no choice. Agnes deserved for her to be there. Agnes deserved so much more. She'd let her aunt down as much as she had herself.

Cole pulled in his driveway and glanced over at his sisters' place. Several lights still shone. Climbing from his truck, he footed it across the open acres of land that separated his cabin from his childhood home, dodging mud puddles and rain. The scent of damp moss hovered like a fog in the cool, dank air.

Aurora greeted him at the kitchen door.

He slipped his boots off and knelt to pet the whimpering husky. "How ya doing, girl?"

The wonderful aroma of chili powder and cumin swirled in the air, and his mouth watered.

"I saved you some," Piper called from the dining room.

He moved through the doorway to greet her. "Thanks." The search-and-rescue call had come two minutes into their weekly family dinner.

Piper swiveled from the computer screen, her back to the desk edging the stairs. "I'm guessing it didn't go well."

Cole leaned against the doorframe. "She didn't talk about it?" He already knew the answer. Kayden kept everything close to the hip.

Piper shook her head. "Nope. Just headed for the shower."

"You know Kayden. . . . When something hurts, she needs her space. Give her a day and she'll be back to her annoying self." He forced a chuckle, but he wasn't fooling either of them. It was hard making more recoveries than rescues, nine times more to be precise. Being on search-and-rescue detail wasn't easy, but it was the job they all felt called to do.

"Do I want to know?" Piper's eyes held the innocence he loved so much about her.

"No, but you're going to hear anyway." It was inevitable in a town Yancey's size—six hundred and three at last count. "Do you want it to come from me?"

Piper nodded her affirmation, but her eyes pleaded otherwise.

He exhaled. "It was Henry Reid's plane. Agnes Grey was on board."

"And?" She nibbled her bottom lip.

"I'm sorry, kid. We didn't find Henry. Agnes died at the hospital."

Her head bent, and Cole moved to stroke her shoulder.

"Poor Miss Agnes."

"I know." Saying it'd been a rough night didn't come close.

Piper wiped her eyes and looked up. "You must be starving. Let me fix you a bowl."

He squeezed her shoulder. Always so concerned about others. "I got it."

"You sure?"

"Positive. You finish what you were doing." He indicated the computer screen. "What are you looking for this time?"

"A book."

"Another mystery?" She'd read thousands.

"Princess Maksutov's diary."

Cole lifted the lid off the Crockpot and pulled a bowl from the cupboard. "That's a different title. Who's that by?" He filled a hefty bowl with chili, topping it off with diced onions and shredded cheddar, then grabbed a bottle of water from the fridge.

"Princess Sofia Ioannovna Maksutov."

Balancing the bowl in one hand and the basket of corn bread in the other, a bottle of water tucked under one arm and a bottle of honey under the other, he made his way back into the dining room, Aurora fast on his heels. "Why would you want some chick's diary?"

"It was stolen from the historical society's display at the library. Poor Mrs. Anderson's all in a dither."

"You don't say?"

"She has good cause this time. Someone reached in the display case and stole it."

"Stole what?" Gage asked, entering from the kitchen. After returning from guiding a three-day white-water-rafting excursion only to be called in to assist with the night's rescue, Gage still hadn't managed to shave, let alone eat.

Aurora sprung up and bounded toward him, licking his scruffy face as he bent to pet her.

"I was just telling Cole how someone stole Princess Maksutov's diary."

Gage rumpled his brow. "Who?"

Cole shrugged.

"She was the wife of the last Russian governor of Alaska," Piper explained. "She's buried in the old Russian cemetery."

Gage snagged a piece of corn bread from the basket. "Why would anyone steal Princess Macksue's diary?"

"Princess Mak-su-tov." Piper enunciated each syllable. "And I have a theory."

"Shocking." Gage feigned surprise as he sank down into the chair opposite Cole.

"What's shocking?" Kayden asked, padding downstairs in her sweats, her damp hair leaving drip marks on her T-shirt.

"Piper's got a theory." Cole pulled a chair out for his sister.

Kayden bypassed the chair and leaned against the sideboard instead. "Let's have it, Nancy Drew."

"Very funny." Piper swiveled back to face the monitor. "I think someone stole it to turn around and sell it."

"Would it be worth anything?" Gage asked, slathering his corn bread with honey but somehow managing to get more of it on himself than the bread.

"Sure. It's close to a hundred and fifty years old. It had gold filigree on the cover and edging the pages. To certain collectors it might be worth a small fortune. I bet someone stole it and is planning to sell it on eBay."

"That wouldn't exactly be bright." Cole shook his head

as Gage attempted to wipe the honey from his hands with a paper napkin.

"Please." Piper rolled her eyes. "We're talking about someone in Yancey. Not exactly mastermind criminal stock."

"True." Theft in Yancey wasn't the norm—a few drifters, the occasional misdirected teen. Cole's heart sank. *Not Jesse. Not this time.* He'd been working with Jesse Ryan in youth group for months. He thought the kid had finally turned a significant corner in his life. "Any leads on who might have stolen it?"

"Sheriff Slidell doesn't seem very concerned. He had Landon file a report, but I doubt he'll do much else, which is why I'm scanning eBay and the like. If it comes up for sale, Slidell can track down the seller and we can get it back where it belongs."

"I'm sure Slidell will appreciate your efforts," Gage said, struggling to pull off the tiny bits of napkin stuck to his hands.

Piper huffed. "He can appreciate all he wants."

Cole swallowed a chuckle along with another bite of chili. Piper was adorable when she set her stubborn mind to something—and the pursuit of justice ranked high on her list.

He took a swig of water, praying Jesse wasn't involved. His gang had been responsible for several thefts and much of the vandalism in Yancey in the past year, but Jesse had been straight the past two months. He'd given Cole his word.

The man bent at the water's edge, ignoring the biting rain. They were all gone now—helicopters, emergency personnel, passengers.

Tossing a rock in the ocean, he watched it skip erratically atop the choppy waves before sinking into the black depths, just as the plane had.

One single act had ensured his future.

His heart had nearly stopped when they'd pulled her from the wreckage, but she'd died in the end.

He smiled with satisfaction. His problems were over. A few more days and he'd finally get what he deserved.

Standing, he watched the storm whip across the sea, pounding frothy waves against Tariuk Island's rock-strewn shore.

If anyone else got in his way, he'd deal with them as he had the old lady.

It was his time now.

3

"Are you sure you have to go?" Carrie slumped on the bed, her knee butting against Bailey's red canvas duffel, now stuffed to the gills with clothes.

"It's Agnes. I'm all the family she had." She shoved a pair of jeans in. Had she already packed jeans? Had she remembered to pack a sweatshirt?

She sighed, unable to put any serious thought into what she ought to bring. Her mind still swirled with the devastating reality of the news. Agnes was gone—and she was going back to Yancey. Gus had called back, letting her know the funeral was set for Tuesday.

Her stomach churned, and she forced down another saltine.

"That's not technically true," Carrie said.

"What's not?"

"You aren't her only family member." Carrie worked on refolding the discarded pile of clothes Bailey had decided not to take.

"I am for all intents and purposes." Wrestling with the zipper, Bailey managed to close the bulging duffel, then hefted it over her shoulder, carrying it to the living room. She plopped it on the sofa and turned to look for her book.

Carrie padded after her. "You don't think *she'll* be there?"

Bailey's shoulders dropped. She prayed not. Going home was horrific enough without the added trauma of seeing her mother. "Evelyn was never around while Agnes was alive. Why show up now that she's dead?"

"They were sisters."

"Family doesn't exist for my mother." Bailey found her book and slid it in the duffel's front pocket. "She lives for no one but herself. Always has. Always will."

"Why don't you let me come with you? I'm sure I could get some time off. You should have someone there with you. Someone other than your mother."

Bailey hugged Carrie. "Such a good friend, but you said yourself if you take any more time off, you won't have a job to come back to." Which was true, but it wasn't the main reason Bailey wanted her best friend to stay behind. She'd met Carrie after becoming a Christian. Carrie was part of her new life, not her past, and she needed to keep the two separate.

"I'm sure if I explain . . ." Carrie started.

"Not necessary." Bailey turned and headed for the kitchen. "I've got some Ben and Jerry's in the freezer I need to finish off before I leave. Wanna help me?"

Carrie smiled. "Way to change the subject."

"Is that a no?"

"Yeah, right." Carrie made a beeline for the freezer. "I call dibs on Chunky Monkey."

A pint of Chunky Monkey later, Bailey saw Carrie out and then cut the lights. Bone-tired, she crawled into bed, not ready to face what lay ahead.

Yancey.

She was going back to Yancey in the morning.

Tears tumbled down her cheeks.

Lord, I can't do this.

You don't have a choice, came the soft reply.

4

Lights danced like fireflies against Tariuk Island's rugged mountains, illuminating the darkness surrounding Bailey.

A cool breeze riffled through her hair, loosening tiny wisps from her tightly woven bun. She struggled to pin them back in place but gave up and gripped the ferry rail as Yancey came fully into view.

The lights spread out to reach her, glimmering reflections skimming across the surface of the water, only to be dashed against the ferry's bow.

She wanted to run, to bolt the other way, but the ferry stayed its course. It was drawing her in, pulling her on a path she didn't want to travel.

Can't breathe.

She forced herself to swallow a gulp of air. Tears smarted her eyes. She wouldn't cry—she'd promised herself.

It didn't matter what they thought. What *he* thought. She was a different person.

The crisp sea air splattered her face like a blanket of reality. Who was she kidding? In their minds she'd forever be Easy Lay Bay. The passing years, a doctorate, and all her streamlined suits weren't going to sway their opinion of her—truth was, there were days she still had to convince herself.

The ferry docked beside a silent marina. She'd chosen the last of the day, hoping the streets would be deserted, praying she could slip into town unnoticed and stay out of sight until the funeral. Then it was just a matter of getting Agnes's stuff in order and hightailing it back to Oregon.

Clutching her bag, she ambled down the gangplank, the cool night air biting at her tearstained cheeks.

"Bailey, is that you?"

She froze midstride.

Gus Holbrook hobbled forward. In the dimness of the dock lights he looked much as he had a decade ago. A few more gray hairs poking out of his weathered ball cap, perhaps, but it was still the same old Gus.

She wiped her face with the back of her hand and struggled to compose herself.

"Let me get that for you." He reached for her bag.

She tightened her grip on the strap. "I've got it."

"Suit yourself. Truck's over here." He gestured to his rusted orange pickup. It was hard to believe the old thing still ran.

"That's kind of you, Gus, but I can walk." She didn't like being dependent on others, especially not in Yancey.

"Nonsense." Gus harrumphed. "I'm not leaving till you climb in that cab, young lady."

She sighed. She didn't want to hurt his feelings. He'd always been kind to her—one of the few. She bit her bottom lip. It would get her through town faster. "All right, Gus. Thanks."

His craggy face lit with a smile.

She held her bag on her lap as they started the short drive from the docks to town.

Nestled between the ocean and the mountains, Yancey was viewed as an idyllic island village by the numerous tourists that flooded its shores every cruise season, but to her it symbolized only regret and shame.

She stared out the windows, amazed at how little had changed in the ten years she'd been gone. The library remained in the refurbished Russian farmhouse at the top of Main Street, setting the tone of a town steeped in history.

Turning right on Main Street, they passed the same shops she'd frequented as a teen—Jenkins' Flower and Fudgery, the General Store, Baranov Books. But it was the store next to Baranov's that caught her eye. *Last Frontier Adventures* was painted in bold blue over the entrance to what had once been Ben's Bait and Tackle—the shop Cole McKenna's family owned. She was dying to ask Gus what happened—had they sold, changed location?—but she couldn't allow herself to go there, couldn't spend her first night in town asking questions about Cole McKenna.

The shop was dark, but the streetlamps illuminated the posters lining the front bay windows—images of people white-water rafting, rock climbing, and scuba diving. Beneath the pictures sat a display of equipment needed for each endeavor. A pair of flippers tugged at her heart. Cole had taught her to dive.

She closed her eyes, and images of that day flashed through her mind—acclimating to the sensation of breathing through a mouthpiece, sharing the rush of going beyond natural limits to a hidden world beneath the ocean's surface with the boy she loved.

"Funeral's set for ten on Tuesday at New Creation." Gus broke through her memories.

Again she swiped moisture from her eyes. In town less than a half hour and she'd cried twice. She was pathetic.

"We can go over the will Wednesday afternoon, if that suits."

It was hard to believe Agnes was gone. The woman had seemed invincible. "That'll be fine," she said, working to keep her voice even, to show no hint of the sadness barreling through her.

They passed the town square. Blue ribbons and glittered signs posted throughout signaled the upcoming Summer Festival and Bailey winced. She'd made one of her numerous and more infamous mistakes with Tom Murphy behind the dunking booth.

Her stomach lurched.

This is too hard. Too painful.

"You'll have to stop by the diner tomorrow. I'll make you a hearty breakfast to kick off your first day back home."

She wasn't home. Yancey could never be home. "Still got the diner?"

"Yep. It was Martha's dream. After she passed . . . well, I couldn't just close it. I'm sure people think it's odd after all these years, but I can't bring myself to give it up."

"A lawyer owning a diner. I suppose that's not so unusual."

He chuckled. "I suppose not. Life in a tourist town—everyone plays a variety of roles." He looked over, studying her in the gleam of Main Street's lone stoplight. "Speaking of roles . . . I imagine it'll take you a while to sort out the shop and decide what you want to do."

She steeled herself for Gus's displeasure. "I've already decided."

The light turned green, but Gus didn't move. "You have?"

"Yes. The light . . ." she said, gesturing toward it as green reflected across their faces.

Gus accelerated, the old truck clunking and sputtering. "You were saying . . ."

"I've decided to sell."

"You're selling the Post?" Sadness rang in his tone, but not surprise.

Bailey shifted from the window, a cool draft seeping through the worn-out sealing. "I want to find a buyer who will agree to keep it the Russian-American Trading Post."

Much as Gus couldn't destroy Martha's dream, she wouldn't destroy Agnes's by closing the shop, but she couldn't stay in Yancey. Finding a buyer was her only option.

"That's not exactly going to be easy. The Post was Agnes's baby. It'll be impossible to find someone who'll love the place the way she did."

"Perhaps, but as long as the buyer keeps it the Trading Post, it'll be fine." She'd know she'd done right by Agnes. "Can you put out the word? Try and think of someone who'd be a good fit?" Surely someone else in town shared Agnes's love for Russian history. She did. There had to be more than two of them.

Gus pulled to a stop in front of the Post and cut the engine. It took the truck another moment to respond and stop gurgling. "I'll see what I can do."

"Thanks."

He inhaled. "I had hoped . . ."

She arched a brow.

He shrugged. ". . . that maybe after you'd spent a few days you'd decide to stay."

"That's sweet, Gus, really, but impossible."

A weary smile spread across his wrinkled face. "Nothing's impossible . . ."

"With God," she finished Agnes's favorite saying.

Her chest tightened. Even God couldn't fix her past.

"I think you'll find the place hasn't changed much," he said as he hefted himself from the cab.

Small towns never did.

He lumbered around to her side and opened the door, the hinges creaking with age. "We managed to talk Agnes into letting us repaint the place last year."

She stepped from the truck and nearly lost her footing. The two-story white panel shop with apartment overhead knocked her back thirteen years, all the feelings of an abandoned fifteen-year-old girl crashing over her anew.

Her mother's excuses for dumping her off resounded in her mind as she stared at the white lace curtains framing the over-sized shop window. It was too dark to see the items on display, but the arrangement remained simple.

Her gaze traveled up to the apartment windows overhead. The same white eyelet curtains hung behind two lit electric candles.

"The candles," she murmured, her breath catching in her throat.

Gus stared up at them, his eyes misting. "Main Street didn't seem right without them lit."

She nodded, fighting back tears. She wasn't the only one hurting. Gus had carried a torch for Agnes as far back as Bailey could remember. He'd lost his wife years ago, and as far as she knew, Agnes had been the only woman to catch his eye since. It was all very sweet and innocent. From her and Agnes's frequent phone conversations, Bailey knew the two had still sat beside each other every Sunday and Wednesday night at church and shared supper most Sunday afternoons. No whirlwind romance, by any means, but a deep abiding friendship and, Bailey believed, love.

Gus cleared his throat. "The sign's new."

"Oh?" She glanced up at the oval-shaped burgundy sign with raised gold lettering that read *Russian-American Trading Post* and then back at Gus, confused. "It looks the same."

Gus let out a strangled chuckle. "She agreed to let us get her a new sign if it was identical to the original. Dale Green had to make it from scratch. Took him three times to get the color exactly right." He shook his head. "Gal was so headstrong." He turned his head and sniffed.

Bailey remained rooted in place. *Should I say something?*

She reached out her hand and promptly drew it back again.

Gus fumbled with the keys. "I think you'll find everything in good working order."

He opened the door and switched on the lights.

Bailey remained fixed in the entry.

Crowded pine bookcases and file cabinets flanked one wall; items on display for sale in a glass-enclosed case flanked the other.

Agnes's worktable commanded the center of the room, a chair on either side—one for Agnes and one for her.

Her heart hammered in her throat.

Gus gestured to the stacks of files covering every inch of the workspace. "She must have been in the middle of sorting files when . . ." He pulled off his cap and clutched it in his arthritic hands. "Some of the gals from church put some food in the icebox for you when they heard you were coming."

She wondered how long it had taken for the news of her pending arrival to filter through town—a day? More likely, a few hours.

She nodded, fighting to stall the tears. She remembered those women—their admonishing glances, their hushed whispers.

Her stomach quivered.

A shadow scampered across the floor, followed by mewing. She looked to Gus and he smiled.

"Is it . . . ?"

Butterscotch poked his head around the stairwell.

Bailey bent, signaling for him to come. "Hey, Scotch." She held out her arms.

The cat mewed and sniffed the air tentatively.

"It's Bay," she whispered, and he darted into her arms, purring.

He was soft and warm and every bit as cuddly as she remembered. "How you doing, old friend?" She rubbed the silky fur between Butterscotch's ears, and he purred.

"I stop by every day and feed him. Tried taking him to my place, but that foolish cat would have none of it. Bolted out the door every chance he got."

"I'll take care of him."

"Sure looks happy to see you."

"Yeah, I suppose he does."

"He isn't the only one. It's good to have you home, girl. Agnes would be so happy."

Bailey swallowed. She only wished they'd had more time.

"Well, it's late." Gus sighed. "I should get out of your way and let you get some shut-eye."

"Thanks for the ride."

"Don't mention it. If you need anything . . ."

"I know who to call."

She locked the door behind him and, cradling Butterscotch in her arms, climbed the stairs to the apartment overhead.

The soft glow of the candles illuminated the cozy living space. A half-done puzzle of Big Ben covered the small table, an empty tea-stained mug resting beside it.

Butterscotch meowed.

Biting back tears, she turned to the bedroom she'd called home for a handful of years and flipped on the light.

The same pink, ruffled comforter lined the bed, the same half-empty perfume bottles and jewelry boxes lined the dresser. She trailed her hand along the items, her fingers stilling on the gilded-silver-and-enamel music box.

She lifted it and sank onto the edge of the bed. Butterscotch curled up beside her. With a shaky breath, she opened the lid and Tchaikovsky's theme from *Swan Lake* spilled out.

Tears budded in her eyes. A gift from Agnes her first night in Yancey.

Nestled inside lay the locket Cole had given her. She remembered that day, that moment, as if it were yesterday. The warmth of the sun after a day spent diving, the sand between her toes, the look in his eyes—full of hope and anticipation—as he'd presented it to her, his hands sure as he placed it around her neck.

Tears tumbled down her cheeks. Two gifts from the two people she'd loved in Yancey. And now she'd lost them both.

5

Slipping off his dive mask, Cole swallowed a gulp of sea air. The sun's rays penetrated his dry suit, its warmth radiating along his cool skin.

Landon sank down beside him, tossing him a Gatorade and a granola bar.

"Thanks." Cole stretched out, his body aching from the day's heavy labor. Fortunately, all that remained was harnessing and refloating the fuselage. Henry Reid's body had been retrieved, leaving only Mark Olsen's unrecovered. Cole hated leaving a man behind.

Landon angled his head back and shut his eyes.

"Don't get too comfortable," Cole instructed. They'd be heading back down soon.

Deputies Tom Murphy and David Thoreau chuckled voraciously at the boat's bow. What they found so funny about today's events eluded Cole.

"She looked great. And still single," Tom said.

"Maybe you should drop by, offer to take her out for a drink."

"We know where that'll lead."

Thoreau nudged Tom. "Exactly. Come on, you know us married guys have to live vicariously through those of you who haven't been taken prisoner yet."

"I'll see what I can do."

"Details, my man. That's all I'm asking for."

Landon tossed his empty Gatorade bottle in the waste bucket. "What are you two jabbering about?"

Tom lifted his chin. "Haven't you heard? Easy Lay Bay's back in town."

Cole's jaw flexed. "Don't call her that."

Tom and Thoreau exchanged a knowing glance.

"Why not?" Tom hopped down from the bow and swaggered toward Cole. "Oh, that's right. I forgot. You two had a thing way back when."

Tom's tone and choice of words made what he and Bailey had shared seem dirty, when it was far from it. Or at least he'd believed so until she'd broken his heart and never looked back. "We were friends."

"Friends?" Tom tilted his head in Thoreau's direction. "Well, we all know how *friendly* Bailey could be."

Cole crushed the empty Gatorade bottle in his fist. "It wasn't like that."

"Then you must have been the only one she wasn't like that with."

Cole stood and grabbed his gear. He was too old for childish games. "If Bailey's back in town, it's for her aunt's funeral. Show some respect."

To his astonishment Tom let it drop, and Cole returned to the water, hoping to drown all thoughts of Bailey Craig in its depths. In a few days she'd be gone and he could go back to pretending she didn't exist.

Cole sat at the stern, bone-tired and ready to be back on shore.

They'd floated the plane successfully and the wreckage was being towed back to shore by their support vessel a few leagues ahead of them. Retrieving wreckage wasn't his favorite job, but it was a necessary one, and since he was the most qualified diver on Tariuk Island, his help was needed.

That's the way things worked in a small town, at least how they worked in his town. Everyone helped out—whether it was volunteering with search and rescue, assisting in towing disabled vessels to shore, or running a booth at the Summer Festival.

His parents had fostered a love of service in him and his siblings since they were young.

"Work hard. Serve diligently. Do something you love." His father's wisdom had blessed him well. He and his siblings worked hard—running shore excursions for cruise liners docking in Yancey, facilitating corporate retreats, anything that allowed them to run a business they believed in while performing jobs they loved.

He sank back to enjoy the remainder of the trip to shore. The ship was quiet for a change, and he'd swapped his dry suit for a pair of sweats and T-shirt.

Water lapped rhythmically against the hull, and a crisp breeze floated over the bow with each dip. The sun, lowering toward the horizon, pulled the warmth of the air with it. He was ready for a hot shower and a hearty meal.

An enormous beam trawler muddled past, hauling its day's catch to shore. Their vessel, miniscule in comparison, bobbed in its wake. The fresh scent of shrimp mingled with the salty sea air, reminding Cole of family fish fries on the beach.

"Deputy Grainger," Fred hollered from the wheelhouse.

Landon got to his feet. "Yep?"

"Call for you on the radio. Sheriff Slidell."

A minute later, the boat banked hard starboard, nearly knocking Cole from his perch.

Landon emerged from the cabin. "Emergency call from a trawler. We're closest."

Cole sighed. The day was about to get even longer.

Alaskan Dreams, a seventy-foot privately owned trawler, sat anchored twenty miles off Tariuk Island's shore, its fishing net strung high.

As their boat buffeted against the trawler's side, Cole's gaze narrowed on the net. Something was caught with the fish.

He squinted and felt the blood drain from his face. A diver's body hung among the wriggling pollock.

Sid, the captain and owner of *Alaskan Dreams*, met them as they climbed aboard, his white captain's cap clutched tight in his fists, his knuckles the same shade as the battered material.

Cole's gaze traveled back to the diver. Long blond hair trailed from her mask, the strands ensnared in the thick orange netting. Nausea rumbled in his gut as Bailey's sweet face flashed through his mind. No. It couldn't be. She was just on his mind because of Agnes's passing. It couldn't be her.

"We thought it best to leave everything—" Sid's voice cracked. "To leave the lass as we found her." He shuffled his feet, his eyes averted from the victim. "Some of the men thought we ought to cut her free, but—"

"You did good, Sid." Landon clapped a reassuring hand on the elderly man's back. "You did the right thing."

Sid nodded, a flicker of relief easing the ache on his weathered brow.

Landon pulled out his notepad. "I'm going to need some information."

Pat Wharton, one of the deckhands, leaned against the rail beside Cole while Landon and Sid conversed in the wheelhouse.

"I've heard tales of nets dredging up the dead," Pat said, his coloring green. "I've just never seen it myself."

Unfortunately, working dive rescue, Cole had seen the sea give up more than its fair share of the dead, and contrary to popular opinion, it never got easier.

The pungent odor of pollock and decomposition hung thick in the air, the sea unable to wash away the stench.

Time passed slow as molasses and fast as a firecracker, bringing with it the distinct sensation of crisis and all its distorting properties. The need to respond, to be of help, nearly suffocated Cole. He dealt better in action. Standing on the sidelines was quickly bringing him to his knees.

What if it *was* Bailey captured in the net? He fought the

suffocating urge to race to it, to tear her free, but there was protocol to follow, rules of investigation to adhere to. It couldn't be Bailey. His mind was playing tricks on him. He needed to wait, to be patient. If only his heart would stop racing.

After what seemed an eternity, Landon ordered the net released.

Hundreds of speckled fish wriggled across the deck, their mouths opening and closing, their gills desperate for oxygen.

"They'll all have to be tossed back into the sea," Sid said, and the truth of it washed over the crew's faces—their day's work gone in the blink of an eye.

The renewed scent of pollock blanketed the air, clinging like a thick, soupy fog to the fibers of their clothes.

Landon knelt at the base of the net. "Cole, give me a hand."

Finally he could be of some use. He rushed forward, afraid of what he might find, yet feeling foolish for even thinking it.

"Her body's caught in the cod end of the gear. We'll need to cut her loose."

Cole squatted beside Landon while Tom and Thoreau looked on. For once the two remained silent.

Painstakingly, they worked to free her from the thick orange netting, and then Landon took another round of photographs before removing her mask.

Cole's chest tightened, and he released a shaky expulsion of air. It wasn't Bailey, wasn't anyone he knew, but the fact brought him little relief. She was young. No older than Piper.

Her eyes, a faint blue surrounded by cloudy white, stared up at him.

Landon called for Tom and Thoreau to bring the body bag, and Cole remained ready to help lift her into it.

"On three," Landon instructed.

Cole nodded.

"One, two, three."

They lifted and the woman's gear shifted, her air tank swinging loose.

Tom bent and retrieved it.

Cole and Landon placed her gently in the bag, then stood.

"We'll need Cole to check the gear," Landon began, as he had so many times before.

A strange smile curled on Tom's lips. "I don't think that's a good idea."

Landon cocked his head. "Why not? We always use Cole to check the equipment in this type of case."

Tom shifted the tank so the writing faced them. "Not when it's his own equipment."

Cole gaped at the yellow lettering stamped across the tank— *Last Frontier Adventures*. He took a staggering step back.

She'd rented her equipment from his shop.

6

Sheriff Slidell met the boat at the dock. Booth Powell, Yancey's medical examiner, stood to his right, making Slidell's five-foot-ten, one-hundred-ninety-pound frame look puny. Booth was thin as a rail, but a towering six feet five. Long and lean, he said his nimble fingers perfected him for a job he loved.

Rather than viewing his profession as morbid, he often commented that he regarded himself as one of the heroes destined to see justice done. If his autopsy could rule out unnatural death and give peace to grieving families, it made his day. If, on the other hand, his report indicated foul play, it was the first step in finding the killer.

Cole wondered which it would be in this case.

Had the young lady in her twenties died of natural causes? Suffered a heart attack under the sea?

Had foul play found her? A dive buddy caused her harm?

Or . . .

His heart lurched.

Had his equipment played a role in her death? He hadn't personally rented the gear to her, but someone at the shop had. Safety First was their motto and they all took it to heart. Had something gone wrong? One of them slipped? Paid too casual attention during an inspection? Been less than stringent before renting the gear?

"What do we have here?" Booth's deep Louisiana twang pulled Cole from his thoughts.

It was amazing that after twenty years in Yancey his twang still remained. Booth said it was in the blood and no change of location could alter that.

Booth bent and unzipped the body bag, taking a cursory glance at his new charge. "Young." He shook his head in dismay.

Sheriff Slidell hovered over Booth's shoulder. "She's not local."

"Someone local knew her." Satisfaction danced in Tom's voice.

"Oh?" Slidell straightened.

"The deceased's tank is from Cole's shop."

Slidell's head swung in Cole's direction. "Is that right?"

"Stamp says it's one of mine," Cole answered straight and to the point. If he could be of help, he would.

Slidell nodded. "Well, then, we'll need someone else to run the equipment check."

"I understand." He knew the protocol. "Owen Matthews up on Kodiak Island is a good man, good diver. He does equipment checks for the police department up there when the need arises."

"All right." Slidell noted the name. "I'll give him a call."

Booth zipped the bag and stood. He relayed instructions for the woman's body to be transported to the morgue.

The waiting paramedics lifted the gurney and loaded it into the back of the ambulance.

Booth ambled to his SUV, and Slidell followed.

Cole waited for the ensuing exchange. With Booth and Slidell, there was always an exchange. Slidell expected things done on his timetable, and Booth refused to be rushed.

"What can you tell me?" Slidell asked as Booth tossed his bag in the rear of his Blazer.

"Now, you know good and well it's too early for me to give you anything other than supposition. You'll have to wait for my report." Booth shut the hatch and signaled for the ambulance to head out.

"How long?" Slidell asked.

Booth climbed in the SUV, his head nearly hitting the ceiling, and shut the door. He took his time lowering the window.

Red crawled up Slidell's neck. He lurched to rest his arm on the sill. "You didn't answer my question."

Booth started the engine. "Henry Reid's first in line. She'll be next."

Slidell didn't move. "How long?"

"Forty-eight hours." Booth glanced at Slidell's arm and then back at the man.

After a moment, Slidell stepped back.

Cole watched the gravel fly in the Blazer's wake, then turned to Landon. "What does he mean Henry Reid's first in line? We just retrieved him from the ocean's floor and now Booth's planning on picking up where the fish left off?"

"NTSB ordered the pilot's autopsy, if we recovered the body."

"They think Henry might be the cause of the crash?"

"They want to rule out a heart attack, check his blood-alcohol level . . ."

"You and I both know Henry's been sober ten years. You really think he fell off the wagon and dove his plane into the Gulf of Alaska?"

"No. I don't."

Cole leaned against Landon's patrol car with a sigh. "Does Ginny know?"

"I'm sure Slidell's informed her." Landon lifted his chin. "Speaking of Slidell . . ."

The police chief leaned on the hood of the car. "Tom tells me you didn't recognize the deceased."

"That's correct."

"But the tank is from your shop?"

"Yeah, but I haven't worked the desk in a month."

"Who has?"

"Kayden had the first two weeks, Piper and Jake the last two." This time of year the excursions he and Gage ran were in highest demand, so the girls and Jake ran the shop. Winter months, things reversed.

Slidell's brows shot up. "Jake, you say?"

"And Piper," Cole reiterated, but it was no use. He might as well have been talking to the wind. Slidell had heard Jake's name and nothing else.

"Why don't we take a ride over there and see if Jake can give us some answers."

7

Landon followed his boss and Cole into Last Frontier Adventures, the shop Cole owned and operated with his siblings. In place of a bell, "Wipe Out!" signaled their entry.

Another of Piper's touches.

Beach murals and surfing posters donned the walls. Polynesian leis topped the displays and the scent of cocoa butter swirled in the air.

If it weren't for the dry suits necessary for cold-weather diving, he'd think he'd just entered a tropical dive shop.

Piper looked up from a transaction with a customer and smiled.

Landon prayed she wasn't the one who had rented out the equipment. Not that he suspected anything would turn up wrong with it. The McKennas were very careful with their equipment. But knowing Piper's tender ways, if she'd met the deceased woman, it would break her heart to learn she was dead.

"You're all set," Piper said, handing Nancy Bowen her receipt and booklet. "Class starts on the fifth. Be here by seven."

"Bright and early." Nancy turned with a smile. "Cole, Sheriff." Her smile widened. "Landon."

He tipped his hat. "Nancy."

Color danced in her cheeks. "I just got the last slot in Cole's wreck diving class. Piper tells me you'll be assisting?"

Piper rose up on her toes to grin at him over Nancy's shoulder.

"Oh, she did, did she?" He oughta thump her. If she wasn't his best friend's kid sister . . .

"Landon?" Nancy said.

He looked down at her, standing a mere foot from him. He didn't want to hurt her feelings. She was a sweet gal. He just didn't feel the spark he hoped to with a potential spouse.

"Was she right?"

"Hmm?"

"Was Piper right?"

Piper gloated behind Nancy, waiting with gleeful expectation for his answer. "Yes, I'm assisting on that class."

"Great. I'll see you then." She moved past him to the door while he glared at Piper. Unfortunately his attempt to look menacing only seemed to amuse her more.

"Wipe Out!" signaled Nancy's departure.

"Piper, I oughta—"

"Thank me?" she suggested sweetly as she moved around the counter to greet Cole with a hug.

"Hey, kiddo." Cole pressed a kiss to her brow. "I think you better stop playing matchmaker for Landon."

"Why? Just because he's grumpy?"

"Take it as a hint," Landon said through gritted teeth.

"Wipe Out!" chimed again as the door opened. Gage entered, followed by a slew of people—sun on their cheeks, hair tousled from a morning spent riding rapids.

"Good trip?" Cole asked.

Gage shifted his sunglasses to rest on his head, pale skin denoting the area they'd covered. "A blast."

Everyone chattered around them like a tiny swarm of buzzing bees.

Gage's perceptive gaze shifted from Cole to Slidell to Landon. "Everything okay?"

Landon nodded. "Slidell's just got a couple questions for Piper and Jake."

"All right. Well, I'm going to pull the trailer around back."

"We'll be out to help soon," Cole said.

"No worries." Gage whistled to get his group's attention. "If you'd all like to follow me, we've got some fresh lemonade and homemade muffins waiting for you."

The noise of the crowd rose in crescendo as they shuffled past, then slowly decreased until all that remained was a low murmuring emanating from the back garage.

Piper's brown eyes focused on Landon. "What's going on?"

Slidell cleared his throat. "I've got some questions for—"

"Wipe Out!" chimed again, and Slidell's face contorted with irritation.

"Tourist season." Cole shrugged. "We're lucky if we get a few minutes downtime all summer."

Kayden entered with a brown paper bag in one hand and a loaded drink tray precariously balanced in the other.

Slidell swooped past Landon. "Let me help you with that." He tugged at the drink carrier.

"I'm fine, really."

"I insist." He wrenched it from her and offered to carry the bag too.

"Signing up for another flight-seeing trip?" she asked.

Landon chuckled under his breath. Slidell signed up for anything and everything Kayden was part of.

"Nope. Afraid not." Slidell set the drink tray and bag on the counter. "I'm here on official business."

"Oh?"

Jake Westin emerged from the rear carrying a bin of kayak helmets.

"Ah." Sheriff Slidell strutted forward. "Just the man I wanted to see."

Jake set the tub on the counter and gazed at Slidell with the usual amount of indifference.

Though Jake had lived in Yancey for nearly a year, Slidell still treated him like a vagrant.

"I need to talk with Jake. Ask him a few questions."

Kayden flashed Cole an I-told-you-so look. "What'd he do?"

Cole grimaced. "He didn't do anything. Slidell needs to speak with both him and Piper about an air tank we rented out."

"Oh." Her superior air deflated. Clearly she thought she'd gotten the proof she needed to finally prove Cole wrong.

"What's this about an air tank?" Piper asked.

Landon swallowed, knowing the news would shake her. "A diver's body was found."

"Wearing one of your tanks," Slidell added before Landon could finish.

Landon heard Piper's gasp across the room.

Her eyes widened. "One of ours? Who was it?"

"She wasn't local," Landon said, hoping she'd find some solace in that.

"What do you need from us?" Kayden asked.

Slidell pulled his notepad from his shirt pocket and flipped through it until he found what he was looking for. "I've got the serial number off the tank. I need a name and any information you've got to go with it."

Jake linked his arms across his chest. "And, of course, you naturally assumed I'm the one who rented it to her."

"No one is assuming anything," Landon said, trying to diffuse the mounting tension between his boss and Jake. He didn't blame Jake for being irritated; Slidell had jumped to all the wrong conclusions again. But being confrontational wouldn't help matters.

Slidell, true to form, got within an inch of Jake's face. "You've been working the desk."

Jake didn't flinch. "So has Piper."

"I'll grab the ledger," Piper offered, always the peacemaker.

Kayden stood to the side, apprehension firm on her face.

Piper laid the book open on the counter. "Whenever you're ready, Sheriff."

He relayed the serial number.

"Got it. Twenty tanks rented out on the twenty-ninth. Due

back day after tomorrow." Piper's eyes scanned the page. "She was so young."

"How young?" Slidell asked.

"Eighteen, nineteen."

"So you remember her?"

"Yeah. She was really sweet." Piper retrieved the corresponding card from the file box and handed it to Slidell.

"Liz Johnson," he said. "What else can you tell me about her?"

"Not much. She was friendly, like I said, but kind of . . ."

"Kind of . . . ?" Slidell prodded.

"Evasive, I guess you could say. Private. We get a lot of people like that."

"Who was she with?"

Piper shrugged. "No one."

Slidell arched a brow. "The young lady rented twenty tanks for herself?"

"Said she was meeting up with friends. It was her job to get the tanks."

"She give any names?"

Piper shook her head. "Nope."

"Mention where she was from?"

"Said the West Coast."

"Say why she was diving?" Slidell's tone grew more clipped with each question.

"A pleasure trip, if I remember right."

"Twenty tanks' worth? That's a lot of diving." Slidell snorted.

"For all we knew, she had nine friends," Jake said. "We don't grill our customers."

Slidell hitched up his pants. "Maybe you should."

"We try making conversation," Cole explained. "Some like to talk. Others don't. That's their prerogative."

"I see." Slidell flipped to a clean page. "You got a credit card slip?"

Piper looked at the ledger and shook her head. "She paid cash."

"Cash? Didn't you find that a little suspicious?"

"A lot of divers prefer to work in cash," Cole said. "To not be tied down with credit cards. Gives you a certain level of anonymity."

Slidell's lips thinned. "Makes you harder to trace."

"It fits the lifestyle," Kayden said.

"What lifestyle is that?" Slidell pinned his gaze on Jake. "Drifter?"

Landon cleared his throat. "You'd think one of her friends would have reported her missing." His chest tightened. "What if she wasn't the only one? Maybe we should be sending out a search party."

Slidell frowned. "For who? We don't even know for sure anyone was with her."

"You said yourself it's highly unlikely twenty tanks were for one person," Landon pointed out, trying to keep his tone respectful. It was a difficult position to be in when you respected the office but not the man.

Slidell turned to Piper. "You didn't see anyone else around?"

"No."

"How'd she carry all the tanks?"

"I helped her load them into the back of a pickup," Jake said.

"Don't suppose you got the license plate?"

"It was out of state."

"Which one?"

"Washington."

Slidell's eyes narrowed. "Interesting you remember."

"I'm observant."

"Right." Slidell drummed his pen against the pad. "Well, I guess that solves where she's from."

"Not necessarily." Jake leaned against the counter. "It could have been a rental."

"Why don't you leave police work to the professionals," Slidell scoffed.

"He's right," Kayden said, and everyone's shocked gaze

flashed to her. "What?" she snapped. "I'm just saying they could have rented it."

Slidell smiled at her. "I'll check into it." He closed his notepad. "I suppose that's all I need." He glared at Jake. "For now."

As Jake approached Kayden, Landon wondered how heated a discussion was about to unfold.

Jake offered a smile of truce. "Thanks."

She looked up, surprised. "For what?"

He slid his hands in his jean pockets. "For backing me up on the license-plate thing."

Kayden leaned against the counter, crossing her arms. "I was just pointing out the obvious."

The sheltered expression settled back on Jake's face.

Cole leaned in to Landon and whispered, "I love my sister, but I sure wish she didn't always have to be hard as nails."

Landon nodded. Kayden and Piper were such opposites.

"Forget I said anything," Jake said.

She turned her back. "Already forgotten."

Following their rescheduled family dinner, Cole followed the familiar creak of the front porch swing to find Kayden stargazing, just as their mom had done every night until her last. When the pain had so contorted their mother's body that her legs failed her, Cole would carry her out bundled in her favorite quilt. As she had stared up at God's handiwork—the shimmering canopy of stars overhead—peace would fill her face. Peace despite the pain.

He wondered if Kayden sought such peace, returning every night as she did to the porch swing—picking up where their mother had left off.

Since they were young, the rhythmic creak of the swing had been their lullaby, the music they drifted off to sleep by. Even now it brought an inexplicable soothing to Cole's soul.

He took a step back, content to let Kayden enjoy her nightly ritual a bit longer, but a weathered plank groaned beneath his movement.

Kayden turned with a start.

"Sorry." He shrugged.

"It's fine." She pulled her knees to her chest.

He sank down beside her.

"Nice night." The moon was so full and bright it seemed but a handsbreadth away.

"Yeah, but I'm guessing that's not what brought you out here."

She knew him too well. He took a deep breath, bolstering for a fight. The sugary scent of lilac filled his lungs, and he savored the sweet smell of summer before responding. "I wanted to talk to you about Jake."

Her shoulders stiffened. "What about him?"

"You were pretty quick to assume the worst about him."

Her lips pursed a moment before she spoke. "We don't know anything about him."

"I know he's not tampering with our equipment, if that's what you're thinking."

"Sheriff Slidell seems interested in him."

"Slidell doesn't like competition."

Her eyes narrowed. "What do you mean?"

"Everyone in town knows Slidell has a thing for you, and evidently he thinks Jake's competition."

"Then he's crazy. I feel nothing for Jake but indifference."

"That's obvious. But why do you have to be so hard on him?"

"You think I should be like you, inviting a perfect stranger into our family, no questions asked?"

"He's not a stranger. I've seen him every day for close to a year."

"He showed up in Yancey with nothing but a duffel bag. He has no family that we know of, no past. He's a drifter."

"And that's so bad?"

"He could be a serial killer for all we know."

Cole chuckled. "You've been reading too many Patterson novels."

"I'm serious."

He inclined his head, his eyes meeting hers—they were always so full of fire. "When are you anything but?"

Piper stepped onto the porch, a bowl in hand. "Anything but what?"

"Nothing," Kayden said. Then her eyes narrowed. "What are you eating?"

"Hot fudge sundae with gummy bears."

"Uh. That's so bad for you."

Piper got a big spoonful and danced it around. "Afraid it will make you sweet?"

A smile cracked on Kayden's face. "You're a mess."

"Who's a mess?" Gage asked as he joined them on the porch.

"Piper," Kayden said with a sigh.

"Kayden's on her high, healthy horse again." Piper took another bite.

Gage mocked surprise. "Well, that's a first."

Kayden stood. "I'm going for a run before it gets too late."

"I'll go with you," Gage offered.

"Fine. I'll go change." She disappeared into the house.

"So." Gage squatted on the porch step. "I forgot to tell you, I saw Bailey Craig today."

Cole's heart fluttered. "How was she?"

"Didn't get a chance to find out. She bolted out of the general store and back to the Trading Post before I could cross the street. Gus said the funeral's tomorrow morning."

"Yeah."

Gage arched an assessing brow. "You going?"

"I am." He'd planned on paying his respects to Agnes all along, but God had laid another reason on his heart. Tomorrow would be one of the hardest of Bailey's life—laying her aunt to rest beneath the entire town's scrutiny.

He'd go and be a friendly face, though he doubted she'd consider him as such.

And he'd make sure Tom and Thoreau behaved if they showed. He wouldn't put a lewd advance past them, even at a funeral.

"I'm going too." Piper's hand rested on his shoulder. "I want to say good-bye to Lady Grey."

Cole clapped his hand atop hers. "That'll be nice. I'm sure Bailey can use the support."

Gage leaned against the railing. "I doubt she'll find much in Yancey."

Cole swallowed. "I'm sorry to say I think you're right."

"Then it'll be our job to befriend her," Piper said, forever the optimist.

Cole rubbed the back of his neck. He'd tried that once and it had nearly killed him.

"Befriend who?" Kayden asked, now clad in running attire.

"Bailey Craig," Piper said. "She's back for Agnes's funeral."

Kayden rose onto her toes, stretching her calf muscles. "Bailey Craig . . . I'd forgotten all about her."

Cole sighed. He hadn't.

8

Bailey yanked off the gray skirt and slipped the black trousers back on. The temperature had dropped nearly fifteen degrees overnight, and she hopped with jacket in hand to the pink shag rug in front of the full-length mirror.

She slid her arms in the cropped suit jacket and studied her reflection, wondering if the sleek black ensemble and a pair of sensible pumps would convince everyone in Yancey she was no longer the wild and reckless girl who left town right after graduation.

She smoothed the French twist she'd fashioned and slid another bobby pin in to secure it.

Her shoulders slumped, and she sighed. Who was she kidding? The proper hairstyle and attire wouldn't be enough to dispel her tarnished image. She'd forever be the town tramp in their eyes.

On her lone venture outside the shop to grab a bottle of OJ, she'd run smack into her past. Tom Murphy had been quick to invite her over for a drink, the leer in his eyes evidence of where he expected it to lead.

She'd promptly refused amidst the curious glances and whispered murmurings of the other customers.

Her heart hammering in her throat, she'd bolted back to the Post and hadn't left since.

She stared at her reflection. Dark shadows pooled beneath her puffy eyes and she dotted concealer on. It would do no good to let anyone see how much she was hurting. It never had.

She took a deep breath and exhaled slowly.

A few more days, a week at most, and she'd be back in her own comfy bed, not tossing and turning all night on the sofa— she couldn't face sleeping in her old bedroom, or Agnes's—her thigh littered with black-and-blue splotches from the sofa's prodding spring.

Back in Oregon she'd be surrounded by university colleagues and neighbors who knew she was a no-nonsense gal, devout in her faith, ordered and proper, an upstanding citizen with high moral standards.

Her bottom lip quivered.

None of that mattered today.

Her knees giving way beneath her, she retrieved the music box from the vanity table and sank on the edge of the bed.

Today was for Agnes.

Her tears bounced off the spray of roses donning the enameled lid.

Wrapping her arms about her waist, she rocked back and forth, her chest heaving with sobs.

Oh, Agnes. I miss you so much.

A cool summer breeze riffled through the dandelions smattered among the gravestones behind New Creation Church.

Pastor John spoke of God's gift of redemption through Jesus Christ and of His grace. Of Agnes being with the angels and in Christ's arms.

Bailey stiffened, wondering what would happen when she got to heaven. Christ had forgiven her. But would He embrace her?

The wind mingled sea air with the sweet scent of tulips donning the casket.

Bailey tugged at her jacket sleeves, rubbing the material until a warm friction ensued—anything to keep her distracted and the tears at bay.

The morning tide sloshed against the shore, leaving white foam bubbling on the sand. Spray billowed through the tufts of sea grass.

Agnes loved the sea. Always had. It seemed almost fitting her life had ended there.

A gull's cry echoed over the crashing waves, and Bailey followed its flight until it faded into the horizon, before casting her attention back on Pastor John.

He'd aged over the years. His hair and moustache were now a silvery gray, his dark eyes dimmer than she recalled.

His gaze met hers, and she sensed a new level of humility, or was it pity?

She supposed anything was better than the stern, disapproving glares she used to receive. Perhaps old age had softened him.

The dip in his voice reined her attention in tighter.

"Agnes requested in her will that we close her funeral by singing her favorite hymn."

Bailey fought to remain erect, willing her knees not to buckle as they swayed beneath her and the burgeoning tears not to fall. No one in Yancey would see her cry. *Ever.* No matter how much she hurt. She'd promised herself years ago and she wouldn't break it now.

Pastor John cleared his throat. " 'Amazing Grace . . .' "

A myriad of voices joined in. " '. . . how sweet the sound . . .' "

Just sing. Sing and breathe. You won't cry. Not in front of them. Her hands shook and her body trembled as the words left her mouth. " 'That saved a wretch like me.' " The words hit home with a bolt that shook her, always did. " 'I once was lost, but now am found . . .' "

Thank you, Jesus, for finding me. For saving me. I know Agnes is with you now and that brings me peace despite the heartache. "Peace I leave with you; My peace I give you. I do not give to you as the world gives. Do not let your hearts be troubled and do not be afraid."

The song concluded and after a closing prayer, Pastor John excused everyone assembled.

Bailey kept her gaze downcast as people shuffled past. So many pairs of shoes moving by. So many who loved Agnes.

In a few minutes they'd all be gone and she could say a proper good-bye, without anyone peering on. She'd tell her aunt how much she loved her and how desperately she'd miss hearing that gravelly voice coming over the phone line, encouraging her, prodding her on . . . even chastising her when she needed a good kick in the pants.

"Bailey." A hand rested on her shoulder.

She flinched, her heart nearly stopping.

It wasn't Pastor John, but she knew the voice. It haunted her often in her dreams.

Her heart sank as she gazed up into those eyes—the same seafoam green ones that first filled her with joy and then with shame.

It'd been futile thinking she could avoid him in a town Yancey's size. He was as much a part of the place as tides were the ocean. Every memory of Yancey was wrapped up in him. Her best and worst.

"Sorry." Cole offered a weak smile. "I didn't mean to startle you."

She blinked. It was all she was capable of.

He extended a hand. "It's Cole . . . McKenna."

She prayed the tumultuous emotions reeling through her didn't show on her face. "I remember." Her voice sounded weak, pathetic.

He held his hand in the air a moment and then slid it in his trouser pocket. "I wanted to tell you how sorry I am about Agnes."

She nodded, the words too thick in her throat to speak.

The boy she'd once loved had grown into a man—a tall, muscular, heartbreakingly handsome man.

"Are you planning to be in town long?" he asked.

She shook her head. *Please, go away. I'm not strong enough for this. Not now.*

The fresh, woodsy scent of his aftershave carried on the breeze, followed closely by the scent of . . . *honeysuckle?*

A petite brunette slid from behind Cole and linked her arm with his.

Perfect. Now I get to meet his wife.

The woman smiled gently, and Bailey fought the urge to wither from sight. Of course she'd be lovely and sweet and everything perfect. She was Cole's. He deserved no less.

"Not sure if you remember my baby sister, Piper." Cole squeezed the woman's shoulder.

Bailey schooled her features, hoping not to reveal any hint of the strange relief sweeping through her.

Piper rested her hand on Bailey's arm. "I'm so sorry for your loss. Our town potlucks won't be the same without Miss Agnes's sourdough fruitcakes." Her eyes glistened with tears. "Yancey won't be the same without her."

"Thank you," Bailey managed. If they didn't leave soon, they'd witness her burst into tears, and that couldn't happen. Not here. Not in front of *him.* "I should . . ." She pointed to the casket.

"Of course." Piper stepped back. "Sorry to have kept you."

"Thank you for coming." She turned to stride away, working to keep her breathing even.

Cole grasped hold of her arm, and she shuddered.

He let go. "Sorry." His eyes held hers, boring into her. "I just wanted to say if you need anything, anything at all, while you're in Yancey, give me a call. I'm in the book."

"That goes for us all," Piper said. "Kayden and I are in the book too."

Bailey swallowed. It hurt to hold Cole's tender gaze. It was too kind. "Thanks. I really should . . ." Without finishing her sentence, she strode to Agnes's casket and remained still until she heard their footsteps fade. Only then did she allow the tears to fall.

9

Piper squeezed Cole's arm. "She seemed so sad."

"I'm sure she is, kid."

He glanced over his shoulder at Bailey standing beside the casket, her back to him—her shoulders finally slack.

She'd remained so stiff during the service—a blank expression on her face, her jaw rigid.

His heart went out to her. For all she was going through and all she'd been through.

She'd always put on a brave front, pretending the crude nickname and teasing gossip didn't hurt her. Maybe it hadn't, but he doubted it.

She couldn't help but feel something at being used by the boys and teased by the girls. Never having any true friends, no real love outside of Agnes. Maybe he should have been kinder. Tried harder. Shown some mercy and forgiveness. But he'd been hurt too. He'd loved her once, and she'd stomped on his heart without any remorse.

But . . .

He sighed.

If he'd been a true friend, he would have tried yanking her back from the slippery slope she was hurtling down, instead of standing by and watching her self-destruct.

Was it too late to make amends? Too late to part on better terms?

She turned, her tear-filled eyes meeting his, and his breath hitched.

She wiped her face, turned heel, and strode away.

Tom and Thoreau were right about one thing. Bailey was still gorgeous, though in a softer, more natural way. Gone was the heavy black eyeliner, the deep red lipstick. Instead, a soft rose blushed her cheeks and supple lips. The only adornment to her striking blue eyes was her long silky lashes that fluttered when she blinked.

She was so much more beautiful now.

"Cole," Slidell hollered from across the street.

He waved, signaling he'd heard him, then turned to Piper, who remained at his side. "I better see what he wants."

Piper nodded. "Okay, I'll catch up with you later."

He planted a kiss on the top of her head. "Thanks for coming today."

"You bet." With a quick wave to Slidell, she headed to her Jeep.

With a sigh, Cole crossed the street, avoiding the flood of tourists plowing up the hill en route to the shops of Main Street. Like a flock clinging to their shepherd, they clumped together, struggling to stay close to their tour guide, the panic on their faces evidence of their fear—fear of missing some factoid of history, a clever anecdote, a shop suggestion. If they didn't slow down, they'd totally miss the beauty Tariuk had to offer—the rugged mountain peaks still laced with snow, the fresh sea air, the colorful shops and people that called Yancey home.

"I hate tourist season." Slidell banked his gum wrapper off the trash can.

"I thought you were on board with the mayor's plan to build a dock on the west shore large enough for cruise ships so the tourists didn't have to be shuttled over by smaller boats."

Slidell folded a fresh piece of gum in his mouth. "Don't get me wrong. What's good for Yancey's economy is good for Yancey, so I'm all for it. But it doesn't mean I like the throng of outsiders stampeding through my streets four months out of the year."

"Always the politician."

"Hey, mine is an elected position. I have to do what's right by the people."

Cole still wondered how his neighbors had voted for Slidell in the first place, but the fact was they were stuck with him for another year. It wasn't that Slidell was a bad man; he simply cared more for his image than for seeing justice done.

"Booth called."

"Okay?" Cole slid his hands in his trouser pockets.

"He's finished the girl's autopsy and found something he wants you to see."

His heart lurched. Had a problem been discovered with the equipment? He prayed not.

Slidell lifted his chin. "Shall we?"

Cole nodded and followed Slidell the three blocks down and two blocks over to the morgue.

Landon and a very impatient-looking Mayor Cox met them out front of the two-story brick building that sat adjacent to the north side of the sheriff's station.

Cox held up his fist, a crumpled wad of paper seized inside. "What is the meaning of this?"

"Care to elaborate, Neil?" Slidell asked.

Cox unclenched his fingers, smoothing out the flyer the best he could. "How could you paste this girl's face all over town?"

"Not hard," Landon replied. "Deputy Earl Hansen made up the flyer at the station. Armed with a box of them and a staple gun, it took me less than an hour."

Cox tapped his foot in a rapid, caffeine-fueled pace. "Less than an hour to scare off our livelihood."

"I beg your pardon?" Landon narrowed his gaze. "Are you suggesting we should impede the investigation of a woman's death so that we don't scare off the tourists?"

"Not impede—simply . . ."

Landon's jaw tightened. "Simply, what?"

Cox's agitated gaze shifted to Slidell. "What are you trying to accomplish with these flyers?"

"We're trying to get a lead on the woman's identity."

"Isn't there a more subtle way to accomplish that? Questioning our townsfolk rather than frightening our tourists?"

"We are working our way through the community," Landon said. "So far—other than Piper and Jake—no one remembers seeing her."

"Fine. Continue with your investigation, but would it kill you to be discreet?"

Color crept up Landon's neck. "A woman's dead."

"I understand that, and while it's very unfortunate, there is no need to go scaring the tourists."

Irritation at the mayor's lack of concern and lack of decency bit at Cole. "A person dies and you're worried about image?"

"I'm worried about the people of this island. A lot of folks' livelihood hinges on tourist season."

"Last Frontier Adventures included," Cole said. "But some things are more important." *Like justice.*

"All I'm asking for is a little consideration for our shopkeepers."

"We'll take that into account, Mayor," Slidell said in a conciliatory tone.

Cole looked at Landon. They both knew what that meant. Slidell would cave to Cox's wishes. He always did. But that didn't mean a concerned citizen couldn't keep flyers posted in his shop window.

"If we're done here . . ." Slidell glanced at his watch. "We've got an appointment with Booth, and we're late."

Cox straightened his tie. "Of course."

"You're welcome to come along," Landon said. "Maybe you'd feel something for the woman if you saw her."

"I don't think that's necessary." Cox took a step back. "I'll leave you gentlemen to your business while I attend to mine." He turned heel and scuttled away.

Landon shook his head. "He's got some nerve."

Cole followed Landon and Slidell into the morgue, the building temperature a solid twenty degrees colder than the outside air.

Nancy Bowen sat behind the front desk. With the receiver wedged between her right shoulder and head, her hands were free for touching up her nail polish. Deep red.

She caught sight of Landon and her cheeks flushed. "I gotta call you back," she muttered into the phone before resting it in the cradle. "How can I help you boys?"

"Booth called," Slidell said, straight to the point.

"You can go on back."

She stood as Landon filed past. "Good to see you again, Landon."

"Nice to see you too."

Her smile spread.

Cole leaned over once they were out of earshot. "Miss Matchmaker will be pleased."

Landon's lips thinned. "Don't you dare say anything to encourage her. I'm ready to strangle Piper as it is."

"Gentlemen," Booth said as they entered the windowless room.

The odor of flesh and death clung to the white tile walls and floor. A soiled lab coat hung on a hook beside the large stainless-steel sink.

"Cole, I'm glad you came along." Booth slipped on a fresh pair of gloves. "There's something I want you to see." He moved to the body on the exam table and lifted the sheet draped over it.

Liz Johnson lay with eyes closed. Her chest was stitched up, her skin gray beneath the fluorescent lighting and marred with black splotches.

Not long ago she'd been alive—laughing, smiling, with no clue she'd soon be lying on a cold stainless-steel table, being observed by strangers as a piece of evidence. A shiver snaked up Cole's spine.

Booth lifted the woman's hand and adjusted the light to fall on it. "I wanted your opinion on what I found under several of her nails."

Cole narrowed his gaze, focusing on the reddish-brown substance imbedded under her nail. "Looks like calcite."

"Mmm-hmm." Booth nodded.

"What exactly is calcite?" Sheriff Slidell asked, irritation lacing his voice. Booth deferred to Cole.

"It's a mineral found in caves. Sheets of it grow on the floors and walls. They're called flowstones."

Slidell hitched up his pants. "Is that right?"

Booth nodded. "Owen Matthews made the trip down here from Kodiak." His gaze shifted to Cole. "Good recommendation, by the way."

"I'm glad." Cole swallowed, almost afraid to ask. "Did he find anything?"

"Actually, yes, he found recent surface damage on her air tanks that is consistent with maneuvering through the tight constraints of underwater caves." He moved to the tanks that rested on a nearby table and pointed to the area.

"Any other problems with the equipment?" Slidell asked.

Cole squeezed his fists, fear niggling at him.

A crooked smile broke on Booth's craggy face. "Matthews's findings were that there was absolutely nothing wrong with the equipment."

An enormous wave of relief washed over Cole. "You're certain?"

"Positive. Matthews said the equipment was in perfect condition, other than the damage he suspects occurred while the victim was squeezing through some tight cave passageways."

"Victim?" Landon said.

Booth nodded, moving back to the body.

"You're certain?" Slidell asked.

"Quite. Cause of death was suffocation."

Slidell frowned. "Was there a problem with her air supply?"

"No. She suffocated as a result of a crushed trachea. I found bruises on her neck consistent with someone grabbing her from behind, as well as defensive wounds on her hands and forearms."

"She fought her attacker," Landon said.

Booth nodded, grimly. "She didn't die quick. Bruises on her shoulders indicate someone held her down."

"So someone grabbed her from behind like this"—Landon used Cole for demonstration purposes, wrapping his fingers tight around Cole's neck—"crushed her trachea as she struggled, then"—he moved his hands to Cole's shoulders—"held her down until she suffocated?"

"I'm afraid so."

Slidell's jaw tightened. "So we're dealing with murder?"

Booth nodded. "Yes, sir, we are."

10

Bailey slipped her jacket over the chair back, her heart still hammering in her throat.

Cole McKenna. The one person she'd longed to avoid, yet ached to see.

Her hands trembled, and she put them to use unwinding her hair. She flung the bobby pins into a mishmash on the desk and stared at them, refusing to close her eyes for fear of picturing Cole, his powerful gaze searing through her.

While his eyes held no condemnation, nothing to fill her with shame, she was brimming over with it—the insatiable inner anguish that said she didn't belong, that she wasn't enough.

Butterscotch leapt on her lap, and she nuzzled him close.

Too many memories lingered in this place, too much pain—raw and on the surface.

Time to put Cole and Yancey behind her for good . . . time to stop wondering what might have been.

Placing the cat in his favorite spot—the right corner of the window display—so he could sun himself, Bailey moved into the kitchen and put on a kettle of tea. She had a long day of work cut out for her; she might as well arm herself with nourishment.

A plate of oatmeal cookies in one hand, a steaming mug of lavender tea in the other, she approached the overwhelming mess in front of her with optimism. The sooner it was done, the sooner she could leave Yancey once and for all.

Starting with the nearest pile, she dove into the arduous task of organizing Agnes's files.

Halfway through the first stack, a knock rapped on the door.

She glanced up, half praying it wasn't Cole and half praying it was.

An elderly man cupped his hands to the glass and peered in. When he spotted her, he smiled.

No doubt a tourist, they flooded the town today.

She rose and unlocked the door. "I'm sorry, we're . . ."

The man was tall, with a robust midsection. His weight was braced against a gnarled wooden cane, his labored breaths coming in uneven bouts.

"Are you all right?"

He nodded, though taking a moment to compose himself. "That's a—" he took another wheezy breath—"long walk up here." His thinning brown hair was heavily interspersed with gray, his beard and moustache completely silver. He coughed, then managed a weak smile. "I forget I'm not getting any younger."

"Please. Why don't you come in?"

She helped him inside and into a chair.

Perspiration clung to his forehead. Pulling a handkerchief from his trousers, he dabbed his face.

He wore a casual dress shirt, white with blue pinstripes, sleeves clasped with a pair of gold cufflinks, and a blue sweater-vest.

His gaze swept across the shop.

The afternoon sun streaming in the front windows lit and warmed the room. Bailey glanced at the clock beside her empty mug and realized she'd been working nearly two hours. She stared at the meager dent she'd managed to make and groaned.

"Looks like you have quite the project going."

"I'm trying to get things in order."

"I see." He hoisted himself out of the chair, his weight readily fixed on the cane. "Well, I shan't keep you long. I am in the market for a tea glass holder." His gaze wandered to the display case. "I see you have several. Perhaps you can help me choose one. It's for my Nessie."

"Your wife?"

"Aye, going on fifty-four years."

"Congratulations."

"Nessie would have been here herself, but she fell and broke her hip last winter, and she's not much for walking since. I told her I'd scurry up here and get her a holder, not to worry."

"Oh." Bailey bit her bottom lip.

"Something the matter?"

"It's just . . . I'm not actually open."

Confusion flitted across his face. "Not open?"

"I'm getting the place ready for sale."

"Sale?" His hand shook and the cane with it. "She's selling the Trading Post?"

"She?" Bailey moved closer to steady him.

He sank back onto the chair. "The dear lady who owns this place."

Bailey swallowed, the words still hard to manage. "Agnes, the owner," she clarified, "she passed away."

"Oh dear." His coloring paled.

"Did you know her?"

"Not well, of course. But Nessie and I have been taking this cruise every August for the last decade. The Trading Post is always our first stop. Nessie and Agnes . . ." He inclined his head to make sure he'd got the name right and Bailey indicated he had. He continued. "The two of them would get talking, and nine times out of ten, the Trading Post was the only stop we were able to make before our ship headed out again." He exhaled with a wheeze. "Poor Nessie's going to be so disappointed. And Agnes . . ." He shook his head in dismay. "Was it cancer? It's always cancer nowadays." He spoke with the anguish of a man who'd lost a loved one to the dreaded disease.

"It was an accident." Bailey cleared the lump in her throat. "A plane crash."

72

"Oh my. I don't care what they say. A ton of metal is not meant to be airborne. That's why Nessie and I only travel by ship, car, or train."

Bailey wrapped her arms around her waist. "Can't say I blame you." As eager as she was to leave Yancey, she wasn't looking forward to the flight.

"Now you're selling the place." He looked around and shook his head. "Another shame."

"I am only selling to someone who will keep it the Trading Post." She felt the need to explain.

"I'm sure Agnes would have appreciated that." His eyes narrowed, and he studied her a bit more carefully. "If you're selling the place . . . were you related to her?"

"She is—" Bailey caught herself—"was . . . my aunt."

"Aunt Agnes." He seemed to like the ring of that. "I bet she was a wonderful aunt."

"The best." Bailey withstood the prick of tears.

The man clutched his cane and grappled to his feet, unsteady enough to make Bailey nervous. He smiled at her, his expression soft and warm. "Well, I've taken enough of your time, my dear. Nessie will understand." He hobbled toward the door.

"Wait." What would it hurt to make one sale?

He paused, a brow arched.

"I'm sure we can handle a sale on our own. I worked here all through high school."

"I don't want to be any trouble. . . ."

"It's no trouble at all."

The man's face lit.

Bailey watched the elderly gentleman cross Main Street. Safely on the other side, he turned and waved.

She returned the gesture and watched until he hobbled out of sight, feeling good she'd been able to help him. She felt confident his wife would love the tea glass holder. It was the best Agnes had in stock—silver, dating to the mid-nineteenth century, the detailing exquisite.

Butterscotch rubbed against her leg, purring.

"Our first sale," she said with a smile that quickly faded. "Our first and only."

It was silly to be surprised that she'd enjoyed playing proprietress. She always had enjoyed helping Agnes around the shop. It was the glances and snickers of the local customers that wore her down.

A crazy idea filled her head. Perhaps she could move the stock back to Oregon and reopen the Post there. Then she could have the best of both worlds—running the Post and not having to face her past every day.

She lifted Butterscotch into her arms. "What do you think, Scotch? It's not such a bad idea."

She carried him to the kitchen and poured him a saucer of milk.

Leaning against the doorjamb, she watched him lap up the milk.

Move the Trading Post. Agnes would think it a horrid idea. It had existed in Yancey as far back as anyone knew. For a town so immersed in history, the Post was a cornerstone of Yancey's identity.

No, her only option was to find a buyer fast. She wasn't strong enough to keep combating the memories, or the pain they evoked.

He tossed his cane on the bed and peeled the gray moustache and beard from his face, rubbing his tingling skin.

"How'd it go, boss?" Kiril stood in the doorway, keeping his distance respectful. "Is she going to be any trouble?"

He pulled the pillow from his shirt and tossed it beside the cane. "I don't think so. It sounds like she's going to put everything where it belongs and sell."

"What about the papers?"

"We'll wait until she gets them back in place from wherever the old lady hid them, then we'll go in and take them."

"And the girl?"

"As long as she stays out of my way, I'll stay out of hers." No sense drawing attention to himself. Planes crashed all the time, no one would tie that to him. Nik and the girl . . . they were inconsequential. And besides, Nik had left him no choice. But if something happened to the old lady's niece, questions would arise. Better to bide his time.

"You still want me to keep an eye on her?" Kiril asked.

He pulled off the wig that had added twenty years. "A very *close* eye."

The girl was bright, with a doctorate in Russian Studies. And she was the only one with access to the old lady's files. While her plan was to organize things and sell, the remote chance existed she'd come across what he needed and recognize it for what it was.

If that happened, he'd have no choice. He'd have to get rid of her just as he had her dear old aunt.

11

Landon tossed what he hoped was the last kernel of popcorn in the trash. Leave it to Cole to start a game of popcorn toss, which—given the fact the group consisted of a dozen teenagers—had morphed into an all-out popcorn war.

At least the kids had a blast. For a few of them, youth group was the only place they could relax and be themselves. Despite the mess, it'd been a great idea, though he'd not readily admit it—it'd only encourage Cole's quest for the messiest game ever.

Cole cut the vacuum cleaner. "All clear over there?"

Landon got to his feet. "I believe so."

Cole chuckled. "You might want to take another look."

Landon glanced down at himself. Popcorn kernels clung to every nook and cranny of his henley. He leaned over the trash and brushed himself off, then straightened. "Next time I'm in charge of games and you're in charge of cleanup."

Cole grinned. "Fair enough." He wound up the cord and slid the vacuum in the storage closet. "It was a good group tonight."

Landon sat on the edge of the empty snack table. "Yeah it was. Glad to see Jesse made it." The kid reminded him of himself. Same drive, same hunger. Same penchant for pushing the limits.

"Zach gave him a lift in."

"That's what Jesse said." Landon eyed his friend. "You really worry about him, don't you?" As youth group leader, Cole worried about them all—always looking out for those in need, always trying to pull the lost back into the fold. But Jesse Ryan seemed to hold a special place in his heart.

"I'm not a big fan of his stepdad."

None of them were. Samuel Hancock married Jesse's mom, Sue, less than a year after Jesse's dad died in a hunting accident. A hunting trip Samuel Hancock had been on.

Once the vows were taken, Hancock let it be known he'd be a lot happier if he wasn't shackled with a kid.

"At least Jesse seems to be on the straight and narrow. I think the time you spend with him has really helped. Most everyone in town had already given up on the kid." He remembered what that felt like.

"He's a good kid in a bad situation. If he can make it a couple more years, finish high school and go on to college, he'll be fine."

"Can his family afford college?" The Hancocks didn't exactly live well. A rusted double-wide on the outskirts of town hardly boded well for college ambitions.

"His dad was smart. He had a stipulation in his will that if he died before Jesse graduated college, a certain amount would be set aside for that purpose. Fortunately, Samuel can't weasel that away from Jesse's mom. We just need to help Jesse stay on the straight and narrow until then."

"He will." They'd make sure of it.

"I hope so." Cole gave a halfhearted shrug.

Landon narrowed his eyes. "What?" What was Cole holding back?

He exhaled. "When Piper told me about the theft at the library, Jesse immediately sprang to mind. He's been spending a lot of time over there, and with the vandalism he and his gang did there last winter . . ." He shook his head. "I feel rotten I assumed the worst."

"Don't beat yourself up. Given Jesse's history, it's a natural assumption." Though he knew how deadly assumptions could prove to be. "But I honestly don't think he had anything to do with it."

"You spoke with him?"

"In a roundabout sort of way." The last thing he'd wanted to do was hamper the trust they'd built with Jesse.

"Thanks, man."

"Don't mention it."

"So . . . if Jesse didn't take it, who do you think did?"

"I still half expect it to turn up somewhere. Mrs. Anderson is notorious for misplacing things."

"Piper's convinced it was stolen."

Landon sighed. "Believe me, I know." He wouldn't say anything bad about the girl, certainly not in front of Cole, but sometimes she drove him nuts—always coming up with theories and trying to tag along on his cases. If she wasn't so annoying, he might actually find it endearing. She was the pesky little sister he never had.

Cole chuckled. "I figured she came to you."

"She's convinced it'll turn up for sale on eBay."

"I know. She's been watching it like a hawk. I blame it on one too many Nancy Drew mysteries."

Landon cracked a grin. "Speaking of books . . . I've got something for her."

He pulled a bag out from the front seat of his truck and handed it to Cole.

Cole peered inside the bag and read the title. *"Butt Out! Breaking the Busybody Habit in Five Easy Steps."* He chuckled. "She's not going to like this."

Landon grinned, feeling like a schoolboy. "I know."

"I'll drop it at the shop on my way home." Cole tossed it on the seat of his truck.

"I'd love to see her expression, but I think it's best I'm not present when she opens it."

"You think?" Cole climbed in his truck and started the engine. "I hate to see the payback on this one."

"I'll worry about that when it comes."

"If you live that long."

Landon laughed.

"Thanks for helping again tonight."

"No problem. I enjoy working with the kids."

"Next week?"

"Sure."

"Great. Now get some sleep. You look wiped."

Landon sighed. "Long day."

"Any luck?"

He shook his head. "Spent all day at the docks, looking for whoever may have rented a slip to our gal or ferried her out there, but no luck. No one recognized Liz's description."

"She had to get the boat somewhere. It stands to reason if she rented the tanks in Yancey, she most likely rented the boat here too."

"I know." Landon rubbed the back of his neck, his muscles tightly coiled. "It doesn't make sense."

"Have you tried Cleary yet?"

"Old Man Cleary?" He was a piece of work. Crusty and ornery, Cleary lived to torment others.

"He still rents out a few slips."

Landon grimaced. "That's right. I'll take a drive out to his place tomorrow."

"Good luck with that."

"Yeah, thanks."

"If you need any help, let me know."

"I appreciate it. I keep thinking someone will report our girl missing, but so far nothing."

"She wasn't diving alone."

"I know, which means her dive buddy either killed her or is unable to report her missing."

"You think there's another victim out there?"

Landon sighed. "I pray not."

Cole entered the shop a half hour before closing.

Piper looked up from the counter and smiled. "Hey, Cole."

"Hey, kid. Where's Jake?"

"Grabbing another box of those all-natural power bars from the back. They're selling like hotcakes. But don't tell Kayden. She doesn't need to know she was right again."

"Trust me." Cole kissed the top of her head. "I know better." He eyed the stack of envelopes and labels strewn across the counter. "Looks like you've got a project going."

"Invites for my birthday barbeque."

"You have a birthday coming up?"

She'd only been talking about it for a month. They were all hoping Reef would make it home this year, but Cole wasn't holding his breath. It'd been five years since he'd seen his brother. Five years too long. At least he always remembered Piper with a gift. It wasn't always on time, but it was always extravagant.

Piper tapped the pencil against her full bottom lip. "I feel like I'm forgetting somebody." She handed him the guest list. "Do you see anyone I'm missing?"

Cole skimmed it and chuckled. "You've pretty much invited the entire town."

She bit her bottom lip. "Okay, it's a lot, but I didn't want anyone to feel left out."

"That's sweet." And so Piper. She put everybody's feelings before her own.

"Anyone you want to add?"

"Actually, there is." He'd send one to Bailey. It couldn't be easy losing Agnes, the closest thing she had to a mother. He knew what it was like to lose a parent, both in fact. He'd send the invite with a personal note, show her not everyone in Yancey was trapped in high school like Murphy and Thoreau. Perhaps it would even give them a chance to part on better terms.

"The more the merrier."

"For what?" Jake emerged from the rear with box in hand.

"My birthday bash—and I expect you to be there. I know you're not Mr. Social, but it wouldn't be the same without you. It's Sunday afternoon. Say you'll come."

"Wouldn't miss it for the world, darling." Jake winked.

"Yay." She clapped, then turned her attention to Cole. Propping her elbows on the counter, her eyes alight with glee, she asked, "Soooo, who are you inviting?"

"Bailey Craig."

"Good idea." He could practically see the wheels turning. Always the matchmaker.

"I almost forgot. I've got something for you."

"An early present?"

"I suppose you could say that. It's from Landon."

Her eyes narrowed. "What'd he send *this* time?"

Cole handed her the bag, and she yanked the book out, her eyes skimming the title.

Jake read over her shoulder and burst out laughing.

She turned and Jake smothered his laugh, pronto.

She stuffed the book back in the bag. "He thinks I'm a busybody. Fine. I'm through trying to help him."

"You've got to admit you've been riding him pretty hard about Nancy." Cole wished he could swallow the words back the minute he said them.

Color flared in her face. "It's not my fault Landon is too stupid to see what a great lady Nancy is. I mean, what she sees in him I'll never know. He's gruff, and messy, and spends entirely too much time at his cabin with his dog. He has no fashion sense whatsoever. . . ."

She paused for breath, and Cole jumped in. "Don't take it out on the messenger."

"You're right. I'm sorry." She blew a stray hair from her face. "He just makes me so mad. But—" she took a deep breath and exhaled, a mischievous gleam breaking on her face—"there's always payback. . . ."

Cole shook his head. It seemed the two lived to annoy each other. They were worse than Gage and Kayden growing up—always trying to one-up the other.

"I'm glad I didn't cross you," Jake murmured, stuffing snack bars into the basket.

"Wise man," she murmured, a grin spreading on her face.

Cole was almost afraid to ask. "What?"

She practically glowed. "I just thought of the perfect payback."

"I don't want to know."

"It's probably best you don't."

"On that note, I'm outta here." He kissed the top of Piper's head. "Try not to be too devious."

"What would be the fun in that?"

With a chuckle, Cole stepped out of the shop and into a gorgeous night. Stars blanketed the charcoal sky, and the temperature hovered at a balmy fifty degrees. The tourists had returned to their ships, and the town once again belonged to the locals.

While most of Yancey was settling down for the night, Cole was far from it.

Seeing Bailey again had triggered something inside him. Something he couldn't wrap his mind around—it danced on his tongue, fluttered across his subconscious, but he couldn't grasp hold. Frustration oozed inside, taunting him. A flame, long dead, had been rekindled.

12

Cole woke to a ringing phone. "McKenna," he answered, blinking the haze of sleep from his eyes.

"Looks like we may have found our gal's boat," Landon said.

Cole rolled onto his back, blinking against the sun's rays slipping through the blinds. "Cleary rented it?"

"Yeah, and it gets better. Coast Guard got a call shortly after dawn about a boat run aground on the reef in Herring Cove. You interested in towing it in?"

"Absolutely." He looked at the clock. "I'll meet you at the marina in a half hour."

"I'll bring coffee."

Climbing from bed, Cole took a quick, brisk shower and then downed a bowl of cereal. Grabbing his gear, he headed across his property to the boat launch.

Owning one of only two boats on the island capable of refloating and towing disabled vessels, he and Gage were called on often—yet another one of their many services. The majority of the time inexperienced sailors were to blame, but occasionally a more serious matter presented itself. He had the feeling today's would fall in the latter category.

The sun hung orange over the horizon, signaling another warm day as he steered the *North Star* around Tariuk's southern shore. Skirting the rock-strewn inlets, he maneuvered his way to the house Gage rented. Situated on the very tip of the south shore, Gage's cabin boasted a decent dock and plenty of privacy. Cole pulled up to the pier and cut the engine. Only the rhythmic lap of the waves and the occasional rustle of leaves broke the silence.

Securing the *Star* to the dock, he walked the pier's length, noting the absence of Gage's kayak. No wonder he hadn't answered his phone.

Sitting down, Cole let his feet dangle over the edge as he relaxed against a piling. He hoped Gage would show soon or he'd be forced to make the trip without him.

Fortunately it wasn't long before the steady stroke of an oar gliding through the water reached his ears. A few minutes later, Gage rounded the bend. Shirtless, his muscles flexed with each rhythmic row. Catching sight of Cole, he waved.

"I tried calling," Cole said as he helped Gage lift the kayak onto shore.

"What's up?"

"I got a call from Landon. It looks like they found our victim's boat. I could use your help towing her in."

Gage wiped the sweat from his brow. "Sure. Just let me grab a shirt."

"Maybe take a moment and swipe on some deodorant."

Gage smiled. "No promises."

A little shy of seven o'clock, they pulled the *North Star* into Yancey's marina and found the place practically empty. All commercial fishermen were long gone and any serious recreational ones had joined them. Fish were most plentiful and easiest to catch at sunrise and sunset. It didn't surprise Cole the call had come in shortly after dawn.

Landon waited on the pier, three cups of steaming coffee in hand and a bag of gear at his feet.

Cole eyed the crime-scene kit. "Something we should know?"

Landon climbed aboard. "I'll explain on the way."

An hour later, Cole maneuvered past the breakers, easy on the draft around Blindman's Bluff and into Herring Cove.

The sloop, one of Cleary's old CAL 2–27s, was run aground on a reef at the far end of the cove.

"Watch where you step," Landon instructed as they climbed aboard the abandoned vessel.

An awful stench assailed Cole—cloying and dense, like rotting hamburger on a hot summer day. "What on earth?"

Landon had said the fisherman who made the call had mentioned a problem on the boat—but what would cause such a stink?

"This can't be good." Gage clapped a hand across his face, turning from the putrid funk with revulsion.

Cole peered into the dark galley and the malevolent odor thickened. His stomach lurched, his gag reflex kicking in.

Landon rested a hand on his shoulder. "You don't want to go in there."

Blood covered nearly every inch of the area he could see. "Dear God."

"Let's seal it and get it towed back."

Landon stretched a large sheet of plastic over the galley entrance while Gage and Cole helped secure it in place.

"Doc Powell said Liz's flesh wounds were all postmortem."

"Yeah." Landon crisscrossed yellow crime-scene tape atop the plastic.

"From the amount of blood . . ." Cole turned his head to take a deep breath of sea air. "I'm assuming we're looking at a second victim?"

Landon nodded grimly.

The galley sealed off, Cole and Gage set to work refloating the vessel.

Running aground on the reef, compounded by the constant up-and-down motion of the wind and tide, had left serious damage to the ship's hull.

Cole set to the task of tacking, leaving the jib sheeted in place while keeping the mainsail tightly trimmed. With the high tide, the boat quickly spun, heeling over and reducing the draft. He released the windward jib sheet and retrimmed the leeward winch.

Once free of the rock and in deep water, Gage hooked the vessel up to their tow package.

"Cleary's not going to be happy," Landon said, leaning against the pilothouse door.

Cole grimaced. "Can't say I blame him this time."

Cleary met them at the docks, his wrinkled face pinched tight. "My ship, my beautiful ship."

"Now, settle down," Landon said. "We'll help you fix it up good as new."

Cleary's dark eyes narrowed. "Is that police tape? What on earth did they do?"

"I'm afraid I can't say."

"Then get out of my way and I'll see for myself."

Landon blocked his passage. "I can't let you on."

"It's my ship."

"Right now it's a crime scene."

"Crime?"

Landon cleared his throat. "I'm not at liberty to discuss any details." He wasn't announcing that it looked as if they had another murder on their hands. News spread too fast. By lunchtime, the whole town would be in an uproar. They were already garnering more attention than he'd wanted. Tourists slowed as they passed the docks, squinting at the ship in question.

"When can I have my boat back?"

"Hopefully soon."

"Come on, Cleary," Gage said, wrapping an arm around the old man's shoulders. "Why don't we go over to Gus's and grab some grub while they get this mess sorted out."

Cleary didn't bat an eye.

"On me," Gage offered.

"All right, but that doesn't fix things. I shoulda known better than rent to outsiders. Who's gonna fix my boat?"

"We'll all see to it," Landon said.

One of the perks of living in a small town, they all looked out for one another. Most of the time.

Gage steered Cleary up the pier as Slidell ambled his way down, Mayor Cox fast on his heels.

"Wonderful," Landon murmured beneath his breath.

"What do we got?" Slidell asked before taking a sip of coffee.

Landon lowered his voice, "I'd say there's a good chance we're looking at another homicide."

Slidell let a few choice words slip. "Are you sure?"

"Can't be positive until Doc Powell runs blood typing on what we found, to rule out Liz Johnson, but seeing her flesh wounds were all postmortem . . ."

Slidell ran a hand through his thick brown hair. "Cleary linked her to the boat. Maybe Doc was wrong about the timing of the wounds she received."

"There's a first time for everything."

Mayor Cox swiped beads of perspiration from his brow. "Better that than the first time for two murders occurring so close together."

For once he and Landon agreed. "It should be easy enough to determine once I get these blood samples to Doc."

"In the meantime, let's try and keep this hushed," Cox implored. "We can't afford the rumor mill churning on this one."

Landon spied the town's worst busybodies hovering near the top of the pier, their heads bent in deep deliberation. "We may be too late."

With a curse, Slidell yanked his radio from his belt. "Thoreau?"

"Yeah, Sheriff?"

"Mabel and Thelma are hovering at the top of the pier. Do what you can to get rid of them."

Thoreau radioed back. "Like that's possible."

"Just do it," he ground out, then turned back to Landon. "Get the boat hauled into our storage garage and start processing it ASAP."

Landon nodded. "Will do."

Slidell glared at Thoreau trying to move Mabel and Thelma along and not having any luck. "Mayor, you may want to give Thoreau a hand. I believe those two are part of your fan club. Why don't you use some of that charm we keep hearing about."

Cole, Thoreau, and Slidell huddled around the workstation Landon had set up in the storage facility.

The odor of blood hung in the air, dispelled little by the large enclosed space.

"Thanks for coming by," Slidell said, shaking Cole's hand.

"No problem. Glad to be of help." He was as anxious as anyone to see what Landon had found. The sooner they caught the killer, the sooner he'd rest easy. One confirmed murder and one suspected one following so close after Henry Reid's crash . . . It was too much death for such a small town.

Slidell inclined his head to Thoreau. "Tell Tom this meeting ain't optional and I hate waiting."

"Yes, sir." Thoreau booked it to the corridor connecting the storage facility to the station.

Cole hunkered into an empty chair.

After a moment's pause, Slidell grabbed one too, the metal legs scraping across the concrete floor. He sank into it with a huff. "All right, Landon. Let's hear what you got. Tom and Thoreau will just have to catch up."

"All right." Landon laid several items on the table before them. "I found the remaining nineteen tanks rented from Cole's shop. I had Doc Powell contact Owen Matthews again, but I have to say the majority looked to be in pristine condition."

Cole sat up a little straighter. "And the rest of them?"

"Still in good working condition but with similar surface

damage to the one Liz Johnson was wearing. Doc says he found particles of sediment, identical to that found under Liz's nails, imbedded in the crevices of the tank's valve, which is why I wanted Cole here. As captain of our dive rescue squad and Tariuk's only qualified cave diving instructor, I thought he may be able to offer some opinion on where Liz and our mystery man or woman may have been diving."

"That would be a man." Tom's boots clipping the concrete echoed in the steel-framed structure. "Cleary just finished giving Earl a sketch." He held the picture aloft.

Cole studied the image. A man—white skin, dark hair and eyes, drawn from a distance in shades of gray.

"That doesn't show us a whole lot," Landon said.

"Cleary said the girl rented the boat. He only caught a glimpse of the man while they were loading their supplies on board."

"Supplies?" Slidell propped his boot on his opposite knee.

"Diving equipment, couple of duffel bags, grocery items. Cleary said they rented it for two weeks, and judging from the amount of gear and food they loaded, they were planning to stay out the entire time."

"Which explains why no one in town, other than Cleary, Piper, and Jake remembered Liz," Landon said.

"He get a name on the man?" Slidell asked.

"Nope." Tom shook his head. "He only dealt with Liz."

"She mention what they were up to?"

"Nope. According to Cleary, they didn't say and he didn't ask. He just assumed fishing. After he saw the dive tanks, he figured diving. Didn't matter to him. They paid cash, up front. Top dollar, in fact. Cleary was thrilled. Truth be told, the boat wasn't even worth the two weeks' rent they paid him."

Cole chuckled. The way Cleary had carried on at the dock, he'd have thought they'd just destroyed a brand-new sloop.

"Cash again." Slidell sighed.

"They didn't want to leave a trace," Landon said. "And that

goes along perfectly with what I found, or I should say the lack of certain items I didn't find."

Slidell hunched forward. "Such as?"

"No identification. No duffel bags. Nothing but the tanks from Cole's shop and—"

"But Cleary specifically said he saw them carry duffels on board," Tom interrupted. "Where are their clothes, their belongings?"

Landon leaned against the workbench. "I have a feeling they were tossed overboard along with the body of our victim . . . or victims."

Tom crossed his arms with an air of defiance. "How'd you reach the conclusion there is another victim?"

"Rain washed away most of the trace evidence outside the galley, but I found hair matted with blood snagged on the starboard cleat. I sent it over to Doc Powell. He did a quick blood-typing test and confirmed the blood on the boat does not match Liz Johnson's."

"Wonderful." Slidell exhaled. "We're looking at a second homicide."

Landon nodded. "I strongly believe so."

"And our body?"

"Somewhere in the gulf."

Tom snorted. "That narrows it down."

"It is what it is." Landon shrugged.

"Why dump all their gear?"

"Harder to prove identity. We only know our Jane Doe's name because Piper had it on the rental slip. Unfortunately Liz, or most likely Elizabeth, Johnson is ranked as one of the most common names out there. The prints Doc provided pulled up no information, and we need something to compare her dentals to. None of the Elizabeth Johnsons in the missing persons database are our gal."

"So either no one knows she's missing or no one's bothered to report it," Cole said, hoping it was the former. Not that he wanted anyone to lose a loved one, but having no one who cared enough to report the woman missing seemed even sadder.

"Cleary said the boat wasn't due back until today. Piper said the same about the tanks," Tom said.

"So it's probably too soon for anyone to realize she's missing," Thoreau chimed in.

"Another day or so should do the trick. I'll keep checking the missing persons database. Maybe something will pop up," Landon said.

"And our mystery man?"

"Without a body, there's no chance for identification. We're posting Liz's picture and the sketch Cleary provided of our man throughout town. Maybe we'll get lucky," Tom said.

"There's always the chance the body will float. Or someone will come looking for them both," Landon said.

Slidell reclined back. "Not exactly comforting odds."

"For now it's all we have to go on," Tom said.

"That's not entirely true." Landon stepped back to the table. "Whoever was clearing the boat of everything personal missed one pivotal item." With gloved hand, he lifted a cell phone. "Found it beneath the cushion of the galley bench."

Slidell rubbed his hands together. "Now we're getting somewhere."

"Yes and no," Landon said, squashing the budding hope. "I called the carrier, and there's no file on record for the phone."

"What?"

"There's no history on the phone. The number doesn't even correlate to any records they possess."

"So you're saying they provide service for a phone they have no contract or record on?"

Landon nodded. "The phone shows the carrier, but according to them the phone and the number don't exist."

"You're saying we're at another dead end."

"Not exactly." A slight smile cracked on Landon's lips. "I've got the last call made from it. A week ago yesterday."

"Same approximate time as Liz's death, according to Booth," Cole said.

Landon nodded. "It was a text."

"And?" Slidell said, his patience clearly waning. "What did it say?"

" 'Let's talk.' "

"That's it?"

"Yes and no . . ."

"Real helpful, Landon," Tom grunted.

"Who was the call placed to?" Cole asked. That, at least, would provide another avenue to pursue, and allow Landon to proceed.

"It's just showing as an unlisted number. I'd like to send the phone to a friend I have up in the Fairbanks Police Department. I gave him a call and he said it takes time, but he can usually locate the actual number."

"Fine." Slidell grunted. "Now, what's this *yes and no* junk?"

"*Yes*, that's all the text contained, but that's not all that was sent." Landon set the phone aside and lifted a glossy print, handing it to Slidell. He handed a duplicate to Cole and a third to Tom. "This picture was sent as an attachment to the text. I know it's grainy. . . ."

Slidell held it up, examining it. "What is it?"

"A painting of some sort," Landon said.

Cole studied the angelic face, rimmed by gold. A cherubim, perhaps. "Actually, it looks like . . ." He paused. What were those called? "An . . . icon."

"An icon?" Landon's brow furrowed.

"You know, the paintings you see in the Russian Orthodox churches." He'd visited several with Bailey and her aunt way back when.

Tom snorted. "What would some old painting have to do with a double murder?"

Cole rubbed his jaw. "I don't know. I'm not even positive that's what it is." But he knew someone who might. Bailey. Did

92

he really want to drag her into the investigation? No. But asking her to take a look at a photo wouldn't be pulling her in. She would simply be providing clarity on the image. She'd worked in Agnes's shop. Surely she would have an idea. What could it hurt to ask? "I know someone who may be able to help us with the photo," he finally said.

"Give them a call." Slidell stood and dropped the photo back on the table. "At this rate, it may prove our only viable lead."

13

Cole considered calling Bailey but decided he might have better luck just showing up in person to make his request. He showered, shaved, and combed his damp hair. Slipping into his favorite pair of board shorts, he pulled a black T-shirt over his head and slid his feet into a pair of flip-flops. Seventy-two degrees in Yancey was paradise.

He parked in an open slot on the far end of Main Street and made his way to the Trading Post. Passing Thelma's flower shop, he fought the strange and sudden urge to buy Bailey a bouquet. This wasn't a date. He was going to her for help on a murder investigation. Besides, whatever they'd shared had died long ago, hadn't it?

He caught sight of her through the front window of Agnes's shop, perched on a stool, file folders surrounding her in a myriad of piles. Her hair pulled haphazardly up in a clip exposed her graceful neck, and a handful of untamable tendrils cascaded across her shoulders. She was dressed simply—a baby blue T-shirt and a pair of gray sweats.

He smiled. She looked comfortable. A complete one-eighty from the other day—tailored suit, hair wound in a twist, sadness clouding her beautiful eyes. Casual looked good on her. Natural.

She stood, walking with file in hand, her gaze fixed on whatever lay inside. She nibbled her thumbnail as she paced, clearly concentrating.

She pivoted and froze, her eyes locking on Cole.

His heart thudding, he waved, feeling like an idiot for gawking.

An emotion he didn't want to acknowledge swept over her face, knocking the wind from him as it had that fateful night.

That night was ancient history. Everything about *them* was. She'd never have that kind of sway over him again, the power to devastate, to bring him to his knees. He'd never give it to her.

The door cracked open, and he lifted his chin. "Hey."

She looked past him at the street, gazing from one side to the other.

"How are you?"

Her harried gaze settled back on him. "Busy."

"Yeah." He glanced behind her to the papers strewn everywhere. "Looks like you've got your hands full."

"I'm trying to get everything in order."

"Before you open shop?" He knew better.

"Before I sell."

"No desire to stay in Yancey?" He didn't blame her.

"None." She crossed her arms, positioning herself in the doorway more as a blockade than someone who wanted to continue a conversation. "Was there something you needed?"

He rested his hand on the doorjamb. "Actually, there is."

Surprise fluttered across her face.

"Can I come in?"

She pulled the door to her. "Like I said, I'm really busy. . . ."

He wedged his hand in the crack. "This won't take long. It's important."

She exhaled, and after a moment stepped aside. "All right, but just for a minute."

He couldn't remember the last time he'd been in the Post. He walked by it nearly every day, waved to Miss Agnes, but he hadn't stepped foot in it since he and Bailey had been together.

The place hadn't changed much, other than the piles of folders and papers, of course.

The same cinnamony scent hung in the air. The same floral paper lined the shelves, though it'd yellowed with age.

With each step the old wooden floor creaked beneath him, though it creaked a little louder than when he'd been sixteen. A multitude of memories flooded over him. The first time he'd walked Bailey home. Their first kiss beneath the eaves of the doorway.

"You said you needed something." She set the folder she'd been carrying on the desk and rested her hands on her hips.

"Yeah." He cleared his throat, forcing himself to forget how sweet her lips had tasted. "I wanted to know if you could help identify this." He pulled the image from the envelope and handed it to her.

She glanced at it and her brows furrowed. "What's this all about?"

He explained the situation. How they needed her help. *They,* not him.

"Why come to me?"

He shrugged. "I figured living with Agnes, helping out around the shop, you'd probably know a lot more about this stuff than the rest of us. That's why I'm here." And the only reason he was.

"I have a doctorate in Russian Studies, teach at a university."

"Really?" Agnes had mentioned she was doing well but had never gone into detail. Though he hardly gave Agnes the chance, always changing the subject when Bailey's name came up. After a while, Agnes took the hint, and it'd been some years since he'd heard her name spoken at all. "Well, it looks like I came to the right place."

Bailey swept her gaze back to the photo. *Ignore the scent of coconut and sea air swirling about him.* She focused on the picture in her hand, still not registering the image. How could she when Cole stood so near . . . his toned body radiating heat, his sandy blond hair dipping seductively across his brow, teasing the end of his long black lashes whenever he blinked those gorgeous seafoam green eyes.

What is wrong with you? Cole McKenna is nothing but trouble. The fact her heart wouldn't stop hammering proved it.

"Any idea?" he asked, his voice as silky as she bet his skin still was.

"Hmm?"

He cocked a smile and her knees buckled.

Get a grip, girl. "It's . . ." She cleared her throat. "It's Russian."

He stepped closer, his elbow a mere inch from hers.

She stiffened.

"Anything else jump out at you?"

My heart at the moment. She stepped back, trying to keep her attention focused on the image. The round face of a young child—or cherubim, perhaps. Downy soft hair rimmed his graceful face. "It's an icon. Most likely sixteenth century based on stylization, but I'd need to see it to be certain."

"Therein lies the problem. We were hoping you could tell us where to look."

"Icons like this were brought to Alaska by missionaries for the churches they built here."

"So we should be looking at the old Russian Orthodox churches?"

"Yes, but I don't think you'll find it. Not anywhere in Alaska, at least."

He arched a brow. "Why's that?"

"Agnes dragged me to every Russian Orthodox church and museum in the state at one time or another. Believe me, if that icon was in Alaska, I'd have seen it."

"So you're saying we're at another dead end?"

"Not necessarily. There is someone I could check with."

"Great. Who?"

"My aunt Elma."

"Your family certainly loves Russian history."

"She's not really my aunt. She is . . . was . . . Agnes's best friend. Elma loves Russian history as much as Agnes did. If that icon is in Alaska, she'll know about it."

"Could you call her?"

"I can't. She doesn't have a phone."

"No phone. Where does she live?"

"Isux. Out in the Aleutian chain. I suppose I could take a day and visit her." It'd get her out of Yancey and would be her last chance to see Elma. Once she left Alaska, she was never coming back. "Okay, I'll see if I can get a flight."

"We could have Kayden take us. She . . . no, maybe not. She's flying up to Anchorage tomorrow—some kind of pilot certification training. . . . But we could fly with her to Anchorage and catch the morning commuter flight to Dutch Harbor from there."

She swallowed. "We?"

"I want to go with you."

Bad idea. Terrible. Borderline catastrophic. "Uh-uh."

"The sheriff entrusted me with this photograph. It's evidence and not allowed out of my sight."

An entire day with Cole McKenna. "I don't know." She shook her head, scrambling for any excuse. "It could be difficult finding a boat ride from Dutch Harbor to Isux. They aren't always easy to secure, especially during peak king-crab season."

"Don't worry. I've got it covered."

"Why did I have a feeling you were going to say that?"

He was awfully quick with solutions—first the flight and now the boat ride. She narrowed her eyes. If this was some attempt to get her into bed . . . no. He wouldn't dally with her then; why would he now?

His lips broke into an alarming smile at her stare, and warning bells clanged to life.

"Maybe this isn't such a good idea."

"Why not?"

"I've got a lot of work to do. I can't afford a day off." What she couldn't afford was a day spent alone with Cole.

"I understand, but right now this photo is all we've got to

go on. It could mean the difference between bringing a killer to justice and never solving the case."

Great. Her shoulders slackened. How could she say no to that?

A young woman's life had been taken, and all Cole was asking for was one day out of hers. "All right, but I want it understood this is strictly business."

"Okay." His brow furrowed.

"I just don't want anyone thinking . . ."

His eyes narrowed. "Thinking what?"

"Never mind." She grabbed a stack of files from the desk. "I'll go, but only to help the victims."

He held up his hands. "I'm not viewing it as anything else."

Of course he wasn't. This was Cole. He didn't dally with girls like *her*. She hefted the files on top of the cabinet, hoping the exertion would cover the flush of her embarrassment. "When do you want to go?"

"Tomorrow morning?"

She pulled out a drawer and stuffed the first file into place. "Fine."

"I'll pick you up around quarter to six."

"No. I'll meet you. Just tell me where."

"We keep the floatplane on our property. You remember where the place is?"

She nodded, unwilling to face him, unwilling to admit how many times she'd thought of him and their summer spent on his family's land—swimming in the ocean, running along the miles of private beach. He'd taught her so many things, and she'd rejected them all.

14

Bailey ambled down the long dirt drive leading to the McKennas' home, a thousand heartbreaking memories drilling through her.

She caught sight of Cole, reclining on the porch swing, a large husky contentedly lounging at his bare feet.

The rising sun filtered shimmering rays across his golden skin and hair. *Man, he's handsome.*

He caught sight of her and smiled. "Morning."

She stopped short. Was she crazy? Spending an entire day with a man who set her heart aflutter and resurrected tinglings that were best left dead?

He rose, the dog slumbering at his feet waking with a long stretch. Both padded across the porch to greet her, Cole sporting a bright fuchsia moustache.

A chuckle slipped from her lips.

His sandy brow cocked. "What?"

"You've got a little something . . ." She drew her finger across her upper lip.

He mimicked the motion and grinned sheepishly. "Smoothie."

Funny, she hadn't pegged him as the smoothie type.

"Let me grab you one."

"It's not necessary." She just wanted to get on with the day. The faster they moved, the faster they'd return and she could extricate herself from Cole's presence.

"There's plenty left in the blender. I'll grab you a cup to take with us." He darted in the house before she could argue.

"All right," she murmured to his retreating back.

The husky paced back and forth between the porch steps and kitchen door, apparently torn between greeting her and the possibility of a treat.

Cole returned with a plastic Seawolves tumbler in hand and a pair of flip-flops tucked beneath his arm. "Kayden's quite the health nut, but these are actually good."

Bailey stared at the fuchsia concoction with apprehension.

"I promise, you'll like it."

Promise was a tricky word. One she avoided both in making and taking. They were too easily broken. She took an apprehensive sip. "Not bad."

"Kayden uses fresh blueberries from Maine. Mixed with the plain yogurt, you get that purple color."

"Ah." She took another sip. Quite amazing, actually. She glanced around, wondering which other family members may be lurking about and how they'd react to seeing her. Piper had been nice, but then again she'd been too young to know what Bailey had really been like back then—what she'd done to Cole, how she'd hurt him. She feared his parents and the rest of his siblings wouldn't be as kind, and she couldn't blame them. "So where is Kayden?"

"She's down at the plane, doing a final check. We should be good to go soon."

Great. She took another sip of her smoothie, trying not to look completely uncomfortable. Cole, on the other hand, looked perfectly at ease. She'd always envied that about him.

"You still live at home?" she asked, hoping her question hadn't come out as badly as it sounded to her.

"No. I've got my own place. If you look through that cluster of trees, you can just see the edge of my porch." He pointed in the general direction, and she caught sight of the cabin. Two-story with a large wraparound porch.

She could just picture it dosed in a fresh-fallen snow, smoke curling from the chimney. "I'm sure your folks enjoy having you close."

"My folks passed on."

Shock rocked through her. "Both of them?"

He nodded.

"I'm sorry. I had no idea." They were young. Too young.

"It was a while back. Dad had a heart attack my sophomore year of college. Mom died three years later, complications of her illness."

She remembered his mom being ill, diagnosed with MS or lupus. Something deteriorating and degenerative. "That must have been really hard. For all of you."

"It wasn't easy. Reef and Piper were still in high school."

"What happened to them?" No way would Cole have let his family be split up.

"I stayed with them."

"You raised them? By yourself?" She didn't know why she sounded so surprised. Cole was a good man. Too good for her. Always had been.

"Gage and Kayden helped too."

"You must all be really close." She longed for that closeness but, unfortunately, had looked for it in all the wrong places. These days . . . she didn't really look for it at all.

Cole raked a hand through his hair with a sigh. "*Most* of us are."

She furrowed her brows, but he simply went on. "Kayden and Piper live in the old house. None of us were ready to sell it. I built my cabin close enough so I could look after them and the land while still having my privacy." He shrugged. "It works for us."

"It must be nice to have a big family." She often wondered if things would have been different if she'd had a sibling. Maybe she wouldn't have always felt so alone.

"It has its moments."

"And your brothers? They're still in Yancey?"

"Gage is. He's got a place on the south shore. Reef . . ." Cole rubbed the back of his neck. "He lives out of state."

She wondered at Cole's hesitancy. "Reef . . . I remember you having a brother with a really unusual name. Hopefully with a name like that he loves the ocean."

"Yeah, definitely shares Mom's love of it."

"She used to be a swimmer, right?"

"Yeah, she was an open-water champion two years running."

"That's really cool." And really sad—someone so athletic being debilitated by a progressive disease.

The whirling of a propeller shook the air.

Cole lifted his chin. "Sounds like Kayden's ready for us."

She followed him around the rear of the farmhouse and across the back lawn leading down to the beach.

Her heart seized at the sight of the boulder bridging the gap between sea and shore. After the night her downfall began, she used to sneak down to that rock after the McKennas were all asleep. She'd perch at the sea's edge, letting her feet dangle over the side, wishing she could turn back time and undo the damage she'd done. But it was too late. Cole would never forgive her, and she was too prideful to ask. Once she'd even contemplated diving headfirst into the black depths and letting the undertow pull her out to sea, but at the last second some strong force had seemingly held her back, filling her with cowardice and, somehow, resolve to go on.

"Bailey?" Cole's husky voice tugged her out of the past and dropped her smack in the present. "You okay?"

"Fine." She swallowed, feeling unsteady.

Concern etched his brow, and he stooped to look her in the eye. "Is it the plane?"

"What?"

"Are you afraid to fly?"

"No. I . . ."

"It's understandable after what happened."

Truth was, flying wasn't her favorite to begin with, and after Agnes's death she liked the prospect even less.

She stared at the floatplane resting atop the water's surface, sun glinting off the silver propeller. "I'm fine."

Something cold and wet slobbered her hand. She looked down at the husky, its tail wagging furiously.

"Guess Aurora's worried about you too."

Bailey ran her hand through the animal's silky fur. "That's sweet, but unnecessary. I'm fine." How many times had she said that over the years when she'd felt completely the opposite?

Cole helped her climb aboard the small Cessna, the husky clambering up after them. Kayden turned from the pilot's seat, her headset already in place.

"Bailey Craig, nice to see you again. It's been a long time."

A lifetime. Kayden was even more beautiful than she remembered—striking brown eyes, long brown hair, and high sculpted cheekbones. "Thanks for taking us—me."

"No problem. I'm headed up there anyway."

Aurora lumbered past Bailey and hopped into the copilot's seat.

Bailey laughed. "Well, that's a first."

"Rori's my flying buddy. Aren't you, girl?" Kayden ruffled the husky's fur. "Other than Cole, she's the only family member who'll go up with me."

"Why's that?" Panic fastened to Bailey.

"Don't worry," Cole assured her with a gentle smile. "Kayden's a great pilot."

"Oh, it's nothing like that," Kayden said. "Reef's in Australia last we heard, Gage isn't fond of heights, and Piper doesn't trust me."

"She trusts you," Cole said.

Kayden raised a perfectly arched brow.

"It just freaks her out that her sister's flying a plane, that's all."

"You'd think she'd be used to it. Dad had me flying since I was ten."

"I'm sure she'll come around one of these days."

"I won't hold my breath." She swiveled back around to the controls. "You two go ahead and strap in. We should land in Anchorage a little after eight."

Despite the four other seats on the plane, Cole sat beside Bailey, his alluring scent of sandalwood conjuring up images of sultry Tahitian days spent lounging on the beach—sun, surf, and Cole right at her fingertips. She grimaced. It was going to be a long flight.

Two hours later, Kayden glided the plane to a smooth stop outside Anchorage International Airport. Following a quick good-bye, Cole secured two seats for them on the 9:00 a.m. flight to Dutch Harbor.

The day was warm, a delicious sixty-eight degrees and the air full of promise.

Bailey tightened her ponytail and studied her reflection in the mirror. Not wanting to give the wrong impression, she'd gone the no-makeup route, but now, in the drab light of the airport bathroom, she wished she hadn't.

Riffling through her purse she found a tube of cherry ChapStick and a sample tube of mascara she'd picked up on her last trip to the mall. She applied both and stood back to study the results.

Nothing stupendous, but the addition had brightened her eyes. Maybe now she wouldn't feel so bland next to Cole and his stunning looks.

She dropped the ChapStick in her bag and sighed. What was she doing? Trying to look pretty for Cole? Not that there was anything wrong with wearing makeup. It was the desire to focus on her looks and others' acceptance of her based on her looks that was the problem. She braced her weight against the counter as unsteadiness roiled through her.

Lord, being here with Cole . . . I know it's silly, but I'm afraid I may slip back into old patterns—into wanting to gain affection by looking good, by being alluring. I've put all that behind me. Please don't ever let me slip back to who I used to be.

Bailey settled into her seat beside Cole, one of only eight passengers on the commuter flight.

Sun poured through the plastic windows, bathing the cabin in warmth.

Cole stretched out beside her, resting his hands behind his head. "I saw you at Grace Community last night."

Her fingers tightened around the bag of pretzels. She hadn't seen that coming. "Yes." She held her breath, wondering what would come next. Would he express shock at seeing "someone like her" in church? Didn't he understand she'd changed? But, then again, why would he? Attending the midweek service had been a bold move on her part, but she wasn't missing worship while she was in Yancey. God was more important than her fear. If only she lived that way all the time.

He popped a pretzel in his mouth. "I tried to catch you when the service ended, but you left quick. I was hoping to welcome you."

"I'm not really one for hanging around and chatting afterwards."

He seemed to consider that for a minute. "How'd you like the service? I think Braden's really got a gift."

"Yeah, he was great." His message from Romans eight had really spoken to her heart. "He's not local, is he?"

"Nope. Moved down from Fairbanks maybe five, six years back." Cole pulled two bottles of cranberry juice from his backpack and offered her one.

"Thanks. Pretzels make me thirsty."

He took a gulp, then set the juice on the tray in front of him. "Did you like the music? I know it's not for everyone, a teen worship band and all."

"They did a really good job, and it was nice seeing young people so involved."

"They're a great bunch of kids with great hearts for God."

"That's what matters. We've got a pretty hip worship band at the church I attend in Oregon."

"That's cool. You like your church?"

"I do."

"Been there long?"

She smiled at his attempt at subtlety. "Close to six years. I've been a Christian for nine. How about you?" She didn't recall him attending church when they were in high school, but then again, she'd gone out of her way to avoid anything having to do with church or authority back then.

"Not long after I came home from college. At first it was simply because my mom asked me to go, to set an example for my brothers and sisters. But after a while something happened. . . . I started to see the truth. . . ."

Just as she had. It had been amazing—like a light going on for the first time, illuminating the darkness.

"And I thirsted for it, you know?" He angled to face her better. She nodded. She did know.

"What about you? What led you to church?" There was no hint of condemnation in his voice, only genuine curiosity.

It was too painful to talk about the ugliness, the brokenness, the depth of despair she'd sunken to before she was saved, but she supposed she could talk about that first step. "Someone invited me to a dorm Bible study." She wasn't exaggerating when she said, "It saved my life." She'd met Christ that night.

"It's why I work with teens at Grace. There is so much in this world trying to pull them down. They desperately need Christ. We all do. And they need to know how much He loves them."

She bit her quivering lip, struggling to quell the raw emotion surging through her. How she wished someone had reached out to her or that she'd listened when Agnes had tried. So much heartache she could have avoided, so much pain spared for her and everyone close to her.

15

Dutch Harbor's rugged beauty radiated awe in Bailey. The massive ocean surrounding the tiny island, the blue sky—larger than life, the spray of the sea, and the vibrant mass of purple fireweed blooming along the shore made it seem a wonderland. "It's breathtaking."

Cole sighed. "No place like it on earth."

"Spoken like a true Alaskan."

He winked, and her traitorous heart fluttered. There'd been a time, a glorious summer, when she'd pushed past the pain of being abandoned by her parents, when her friendship with Cole was flourishing so that she couldn't imagine living anywhere else. But that'd been before . . .

"Hammer man," a guy called.

Bailey turned, and Cole waved at the young man striding toward them. Tall, curly blond hair, deep blue eyes.

"How you doing, Pete?" Cole clasped his hand.

"Can't complain. Got air in my lungs, waves to ride. What brings you to my neck of the woods?" His enthusiastic gaze shifted to Bailey and he smiled. "And more importantly, who is this?"

Cole turned to her and smiled. "Bailey, this is Pete Baker. And, Pete, this is Bailey Craig. An old friend of mine."

Friend? How could he still view her as a friend after what she'd done?

Pete extended a hand. "Nice to meet you, Bailey." His eyes shone full of youth and optimism.

"You too."

Cole slid on his shades. "We need to procure a ride over to Isux."

"No problem. Let's go."

"Are you sure, man?"

"Absolutely."

Pete led them down the dock to a small vestibule with a sign boasting *Best Whale Tours in Alaska.* He reached in the shed and flipped the sign to *Closed,* then scribbled, *Back in a few. Off to Isux* on the chalkboard underneath.

"We're not pulling you away from something?" Bailey asked.

"Nothing that can't wait." Pete smiled. His boat, *Pierless,* sat moored at the end of the pier. He held out a hand, helping Bailey aboard.

It didn't take long to get under way.

"I dove Big Ben last weekend," Pete said as they cast off.

"And?" Cole asked, settling down beside Bailey, waves lashing against the stern in their wake.

"You were right. It was incredible."

"You ought to try Skimmer's Reef."

Pete glanced back from the wheel. "As good of a rush?"

"Even better."

"Cool."

Bailey smiled at the enthusiasm bubbling inside them; they were overflowing with a zest for life.

Somewhere along the way she'd lost that—taking time to enjoy the world around her, to be carefree and a kid at heart. She'd stopped being a kid the day her mom dropped her on Agnes's doorstep. In truth, probably long before that.

"I keep hearing about some spot in your area called Blue Paradise," Pete said. "Ever hear of it?"

"Yeah." Cole shifted to face her, the sun glinting off his shades.

She swallowed the lump forming in her throat, thankful she couldn't see his eyes, fearful of what she might find there. Blue Paradise had been their spot. It was where he'd taught her how to dive. They'd spent practically every day that summer beneath the water's surface, the two of them in their own little world amongst the colorful coral. How could something that had brought her so much pleasure, now resonate inside her with so much pain?

"Is it any good?" Pete asked.

"Yeah." Cole looked down. "It's great."

"How come you held out on me? Trying to keep it for yourself?" Pete chuckled.

Cole swallowed. "I don't dive there anymore."

The heaviness of his words only compounded the weight bearing down on Bailey.

Pete seemed to pick up on the nerve he was hitting and subtly redirected his attention to the sea.

Cole nudged Bailey's foot with his. The touch, though short and completely innocent, sent shock waves through her. "You still dive?"

"I do." She swallowed, fighting the urge to reach back out to him, to feel his skin against hers, however briefly.

"So you've kept up with it?"

"Yeah, I love it. Particularly wreck diving."

"That's cool. Maybe we can go again sometime."

"Maybe." It was a nice thought, but in truth she couldn't bear it—sharing something that had been so special to them, so intimate. Besides, all of her time needed to be spent on readying the shop for sale. Today was for the murdered girl. Tomorrow it was back to work.

A half hour later, they disembarked on Isux's shore.

"Thanks for the lift." Cole tossed the rope to Pete.

Pete wound it around his muscular forearm. "No problem. When do you want to make the return trip?"

Cole looked to Bailey.

She shrugged. "A few hours?"

Pete smiled. "Good enough."

"Are you sure? We don't want to keep you." She didn't want to ruin his entire day's income.

"No problem." He pushed off, water rippling in his wake. "You kids behave, now." He winked, his eyes alight with merriment.

"Interesting friend," she said as Pete faded into the horizon.

Cole slid his hands in his pockets. "Yeah, Pete's a great guy. A blast to dive with, which is pretty cool considering he used to be terrified of water."

"That guy?" Bailey jabbed a thumb over her shoulder. "You're kidding."

"Nope." Cole kicked a pebble onto his foot, playing with it as a soccer player would a ball. "We got him over his fear."

"How'd you accomplish that?" Pete seemed more at home on the water than anybody she'd ever seen. It was hard to wrap her mind around him being the least bit afraid of it.

"Pete came into the shop. Said he was determined to conquer his fear. Said it was ridiculous to live scared of water when he was surrounded by it, so we worked with him, took it real slow. Started with basic swimming lessons, then diving, then surfing . . . You get the picture."

"That's really cool." She always admired those who could tackle their fears head-on. She'd always found it easier to run.

"His wife's really nice too." Cole kicked the pebble up and caught it on his forearm like a hacky sack, bouncing it along the well-sculpted muscle.

She missed being wrapped in those strong arms. She shook off the thought, forcing her gaze from Cole's physique to the dwellings dotting the craggy landscape, and led the way toward Elma's cottage.

"Too bad Nicky wasn't around today. You'd like her."

"Pete's married. I wouldn't have guessed that."

"Yep. Two kids."

"You're kidding? He looks so . . ."

Cole arched a brow.

She shrugged. "He just doesn't look the marrying type."

"Which is?"

"I don't know. More settled."

"Just because he dresses surfer style doesn't mean he's not settled. Sure he and Nicky live an island lifestyle, but they are very happy, very committed. They adore their kids. They're totally involved in their church." He tsked playfully. "You should never judge a book by its cover."

She grimaced. *Or its past.*

"Wildheart." Elma ran toward them, her arms open wide, her dark hair dancing on the breeze. She looked wonderful—same rosy cheeks, same contagious smile.

Cole arched an amused brow. "Wildheart?"

"Leave it," she said, just as Elma engulfed her.

Elma stepped back, examining her. "Look at you, my little Wildheart—all grown up. So beautiful, no?" She set her dark eyes on Cole.

"Extremely."

A rush of heat swarmed Bailey's cheeks, and she prayed it didn't show, but if Cole's grin was any indicator, she was blushing up a storm.

"Are you back visiting Agnes?" She looked over Bailey's shoulder, then frowned. "She didn't want to make the trip?"

Bailey's heart sank. Elma hadn't heard. That's why she wasn't at the funeral. She should have sent word instead of assuming Gus had, especially with the suddenness of it all. "There's something I need to tell you."

"I can't believe she's gone." Elma wiped her tears. "I just saw her."

Bailey inched closer, offering Elma a tissue. "You did?"

"She came, not long ago." Elma blew her nose in the tissue, then clutched it tight. "Maybe a month or so back. She was working on some research."

"What kind of research?"

"About Amgux."

16

Bailey slumped against the sofa, bewildered. Elma's story was the stuff of legends, surely not truth. "You're saying an entire island sank into the sea?"

"Swallowed whole. But don't take only my word for it." Elma rose and lumbered to the antique corner cabinet, retrieving a leather-bound book from inside. "Here's the firsthand account." She flipped to the page and proceeded to read.

"The day's work on Pavel's roof complete, I boarded my boat for the journey home, a bundle of your grandmother's pirozhki tucked safely inside."

Bailey paused, looking to Elma for clarification. "My great-great-grandmother was Russian. She and her husband lived on Chirikof Island, and her parents lived at the St. Stephen settlement on Amgux Island. Her husband, my great-great-grandpapi, who was Aleut, had gone to help repair her parents' roof after a strong storm."

Elma turned back to the worn pages.

"I wasn't far out when the sea gurgled. At first I feared a whale was surfacing beneath me, but it was far more terrible. Like the ancient Leviathan rising from the depths to seek revenge with fire and flames, the sea split and the earth shook.

"The waters rose, tossing me into the churning depths. I watched in utter helplessness as the sea swallowed Amgux whole.

"By God's grace I survived that day. Your mother's kin did not.

"These are the tales of Amgux and your mother's kin before the sea consumed them.

"May these words preserve their memory so they are never forgotten."

"And the photograph we showed you, of the icon?"

Elma reverently turned the yellowed parchment. "Here."

Bailey's eyes widened at the perfect drawing of the image from the cell phone, but with details that indicated the cell-phone picture was only a portion of a larger picture. The young child with golden locks wasn't alone. A dignified woman sat beside him—mirroring his grace and radiance. "Who are they?"

"I don't know. Even my great-great-grandmother didn't know, but she knew it had hung in the church of her settlement. All their greatest possessions from the homeland were kept there."

Bailey studied the image—the elegant lines, the soft shading. "Your great-great-grandmother drew this?"

Elma nodded.

"She was quite the artist."

"Oh yes." Elma stood. "Come."

Bailey followed Elma down the back hall of the tiny home, Cole close behind them.

"These are hers." Elma proudly gestured at the paintings blanketing the walls of the small reading room.

"I'd forgotten all about these." Bailey moved to examine one of the landscapes up close. "I wish I had a fraction of her talent. My drawings all come out looking like potato people."

Cole chuckled. "Mine too. I think I hit my artistic peak in kindergarten."

Elma wrapped her arm around Bailey's waist. "Oh, child, think how boring this world would be if we all had the same gifts. Only beautiful pictures to look at—no music or literature or exquisite desserts."

"Like pryaniki?" Bailey asked hopefully.

Elma winked and shuffled from the room, a smile on her lips. A few minutes later, she returned with a plate of pryaniki.

The soothing scents of vanilla and nutmeg filled the air as Bailey bit into the sweet Russian gingerbread treat. "Ah, I'd forgotten how amazing these are."

"You like?" Elma asked Cole, her eyes alight with satisfaction.

"It's phenomenal." Icing blanketed his lips.

Bailey laughed, hard. Something she hadn't done in years, and it felt wonderful.

Maybe coming back to Yancey wasn't going to turn out to be as horrific as she'd imagined.

Their return flight was nearly empty, giving them a high level of privacy.

Cole dropped an empty water bottle in his pack, then spread the map across the seat-back tray. "You know, it's not that far-fetched. Amgux must have sat somewhere in here." He circled an area off the northern coast of Chirikof Island. "With the amount of earthquakes recorded each year, it's not unreasonable to think one was strong enough to swallow the island whole."

"So the island sank and the church with it," Bailey said, her mind still swirling with the possibility. "And Liz and our elusive mystery man must have found it."

"That's what I'm thinking."

"It's hard to even wrap my mind around the prospect of an island sinking with its church intact." She sank back against her seat.

He smiled. "Stranger things have happened."

She arched a brow. "Such as?"

"A buddy of mine just got back from exploring submerged Mayan ruins in Guatemala—a series of ceremonial temples at the bottom of a volcanic lake. And I took part in a dive in Alexandria, Egypt, earlier this year, where we explored the ruins of a palace and temple complex, a good portion of it still intact."

"You were in Egypt?" His life was the stuff her dreams were made of.

"I've been fortunate. Diving has taken me all over the world."

"How exciting." She wished she were more adventurous, but she feared she'd lose sight of the line between adventurous and reckless. She'd been reckless once and would never return to that. Being adventurous, it made her feel free . . . happy—and that was something she didn't deserve. She felt Cole's stare on her, and she cleared her throat. "It's nice you are able to do something you love for a living."

"It's not the path I planned, but God had something better in mind."

"You mean the skiing?" She'd always wondered why she hadn't heard his name on the news, hadn't seen him on magazine covers. He'd been one of the best downhill skiers around—breaking records every year.

"Yeah, I had planned to compete professionally."

"So what changed your mind?"

Cole lifted his leg and ran his hand along the crescent-shaped scar that outlined his knee and trailed up his thigh.

"What happened?"

"I took a bad fall. Pretty much ended my career."

"I'm so sorry."

"It was for the best. I didn't see it at the time, but looking back, I see God's hand in it all."

She shifted toward him. "How so?"

"A week into my recovery Dad died. I was needed at home. Even more so after Mom passed."

"That must have been hard." Bailey fought the urge to reach out to him, to comfort him.

"It wasn't easy at first, but then we fell into a rhythm. I look at my injury as a blessing—it took away the choice. I didn't have to choose between my career and my family."

"And you never went back? I mean, after all your siblings were grown?"

"To competing, no. My skiing days are done, and I'm good with that. Diving has my heart."

She remembered when she could make that claim.

"I did go back to school, though—finished through University of Alaska's distance program. I got my degree in Human Resources, which has served me well."

"You like running Last Frontier Adventures?"

"Pursuing adventure for a living . . ." A flicker of delight flashed across his face. "It's like a dream come true."

"I saw the shop. Looks like you've really changed it around since the old days."

"Yeah, the bait and tackle shop wasn't quite me. Gage and Kayden and I sat around and brainstormed how we could take the business Dad built and reinvent it to best suit our skills and passions."

"Looks like you did a great job."

"Thanks." He smiled. "What about you? Do you enjoy your profession?"

While she loved Russian history, teaching wasn't her heart's desire. Running a shop like Agnes had, sharing her knowledge and love in a hands-on way suited her much better.

She shrugged. "I do . . ."

"But?" He leaned closer, and her heart fluttered.

"I don't know. . . . I . . ."

He studied her with such interest, such compassion, she found it hard to breathe.

He rested his hand atop hers. "You okay?"

She jerked her hand back; his touch felt too good. "Yeah." She straightened as heat flushed her face. "It's just a little stuffy in here."

"Would you like some water?"

"That would be great."

"No problem." He fished a bottle out of his pack, opened it, and handed it to her.

She swallowed the tepid liquid, waiting for her heart to settle. "Thanks."

"Better?"

She nodded, even though it was a lie.

Landon stepped off Cole's porch and raked a hand through his hair, more spent than he'd been in a long time.

Noise rustled in the woods and he turned.

Light from the main house illuminated a figure—*petite and feminine*. But something else was making the noise, and moving fast in his direction.

Aurora bolted from the trees, her sleek white fur nearly a blur as she leapt on Landon. "Hey, Rori." He bent, ruffling her fur.

A moment later, Piper emerged. "Landon." She planted her hands on her hips. "What are you doing here?"

"Looking for Cole."

"He's not home."

"So I gathered." He straightened and assessed Piper's outfit—white T-shirt, black exercise capris, and a pair of trail shoes. "Going for a walk?" He wished she'd walk with one of her siblings. Her being out alone on their secluded property, in the woods, at night, didn't sit well with him. Especially not with a killer on the loose.

"Trying to." She huffed. "Rori caught your scent and I had to chase her halfway across the property."

"How'd you know it was me and not some intruder?"

"Because Rori was panting with excitement."

"I'm afraid I have that effect on all the ladies." He tugged his shirt collar with a grin. "It's a curse."

Piper's lips twitched and she burst out laughing.

118

"It's not that funny."

"I beg to differ," she said between spurts of laughter.

"Any idea where your brother is? I've got something I need him to take a look at."

"Yeah, I know where he is." She linked her arms across her chest.

He waited, and waited.

"Mind telling me?" he practically grunted. It was like the girl made a sport out of vexing him.

"Well, I wouldn't want to be a *busybody*." She turned and stalked back into the woods.

With a grimace he took off after her, knowing a little groveling would be required and being not one bit pleased about it.

Catching up, he tugged her to a halt. "Piper, it's important."

She exhaled and glanced at her watch, the digital numbers blue in the moonlight. "What could be so important at ten thirty on a Friday night in Yancey?"

"Liz Johnson's sister just called."

17

Piper poured Landon a cup of coffee.

He looked exhausted and she felt half sorry for him. Then again, it was Landon—annoying, irksome, overprotective Landon.

He set the mug down and raked a hand through his hair. "When do you think they'll be back?"

"Probably another hour or two." She frowned, noticing how haggard he looked—mottled black in the shape of crescent moons rimmed his bloodshot eyes and stubble covered his hollow cheeks. "Have you eaten?"

"Today?"

She rolled her eyes. It was a wonder the man didn't turn to skin and bones. "I've got some lasagna left in the fridge. Let me heat you up some. It'll only take a bit."

"All right." He started to straddle the stool and stopped short.

Her lips twitched. "Problems?"

He yanked an evidence bag from his pocket and tossed it on the counter.

"What's that?"

"A key I found on the boat earlier today. I wanted Cole's opinion on it."

"Looks like a locker key."

"That's what I thought, but I tried every lock in Yancey from Burt's gym to the ferry station. No luck."

"Maybe it goes to something on another island or in another

state. Jake said he thought the truck Liz was driving had Washington plates."

"It'd help if there was a manufacturer name or number on the key, but it's blank." He shook his head. "It's like this guy wanted to remain untraceable. And that, quite honestly, scares me."

"Why?"

"Because it means he knew he was going to do something wrong ahead of time."

She pulled the plate from the microwave, the mouthwatering scent of tomato sauce and oregano hovering in the air as she set it in front of him, the cheese golden and bubbling.

"Thanks, Piper. It smells delicious." He bent to take a bite and paused. "You made this?"

"Don't worry. I wouldn't feed you something Kayden made." Her eyes narrowed. "Unless I was really mad at you."

He chuckled and took a bite.

She leaned against the counter, thankful to see him eat. He worked too hard and took horrible care of himself. He needed a good woman, someone like Nancy Bowen.

"The only consolation is," he said, tracking back between bites, "with the amount of blood we found on the boat, it's highly unlikely our mystery man is still a threat to anybody."

"How do you know it was his blood?"

"Since it's already leaked, I guess it wouldn't hurt any for me to tell you. The blood found on the boat doesn't match Liz Johnson's. We're definitely looking at a second victim."

"Okay, but how do you know the blood belonged to our mystery man?"

Landon paused midbite. "We made an assumption." He dropped his fork. "I made an assumption."

"It's a natural one." She skirted around the counter and hopped on the stool beside him. "The only reason I thought of it was because Cole mentioned the mystery man sent a text. . . ."

"He did. It could have been the person on the receiving end of the message that . . ."

"Was killed," they said in unison.

Landon wiped his mouth. "Good work, Piper."

She let the counter support her weight. Had Landon Grainger just paid her a compliment?

Landon finished off the hearty slice of apple pie and sat back satisfied. "That was delicious. When'd you learn to make a pie?"

"I used to make them with Mom."

He winced at the sadness in Piper's eyes. It was stupid of him to bring it up. She'd been young when Libby died. He hadn't thought. . . .

She took his plate.

"I can get it," he offered.

She ignored him and moved to the sink to rinse it off. "So . . . still haven't found Liz's missing truck?"

"Nope." He stood and stretched. It'd been a long day—a long couple of days. "Starting to run out of places to look."

"Have you tried the glades?"

"No. It's next on my list. So far all my time's been swallowed up by taking the boat apart."

"Looks like you did good work." She indicated the key with a tilt of her head.

"Found it taped inside the toilet of all places."

Her face scrunched. "Eww."

Landon chuckled as his radio crackled. He pulled it from his belt. "Grainger." The peace had lasted longer than expected.

"You found McKenna yet?" Slidell grumbled.

"Found one of them." He winked at Piper.

"The one we want?"

"No, but he's expected back soon."

"Back from where?"

"He and—"

"I'll be right there!" Slidell hollered. "It's the blasted phone again. I've got to go. You heading back over here?"

"Be there in twenty."

Piper slipped the clean plate into the drying rack. "He sounds happy."

"About as happy as a bear who stuck his hand in a honey pot and found a swarm of angry bees. Word of the murders leaked out, and the phones have been ringing off the hook ever since."

"You'd think he'd be thrilled with all the publicity."

"This is bad publicity, and he wants nothing to do with it."

"Maybe he shouldn't be sheriff, then. How you handle hard times is a true show of character."

Sadly, in that area, Landon found Slidell wanting. It wasn't easy working for a man he didn't respect. "Thanks for dinner."

"You're welcome. I'll have Cole call as soon as he gets in."

Landon slid his hat on, and Piper walked him to the door.

"Lock the deadbolt behind me," he instructed.

"Yes, sir." She gave a mock salute.

"Cute, pipsqueak." He tugged her ponytail. "I mean it."

"I told you to stop calling me that."

"Fine. Good night, Piper." He shut the door and waited until he heard the lock click into place before leaving.

18

Cole and Bailey entered the sheriff's station to a frenzy of ringing phones uncommon for ten o'clock on a Thursday night, and every hand was on deck bustling about to answer them.

Cole dropped one of Elma's pryaniki on Landon's desk. She'd insisted on sending a bagful home.

Landon looked up and relief swept across his face. "You're back."

"What's going on?"

"Don't you answer your cell anymore?"

"I wasn't on call today." It'd been on vibrate in case of a true emergency, but Landon hadn't paged him with their emergency code. Not to mention he'd been out of cell-phone range the better part of the day.

Slidell stormed out of his office, an unlit cigar butt clamped in his teeth. "McKenna. Where have you been?"

"We—"

"Sheriff," Tom called, "Mayor Cox's on the phone."

"Again?" Color rose up Slidell's neck.

Tom held the phone out to him. "Afraid so."

Slidell waved him off. "Take another message."

"All right." Tom shrugged. "But he says if you don't take his call this time, he's coming down here."

Slidell growled and grabbed the receiver. "Slidell."

Cole looked to Landon. "What's going on?"

Spewing out a few choice words, Slidell slammed down the receiver. That conversation hadn't lasted long. It sounded like Mayor Cox was headed to the station.

"I'll tell you what's going on. Someone"—Slidell glared around the station—"leaked word of the murders."

"Murders, as in plural?" Cole asked.

Landon nodded. "Blood sample collected on the boat does not match Elizabeth Johnson's."

It had been Liz. "Elizabeth?" Had they learned something more?

"I got a call from Elizabeth Johnson's sister today. Poor girl is distraught. She said Elizabeth and some mysterious boyfriend of hers came up here from California to do some wreck diving, and Rachel—that's the sister—hasn't heard from her since. The description matches. We're just waiting on dentals to confirm."

"Mysterious boyfriend, huh?" Cole said.

"Sounds familiar, doesn't it?"

"How'd she define mysterious?"

"Never saw the guy except through a car window. Elizabeth told her he was private and shy. Rachel found it strange."

"She have a name on the guy?"

"Only a first. Nick," Landon supplied. "What description she had of the guy didn't contradict Cleary's."

"We're still going by Cleary's description?"

Landon shrugged. "So far it's all we've got."

"Any luck with the boat? Fingerprints?" Cole asked.

"Too many to even sort through, being a rental, but I did a more thorough search and found a couple more items that might be of help."

Landon spread a series of photographs across Slidell's desk.

Cole studied the images of ornate censers, candle stands, and a remarkably beautiful chalice set. "Where'd you get these?"

"An underwater camera I found stashed on the boat," Landon explained.

Bailey lifted a photograph. "These weren't taken underwater."

Landon shook his head. "No, they weren't."

"But you just said . . ." Slidell began.

"That they were taken with an underwater camera, but not underwater," Landon clarified.

"Why on earth would you take regular photographs with an underwater camera?" Slidell asked, the remaining thread of his patience nearly worn bare.

"Maybe because they expected these things to be underwater," Cole said.

Slidell gnawed his cigar butt. "Go on . . ."

"Let's say our divers—Liz and her mystery man—took the camera diving. They expected they'd only need an underwater camera, but they found submerged ruins filled with air."

"What kind of ruins would have these types of artifacts?" Landon asked.

Cole exchanged a knowing glance with Bailey and smiled. "A church."

"Let me get this straight," Slidell began. "You're saying an entire island, including a church, sank into the sea, and somehow these images are from the inside of that church."

"As crazy as it sounds, yes," Cole said. Based on the evidence, it was the most logical solution, no matter how illogical it sounded.

"My aunt kept fastidious records," Bailey said. "Give me a few days to go through them. Maybe there's something on the church there."

"In the meantime, I can come up with some coordinates for a search grid based on where Elizabeth's body was found in relation to the area of the sunken island," Cole offered.

"If one even exists," Tom scoffed from the periphery. He hadn't managed to keep his opinion to himself yet. *Hogwash* was the term he used to describe what he felt about their theories. But, fortunately, he wasn't the one making the call.

Slidell rocked back in his chair. "Here's what we're going to do. Landon, you work on the traditional leads we've got. Give the sister, Rachel, a call. See if there was an angry ex-boyfriend in the picture—someone who could have followed the happy couple up here. And find out all you can about this mystery man. Contact Elizabeth's neighbors. Maybe someone else got a better look at Romeo. And keep up your hunt for the truck Liz was driving. Maybe we'll get lucky and find it was rented in our mystery man's name, though I doubt it. Bailey, you search Agnes's files. See what you can find. You said this icon, if found, would be worth money?"

She nodded. "A fortune."

"All right." Slidell rubbed his chin. "Cole, you go ahead and make up a series of search grids. We'll give it a few days, if nothing else pans out we'll see if we can't locate whatever started all this trouble."

Landon leaned against the doorframe. "I think it'd be wise to assume whoever killed two people over this isn't just going to walk away. The longer we wait, the more opportunity he has to kill again."

19

"What do you keep looking at?" Piper asked, a little too loud.

"Shh." Cole didn't want to disturb any of the other worshipers as Grace's praise band sang. Leaning over, he placed his mouth a breath away from Piper's ear. "Bailey. At the back. Sitting alone." She looked so small in the long, empty row. A measly couple of days without seeing her and he'd missed her. Missed the twinkle in her eye when she talked about Jesus, missed the gentle smile that occasionally broke past her guard.

He clutched the bulletin. He couldn't go there, couldn't plunge in no holds barred. He'd given it all once, and she'd knocked his knees out from under him.

He'd tried to be enough, tried holding on tight enough for the both of them, but it had proved as futile as trying to rope the wind.

Wind always slipped through, always found a way to go where it wills, and Bailey was no different. She'd changed, but she was still running—and he was tired of chasing the wind.

The song concluded, and Pastor Braden took the stage. "How's everyone doing this beautiful morning? Please take a moment to greet one another."

Cole turned to find Piper's retreating back.

A moment later she returned with Bailey in tow, nudging her down the aisle toward him, an enormously pleased grin tickling her lips.

"Morning," he said, yearning to give Bailey a hug but settling for a chaste handshake.

"Morning." She yanked her hand back.

Was she shaking?

"I'm glad you came today," Cole said once they were outside and had a little more elbow room.

"It was a good sermon." She'd remained stock-still, almost frozen in stiff repose through its entirety.

"Yeah, it was." How did she do that? Make his heart ache to hold her? To comfort her?

"Bailey." Piper waved. She darted across the parking lot at them, her heels clicking along the pavement. "I'm glad I caught you. You're coming to the barbeque today, aren't you?"

"I'm afraid not." Bailey backed toward the sidewalk. "I've got a ton of work to do."

"Even God rested on the seventh day." Piper smiled.

Cole chuckled. "She's got a good point." It would do Bailey good to be around people instead of cooped up alone in Agnes's shop all day. Besides, the thought of spending more time with her was quite appealing. It couldn't go anywhere. *They* couldn't go anywhere. Not beyond a renewed friendship. As long as he had that concrete line fixed in his mind, he'd be all right.

Bailey bit her bottom lip. "I . . . um . . ."

"Just for a bit," Piper said. "Long enough to eat one of Gage's amazing burgers."

Poor Bailey. She looked like a deer caught in the headlights. His sister had that effect. "I can give you a lift or walk you back to the Post whenever you're ready to go," he said, hoping to sway the scales while still giving Bailey an out.

"All right. But just for a little while. I really do have a lot to get done."

"Great." Piper linked her arm with Bailey's. "Cole had a meeting before church, so we drove separately—why don't you ride with me?"

Bailey's heart thudded as they turned onto the McKennas' drive. Kayden and Piper had been kind to her, Reef didn't live in Yancey anymore—*smart man*—but what about Gage? He was closest in age to her and Cole. He knew the down-and-dirty of her past. How would he react to her presence?

She swallowed as they rounded the bend and the two-story house appeared on the horizon, steadfast against the rocky shore, the sea and the sky its backdrop. Bright bunches of fuchsia and yellow balloons danced in the breeze, and streamers fluttered from the porch posts.

"They didn't have to go to all that trouble," Piper said amidst an enormous smile. She pulled to a stop in the crook of the drive.

Kayden stepped from the house, Aurora bounding after her. "Guys, Piper's back," she hollered.

Bailey hefted a bag of soda from the backseat and stepped from the vehicle, praying her legs held. Why couldn't she stop shaking? What did she think Gage would do . . . remind Cole of what she'd done to him, how she'd cast him aside, or of who she used to be?

Gage rounded the corner, a basketball tucked under his arm. He was taller, a good six feet three, long, lean, and chiseled.

A man she didn't recognize rounded the porch after him.

"Gage, you remember Bailey Craig, don't you?" Piper said.

Bailey swallowed. *Please. I know I don't deserve it, but please let him be kind.*

"Sure." He smiled. "How ya been?"

She exhaled, her body shaky with relief. "Good, thanks." How could they all be so kind to her after what she'd done?

"Nice to see you again," Kayden said.

"You too."

"This is Jake Westin," Piper said, wrapping her arm around the man. "But he's an adopted McKenna."

Jake smiled and extended a hand.

130

Kayden sighed. "Not literally."

Jake's smile disappeared.

"Don't mind her," Gage said, squeezing Kayden's shoulders. "She acts like a bear when she's hungry."

"I do not." She reached for the bag in Bailey's arms. "Let me get that for you."

"Thanks."

Cole hefted a cooler onto the picnic table at the base of the porch steps, his muscular forearms flexing with the movement. He'd changed into his usual casual attire—T-shirt, board shorts, and flip-flops.

"Glad you decided to come," he said quietly when everyone else's attention was diverted on unloading supplies.

She glanced in Piper's direction. "Don't think I had much of a choice."

He chuckled. "None at all. I'm afraid when Piper sets her mind to something, there's no stopping her."

20

Bailey kept out of the way, observing the McKenna clan at work—unpacking bags, tucking platters in the fridge, feeding the husky. Everyone worked independently yet in unison.

It was fascinating, and a bit depressing, watching a family actually interacting like a family.

They were each other's home—a home and family, minus the parents. She hadn't thought that possible. Nothing had been right in her life since her parents split—not that much had been right before that.

"Hey." Cole angled to look her in the eyes. "You all right?"

She nodded, burying her emotions and fixing a happy face. She'd become proficient at it. "Fine."

"You say that an awful lot."

Leave it to Cole to call her on it.

"I don't know about y'all, but I'm starving," Gage said.

Kayden shouldered past him with a bowl of chips. "Aren't you always?"

Gage swiped a handful. "I'm a growing boy."

"You got the boy part right."

"A bear when she's hungry." Gage hefted the bag of charcoal over his shoulder. "I better get the grill going."

Jake stood. "I'll give you a hand."

Gage slid on his *Kiss the Cook* chef hat. "You can watch and learn from the master, my good man."

Piper chuckled.

Kayden sighed. "Don't encourage him."

"She can't help it." Gage squeezed Piper's shoulder. "She knows I'm hilarious."

Kayden cracked a grin. "Such a mess."

"Enough talk," Gage said. "Let's get this party started. Cole, you're on patties."

"Got it."

"Piper, you're in charge of ice and drinks."

"On it."

"Kayden, how are the sides coming?"

"Done."

Gage dipped his head. "Of course they are. Let's see. . . . You can set up tables."

"Already started."

"Excellent." He looked to Jake. "Shall we make a fire?"

"I'll keep the extinguisher handy," Kayden said as she strolled from the room.

Bailey slipped into a chair, content to just sit back and observe.

Cole reached for her hand. "No watching allowed. You can help me with the patties."

You can do this. You can take his hand.

It closed around hers, his skin soft and firm. He was warm, and his heat radiated through her. She swallowed hard. "Patties."

"Right." He nodded, not budging.

"You'll want to change first," Piper said.

Bailey jerked in her direction, forgetting anyone else was still in the room. "What?"

"You don't want to make hamburger patties in your nice suit. You can borrow something of mine."

"Oh, it's okay. I'm fine."

"Nonsense. I bet we're the same size." Piper started up the steps, then paused when she didn't follow. "Come on. We'll get you fixed right up."

Bailey looked at Cole.

He smirked. "When Piper makes up her mind . . ."

She chuckled. "I know."

Cole dumped the meat, bread crumbs, and chopped onions into a large glass mixing bowl.

Hearing footsteps, he looked up.

Two sandaled feet with pink toenails appeared first, followed by two long, shapely legs, a pair of cream shorts, a black T-shirt, and finally Bailey's gorgeous face. She'd let her hair down, and it fell in soft amber waves across her shoulders.

"Wow."

She nearly missed the bottom step, her cheeks tingeing pink. "It's just a pair of shorts and a T-shirt." She shifted her weight uncomfortably.

"Casual looks good on you."

"Thanks."

"You're welcome." He couldn't take his eyes off her. She was breathtaking.

She eyed the mixing bowl. "We ready here?"

"Almost, but first I must swear you to secrecy."

"Oh?"

"Yes. What follows is a McKenna recipe that's been in our family for over two years." He widened his eyes with mock gravity. "You must promise never to reveal what you learn here."

"Okay."

He arched a brow.

"Scout's honor."

"Very well, we may proceed."

They added chopped onions and garlic, several routine spices, and then Cole paused for dramatic effect. "Now, for the *pièce de résistance*." He held up a jar of cocoa powder.

"Cocoa? You've got to be kidding."

"I know it sounds weird. . . ."

"Borderline disgusting."

"It's delicious. I promise."

"How'd you even come up with it?"

"Gage, in one of his creating stages. He's quite the chef."

Her gaze flashed to the patio door and she laughed. "He seems quite enthralled with grilling too."

Cole looked over her shoulder at Gage battling three-foot flames with a water bottle. "He calls it grilling with style."

She laughed. "I can see that.

Bailey grimaced as the hamburger slipped through her fingers. "Oooh. Reminds me of Halloween parties."

Cole arched a brow.

"You know, when your friends turn their basement into a haunted house and have all the mystery bowls you have to stick your hands into. Peeled grapes for eyeballs. Spaghetti noodles for brains."

He leaned against the counter. "Sounds like you had some interesting friends."

"That's an understatement." Though, looking back, she'd never really had any close friends growing up, never truly fit in.

She was always the odd girl out, always watching from the periphery, wondering why she was different and what was wrong with her. Why her family didn't resemble those happy ones where the parents actually spent time with their kids, actually seemed to enjoy goofing around together the way Cole and his siblings did.

The old familiar ache in the pit of her stomach returned, and she bolstered herself for the wave of nausea that typically followed.

She forced herself to focus on the task at hand, working the meat into a perfectly shaped patty, and then held it up for inspection.

Cole gave a lopsided grin. "Close . . ."

He moved behind her and reached his arms around her; taking her hands, he helped her shape a bigger patty. For a brief moment she let herself enjoy the warmth and security of his strong arms.

"How we coming on the—" Gage stopped short at the sight of them.

Bailey jolted, rearing her head back. It collided with Cole's face.

He grunted.

She covered her mouth with her hand. "I'm so sorry. I was startled . . ."

"It's okay." Blood streamed across his lip. He pinched the bridge of his nose and tilted his head back.

"I can't believe I did that." She rummaged around for a towel.

"I'll come back." With a smirk, Gage turned heel and slid the door shut behind him.

"Here." She handed Cole a paper towel. "Are you sure you're all right?"

"Good as new." He straightened once the blood clotted and wiped the residue from his face. "Pursuing adventure for a living I get more than my fair share of knocks. Getting a backwards head-butt from a beautiful lady is nothing to complain about."

She bit her bottom lip. "I have no idea how to take that."

"Trust me. . . ." He winked. "It's a huge compliment."

21

The guests arrived in droves.

Bailey followed Cole onto the patio. Clusters of people dotted the expansive back lawn—stretching from the majestic line of evergreens rimming the north side of the property all the way to the sandy beach lining the east side of their land. "Looks like you invited all of Yancey."

"That would be Piper. I only invited one."

"Oh." She tried not to squeak the word. All this time spent with Cole was dangerous. *Very dangerous.* She was beginning to long for things she could never have. At least not in Yancey, and never with Cole.

"Let me introduce you around, or reintroduce, I suppose."

She stepped back. "Nah, that's okay. I'm good here."

He studied her a moment, then nodded.

He understood. Which . . . while good on the one hand was very bad on the other. It meant he'd discovered the chink in her self-reliant armor—she cared what others thought, and that made her vulnerable. Something she'd vowed never to be again.

"I'll get us something to drink."

"Lemonade would be great."

"You got it." He headed in the direction of the smoke. The yard was too crowded to see Gage at the grill, but the scent of charred meat wafted along the breeze. At least there was lots of potato salad.

"Bailey." Gus shuffled toward her with a big grin on his face. "So good to see you here."

"Thanks."

"How's everything coming with the Post?"

"Slowly getting it in order."

"Good to hear." He slathered a chip with dip. "You've got to try this. It's phenomenal." He popped it into his mouth and red flushed his ears.

"Spicy?"

He nodded. "Just the way I like it."

She laughed.

He offered her one.

"No thanks." She was waiting for the butterflies to settle before she added anything to her stomach. "Hey, I've been meaning to ask you, have you found anyone who is interested in buying the Post?"

He took the opportunity to shove another chip in his mouth, then held up a finger to signal he needed a minute.

"Bailey." Landon stepped up beside her. "How's it going?"

"Fine, thanks."

"Looks like Piper overdid it again."

"I think it's nice so many people want to celebrate with her." Bailey's birthdays usually consisted of Carrie and a couple of ladies from church. She couldn't imagine having so many friends and such a loving family.

"Yeah, it's hard to believe she's already twenty-three."

"You've known the McKennas long?"

"Since kindergarten. The year Piper was born, in fact."

"Wow. So you've known her her whole life."

"Yeah." His gaze landed on Piper and he smiled. "I guess I have."

"Landon." A gaudily dressed woman strutted over. "I want to talk to you."

Landon sighed. "Thelma Jenkins, you're looking well." She wore a brightly flowered Hawaiian blouse over a pair of red slacks.

"Don't go trying to change the subject." She waggled her finger.

"I didn't know we were on a subject." Landon shrugged.

Thelma narrowed her eyes, the green sparkly shadow across her lids glittered brightly in the sun's rays. She shielded her eyes, squinting at Landon. "I heard there was another murder on that boat of Cleary's that you all towed in."

"Now, where did you hear that?"

"Never mind where I heard that. Is it true?"

"We're here for Piper's birthday. It's not the time or the place to discuss an ongoing police investigation."

"Don't you give me that, young man. I am a concerned citizen, and I have a right to know if a killer is on the loose. We all have a right to know if we're in danger."

Mayor Cox pressed his way into the conversation. "Danger? Not in Yancey." Bailey had met the mayor as she and Cole were leaving the sheriff's station on Thursday night and was not at all surprised by his eagerness to placate Thelma. He wrapped his arm around the woman's shoulders and steered her away from Landon. "Now, I can assure you, Thelma, you are in absolutely no danger."

Landon exhaled. "Great. The last thing we need is Thelma Jenkins stirring up panic."

"Do you think Mayor Cox is telling her the truth? Do you think she's in any danger?"

"I don't believe those murders were random. As long as she doesn't have what the killer needs, she's safe."

"Somehow that doesn't make me feel much better."

Landon sighed. "Or me."

Bailey sat on the stone bench beneath the poplar trees, alone for the first time all afternoon. *If* being surrounded by a hundred people could be considered alone. She'd tried slinking back in the shadows, tried spending the day on the fringes, but the McKennas would have none of it. Each gently tugged her into the festivities, making her feel welcome and wanted. It was a foreign feeling—strange and addictive. One she didn't want to end but knew it eventually would.

She slipped her feet from the sandals and let the grass tickle her toes as a breeze riffled through it, her mind still lingering on her conversation with Landon. Would finding the sunken church really solve the case? Would finding the icon lead them to the killer, or the killer to them?

"Mind if I take a load off?" Jake asked.

She scooted over. "Not at all."

She had to admit, Jake piqued her curiosity. With the marked exception of Kayden, the McKennas treated him as one of their own, and he clearly reciprocated their affection, but something in his sheltered gaze and guarded manner said he believed he didn't belong. She understood the feeling all too well. And it made her wonder what Jake's story was. Why he'd transplanted to Alaska of all places?

It appeared nobody knew anything about the man before he turned up in Yancey.

He offered her a soda.

"Thanks." She popped the top and took a sip. The day had grown increasingly warm, the temperature pushing eighty. A scorcher in Yancey. She was thankful for the cooler attire Piper had provided.

"Enjoying yourself?" Jake asked.

"Actually, I am." She grimaced at how that must have sounded, but Jake only smiled over the rim of his root beer.

He wiped the foam from his lip. "I'm glad."

Cole waved across the yard, and she waved back.

"He's a good man," Jake said.

Her cheeks warmed and she looked down, fiddling with the tab of her can. *Which is why he'd never have a future with a girl like me.* "They're a great family."

"That they are."

"They seem to count you as part of it."

Jake smiled on an intake of breath. "Most of them." He reclined. "You should be careful or the same thing will happen to you."

Her eyes narrowed. What did he mean? Would Kayden shun her as well? So far she'd been nice, but what if she stayed in Yancey, what if Cole showed interest in her? Would Kayden change her tune?

"Yep. You hang around here much longer and you'll be part of the family, whether you like it or not."

She swallowed the fear pricking at her and forced a chuckle. "That bad?"

"Actually, it's great, but it sure makes it harder to run."

Laughter erupted, and Bailey jerked her head up.

Gage stood drenched a few feet from the grill. He pointed his spatula—beads of water dripping off it—at Piper. "Oh, you did not."

She pulled another water balloon from behind her back and hit Gage smack in the chest, water exploding about him.

"Game on!" He tossed the spatula and took off after her.

A moment later Gage carried Piper, kicking and screaming, over his shoulders like a sack of potatoes down to the water and flung her unceremoniously into the rising tide.

While he was busy enjoying the victory, Kayden and Cole sneaked up behind him and launched him in head over heels beside his sister.

Kayden and Cole exchanged a high five.

"This ought to be good," Jake said, rising to his feet.

He and Bailey joined the crowd at the water's edge.

Piper emerged first, followed by Gage with a big grin on his face.

"I'm going to change," Piper announced, sloshing off toward the house.

Gage pulled off his sopping wet shirt and tossed it at Cole. "You got a shirt I can borrow?"

Cole chuckled. "As long as you don't go for another swim."

"Can't make any promises."

"Cool tattoo," Bailey said of the tiny footprints emblazoned above Gage's heart.

Gage looked down and something shifted in his demeanor. It was slight, but Bailey sensed it all the same. The playfulness was gone.

"Thanks." He trailed a long, lean finger across the dark blue tattoo. "My son's."

"I didn't realize you had a son." Why hadn't Cole mentioned a nephew? "How old is he?"

The weight of everyone's worried gaze bore down on her. She swallowed. "Did I say something wrong?"

"No. It's fine." Gage's hands curled into balls at his side. "My boy died two days after he was born."

Bailey wished the ground would open up and swallow her. "I'm so sorry. That was so stupid of me. . . ."

"Really, it's fine. Don't sweat it." Gage squeezed her clammy hand.

His kindness only made her feel more of a heel, and she fought the urge to flee.

"Come on, guys," Gage said, forcing a smile. "This is a party. Let's get back to it." He clapped Cole on the shoulder. "I'm gonna grab that shirt."

Cole nodded and stepped to Bailey's side as everyone returned to mingling about.

"I can't believe I did that." She ran her hands through her hair.

"You had no idea."

"Still . . ." Why had she kept mumbling on like a fool when something was clearly amiss?

He tilted her chin up, forcing her to meet his gaze. "There was no way for you to know. You've got to give yourself a break."

His eyes brimming with kindness, he steered her back to the stone bench and they sat.

She released a shaky exhale. "I can't image the pain Gage suffered, the absolute heartache."

Cole hunched over and clasped his hands. "It was awful. He still hasn't healed."

How could a parent heal from that? Well, normal caring parents. Hers would have probably found it easier. It would have saved them the trouble of pawning her off fifteen years later. "I don't suppose you ever heal from something like that." It was beyond human understanding.

"No. I don't suppose you do, but I wish Gage could find some measure of peace. I've tried talking to him about Jesus, but he wants nothing to do with Him."

"When people hurt they usually want to run away from God instead of to Him—even though He's what they need most."

Cole held her gaze. "Very insightfully spoken."

She swallowed. "Just been there myself."

Late that night, Piper looked around the darkness surrounding her and took a deep breath before knocking on Landon's door, bracing herself for his initial reaction. He'd be mad and lecture her, but it would all be worth it when she told him.

Harvey howled at her knock, and a moment later, the porch light clicked on amidst the barking.

Landon opened the door, sleep heavy in his eyes. He was shirtless and wore a pair of rumpled jeans he'd clearly just pulled on. "Piper, what on earth are you doing here?" He glanced at his watch, blinked, then his eyes widened. "At one in the morning?" The haze of sleep vanished and he straightened. "What's wrong?"

She struggled to control the thrill bubbling inside of her. "I found the truck."

"You found the truck?" Landon raked a hand through his hair, making it stand more on end. "Where?"

"In the rushes past the salt marsh."

"When?"

"Just now."

He yanked her inside and switched on the lamp. He grabbed a shirt off the back of the couch and slipped it on.

Piper swallowed. Here came the lecture part. She'd let him have it out, and then he'd thank her for years to come. She'd no longer be just Cole's annoying little sister.

"What were you doing traipsing around the salt marshes in the middle of the night?"

"After everyone left the party, Denny took me on a midnight canoe ride to celebrate my birthday. We were out on the water and I saw the moonlight reflecting off something in the rushes. I made Denny go with me to investigate. It's definitely the truck, Washington plates and all." She waited for the thank-yous to roll in.

Instead, Landon crossed his arms. "Does Cole know you were out with Denny in the middle of the night?"

Unbelievable. She'd just handed him the biggest lead in the case and he was interrogating her. "Cole is my brother. Not my father. Contrary to what you think, I do not require his permission for my social life—or yours. I'm an adult."

"A really foolish one."

"I found your truck."

"At what expense? You were alone with a man in the middle of the night, in the middle of nowhere. If anything happened . . ." His jaw clenched. "There would have been no one to help."

She slumped against the back of the couch, figuring she might as well get comfortable for the ensuing reprimand. In hindsight, it would have been wiser to tell him the news in the morning, thus avoiding the whole freak-out factor, but she'd been bursting at the seams with excitement. Now she'd pay for it. "I was with *Denny*. He wouldn't hurt a fly."

"A lot of men don't show their true colors until it's too late," Landon's tone grew empathic.

She laughed at the absurdity of the idea. "Denny still lives with his mom, for goodness' sake."

"This is no joke, Piper." Gripping her by the arms, Landon hauled her from the couch and pressed her against the wall.

"Landon." She wriggled, but he held her firmly in place, his fingers boring into her upper arms. Irritation swarmed through her. She was not some child he could scare into submission. She wriggled again, to no avail. "This isn't funny."

"Exactly. That's what I'm trying to drill into that thick skull of yours." His face was an inch from hers, his breath hot on her skin as he spoke. "I could do anything I wanted to with you right now and there'd be nothing you could do to stop me." His voice was hoarse, the words heated and throaty.

She wasn't frightened, but she suddenly felt very off-kilter—like she'd just stepped off the Tilt-A-Whirl and hadn't found her footing.

The intensity burning in his eyes was new, and while it didn't change her perception of him, it did alter it. Landon was suddenly a man—virile and strong, and very in control of the moment.

"I could scream."

He cocked his head. "And who would hear?"

No one. She swallowed the lump forming in her throat, despising Landon for putting her in this position, for treating her like a child. "Fine, I get it, but—"

"No buts. You've got to make smarter choices." He released her arms but didn't step back. "This, for example"—he indicated the two of them—"isn't smart. You're at my house, and I'll bet no one knows you're here."

She laughed, hoping it would diffuse the tightness in her belly, the heat scourging through her. "Now you're being ridiculous. I know you of all people would never harm me."

"How do you know?"

Because he was her fourth big brother—worse than all the rest. He'd always been there, grafted into their family as far back as she could remember—bossing her around, teasing her, infuriating her, but . . . at the same time, always looking out for her. "Because I *know* you."

Something flickered in his eyes, and he lifted his chin a notch. "Can you say the same about Denny?"

"No, but . . ."

He exhaled, shaking his head. "Again with the buts. Piper, just because you grow up in the same town as somebody doesn't make them safe. Ted Bundy's neighbors thought he was a polite, charming guy. They never suspected he was a sociopathic serial killer."

She sighed. Put that way, perhaps a midnight canoe ride hadn't been the brightest idea—perhaps it'd even been a bit reckless. But sometimes she liked reckless, and Landon would never understand that. He was a cop. He thought like a cop and lived like a cop. It was his job to be wary, to be vigilant. She had no desire to live that way—always expecting the worst, always having to be on guard.

In frustration she pushed past him, and he did nothing to restrain her. "Don't you even want to go see the truck?"

"Of course I do." He shook his hands out.

She narrowed her eyes. Was he trembling? Had she angered him that much?

"I'll take you home and then head over there." He sat on the edge of the couch and yanked on his boots.

"I'm going with you." She'd been smart enough to keep her hands off the truck when she discovered it, but she was going to be there when Landon took a look inside. It was her find and she had a right to see where it led.

Landon grabbed his keys off the hook and held the front door open for her. "No, you're not."

She walked through. "Yes, I am."

"This isn't up for debate." He opened the truck door for her, and she climbed inside.

"You need me to find it," she said smugly, knowing she was pushing too far but unable to stop.

Gritting his teeth, he slammed the door. He stalked around the vehicle, climbed in, and without a word, started the engine and backed down the drive.

Halfway down the road, he spoke, his tone firm, his words

146

clipped. "You show me the truck and I take you home. I can handle the rest on my own."

"Fine. I'll call Denny and tell him we can finish our date."

Landon's grip tightened on the wheel, his knuckles bulging. She crossed her arms. *Checkmate.*

22

Landon followed Piper, ahead of him with the flashlight, through the mess of reeds past the salt marshes in the area they dubbed "the glades." The farther from civilization they walked, the angrier he grew. Looking out for his best bud's sister hadn't been as easy as he'd first thought, but he had no choice. It was what best friends did. If someone hurt either of Cole's sisters, it was like someone hurt him. Kayden—she'd been the easy one. She was smart when it came to her safety, not to mention frighteningly tough. *Piper* . . .

He sighed. She was a different matter entirely. If things kept heading in the same direction, she'd send him to an early grave. The girl was bright—sometimes too much so. She possessed a rapier wit, but when it came to her safety, she was irresponsible at best, downright reckless at worst.

Cole would light her up when he heard about her latest stunt, but it would make no difference. It never did. The girl was as stubborn as the day was long, and Landon feared she'd never learn until it was too late.

Granted, he'd probably gone overboard comparing Denny Foster to Ted Bundy, but he'd been trying to drive home a point— being alone with a man in a secluded setting wasn't smart under any circumstances, especially not on a third date.

His blood near boiling, he pressed into a faster stride, nearly clipping Piper on the heels.

"Scared of the dark?" she quipped.

A bullfrog croaked.

"Just keep moving." He pressed a hand to her back. "I don't want to be out here all night."

"You're cranky when you're tired."

"You keep being a sass and you'll see cranky."

"Ooh, I'm shaking in my sandals." She laughed, then abruptly stopped.

He nearly bowled her over before regaining his balance. "Brake lights would be nice."

"Sorry. I'm stuck."

"What?"

"My feet are stuck."

He took the flashlight from her and swooshed the beam across her feet, both several inches deep in mud and gook.

He smirked. "Told you, you shouldn't be sassy, pipsqueak."

She rolled her eyes. "Very funny. Now, give me a hand and quit calling me that. It wasn't funny when I was twelve and it's certainly not funny now." She braced herself against him and lifted her right leg. Her foot broke through the strap and she nearly toppled backward into him.

He steadied her. "Easy now."

"Argh! Those were my favorite sandals." She let out a huff and bent to pull the broken strap. With a sludgy suction noise, the sandal flung free, spraying Landon with a fine mist of mud.

Her lips twitched.

"Don't you dare."

She burst out laughing.

Wiping the gunk from his face, he fought the urge to wring her neck. "Let's try this my way, shall we?" He bent, slipped her foot from the remaining sandal, and scooted her behind him. Tugging the broken strap gingerly, he pulled it free and handed it to her.

"Thanks." She held it aloft as mud oozed off. "I guess it's barefoot from here."

"No way. Kids use this area as a partying spot. There's likely broken glass spread all over the area, not to mention the wildlife we might encounter."

"So what do you suggest? I hop on one foot?"

"That could be interesting." Balancing on one leg, she already looked like a lopsided flamingo. He cracked a grin.

"Get real," she sighed. "I think I'll take my chances barefoot."

"Not happening."

"Then what do you propose?"

Landon hefted Piper higher up on his back, fighting off the chill of the rain drenching them. This night had gone from bad to worse. Traipsing through the mud to the chorus of bullfrogs in pouring rain with Piper on his back was far from his ideal. He could have been home—warm, dry, and in bed. Instead, Piper had been out doing what she shouldn't, with someone she should have known better than to trust, and again, he was paying the price. At least it wasn't a total loss. She'd found the truck. He had to, no matter how begrudgingly, give her credit for that. He just hoped it would hold the answers they'd been searching for . . . if they ever reached it.

"How much farther did you say?"

"Not far."

"You said that twenty minutes ago."

"It's not my fault the rain is slowing you down."

"The rain and an extra hundred and twenty-five pounds. Or . . ." He hefted her up again. "Is it more?"

She tightened her grip on his neck. "A hundred and twenty-three, thank you very much."

He chuckled, despite the pressure on his Adam's apple.

"There." She released her death grip and aimed the flashlight a few yards in front of them.

Landon smiled at the beam bouncing off the metal bumper.

"Well," Piper said, shivering on the truck bed. It was now

half past three, and she was soaked, cold, and tired. But at least the rain had stopped.

"There's not much here." Landon slammed the truck door. "So what now?"

He wiped his brow. "Now we hike back out of here. I take you home and get Kayden to fly me to Anchorage."

"Anchorage? What for?"

He smiled. "To catch the early-morning flight to Washington. Turns out this night wasn't a total loss. I found a worn sticker on the inside of the glove box for Jim's Auto Shop in Bellingham, Washington."

23

Landon left Jim's Auto Shop with little more information than he had when he entered. Jim had refurbished and sold the truck on the side. The buyer had paid cash and said he'd take care of filling out the title.

Jim vaguely recalled the man—tall, dark hair, maybe late twenties. The truck was purchased July thirteenth. Two weeks before Elizabeth turned up in Yancey. Elizabeth's sister, Rachel, said Liz left for vacation on the twenty-third, which meant Mystery Man purchased the truck well in advance, possibly leaving it at the local airport for their pending arrival.

Rachel didn't know how her sister was traveling, but working with time constraints, flying seemed the most probable mode of transportation, at least as far as Bellingham. They must have taken the ferry from there.

So far the key had failed to match any locker at the local ferry stop or airport. Landon handed Piper a bagel sandwich and a bottle of OJ he'd procured in the airport restaurant.

She bit into it and sighed with satisfaction.

He smiled. Piper had missed some mud splatter during her rushed cleanup, and was drowning in his UAF sweatshirt, but she looked adorable.

"Maybe they came by bus," she said between bites.

"It would have taken too much time. We know they left Cali

on the twenty-third, and arrived in Yancey by the twenty-ninth at the latest. Plus you've got to allow five days for the ferry."

"Maybe they flew into Seattle. It's a much larger airport with a ton more commercial flights and only an hour and a half from here. Given Mystery Man's penchant for making his trail hard to track, it wouldn't surprise me."

"Or me. They could have easily taken a bus from Seattle to here and retrieved the truck."

"You'd think Elizabeth would question why he wanted to go in such a roundabout fashion. It had to seem strange."

"People will overlook a lot for love."

She angled her head to face him better and smirked. "Spoken from experience?"

"Now, don't you go worrying your pretty little head about my love life again."

"That reminds me. Don't think I've forgotten about your little present. Expect some serious payback."

He winked. "I'd be disappointed with anything less. Now let's go check out the Seattle airport."

After a day and evening spent in a frustrating search of Agnes's file on the Kodiak Archipelago Legends, Bailey finally located it—in the bathroom of all places, tucked between copies of *Better Homes and Gardens* in the magazine rack. She could only assume Agnes had been reading the material during one of her nightly bubble baths and forgotten it in the pile.

Had she not been leafing through the magazines for her own bath, she never would have found it. Unfortunately, it wasn't the only misplaced file. After painstakingly clearing, sorting, and refiling the stacks from the worktable, she'd noticed several files missing from the master ledger. It wasn't like Agnes to misplace things or to leave files lying about in the bathroom.

While her aunt's storeroom was bursting at the seams with

items she simply couldn't say no to, her bookkeeping and filing were meticulous.

Bailey stepped from the tub of tepid water, having read the file from cover to cover.

Pulling on a long-sleeve cotton T-shirt and a pair of flannel bottoms, she pulled her damp hair into a misshapen bun, flipped off the hall light, and headed down to the kitchen to make a cup of tea.

She picked up the phone as the water heated and dialed Cole. It was late, but she was anxious to share her find and decided there was a good chance he was still awake.

He answered on the third ring. "McKenna?"

"It's Bailey."

"This is a nice surprise." His voice was warm and rich, like melting chocolate.

She poured steaming water into the mug. "How's Gage?" Everyone had assured her he was fine and that she shouldn't think twice about it, including Gage. He'd rejoined the party wearing dry clothes and his trademark exuberant smile, and the party had proceeded as planned. A day had passed, but she still felt awful.

"He's fine. Now, stop worrying about it or I'll sic Piper on you."

She chuckled. "All right. I'll stop."

"Good."

She moved to the kitchen table and lifted Butterscotch onto her lap. He nestled into the folds of her pants and purred contentedly.

"I finally found Agnes's notes on the sunken island."

"Great. Any help?"

She swallowed a sip of tea. "Actually, yes. Looks like she did an extensive amount of work on the subject in the days leading up to her death. She cites a series of letters from the Yancey Historical Society as her primary source."

"Guess we should take a look at those letters."

"Exactly what I was thinking."

"I can meet you over there tomorrow when they open."

"Sounds good." She took another sip, debating whether to say more. She wanted to, but could she really trust Cole not to laugh at her?

"Bay?"

"Sorry." She set the mug down. "I've just been thinking. . . ."

"About?"

She exhaled, praying she didn't sound as paranoid as she felt. "How several of Agnes's files are missing."

"How can you tell?"

It was a fair question. The last time he'd been in, the place had been a disaster.

"I straightened up. There are definitely a handful missing off the master ledger, and several seriously misplaced."

"Which ones?"

"The Kodiak Archipelago Legends for starters."

Butterscotch's body tensed. Fur rising, he hissed and leapt from her lap and bolted out of the kitchen.

"What was that?"

"Nothing. Butterscotch is just being weird." The cat certainly had his moments, though that didn't explain the sudden chill washing over her. Now she really was being paranoid.

"You were saying?"

"Never mind." She put her mug in the sink. "It's nothing. Just . . ." She bit her bottom lip and leaned against the counter. "It's just that it doesn't feel like Agnes. She was so meticulous. Everything in its right place, you know?"

"It's been a long time."

"What's that supposed to mean?" That she didn't know Agnes?

"I'm just saying people change."

She twirled the phone cord around her finger. *So much for change.* Agnes still used rotary phones. "I guess I just wish she hadn't."

Maybe then she wouldn't feel so guilty about not visiting,

about always making Agnes travel to her. If she hadn't been such a coward, hiding from her past, she could have had more time with Agnes. Now it was too late.

Something clattered in the next room.

Butterscotch screeched.

"Hang on a sec. . . ."

"Anything wrong?"

"Probably just the cat getting into mischief."

Carrying the receiver with her, she moved into the shop, turned on the light, and found a chair knocked over.

"What's going on?"

"Butterscotch just tipped—" The words stalled in her throat as her gaze fell to the open front door.

Butterscotch perched just inside the threshold, hissing.

"Bailey?" Cole's voice echoed her fear.

"The door's open."

"What?"

"I must have forgotten to lock up." But she hadn't.

"I'm coming over."

"That's not necessary."

A click sounded on the other end.

Her heart hammering in her throat, she scooped up Butterscotch and peered outside.

Nothing but shadows.

24

Bailey bolted the door and checked all the windows, twice.

She carried Butterscotch to the kitchen and poured him a saucer of milk.

Leaning against the counter, she watched him lap it up. Now she just needed to figure out a way to calm herself down. Landon was right about Thelma's uncanny ability to stir a panic.

A knock rapped on the door, and she jumped, nearly kicking over Butterscotch's bowl. Her heart skittering in her chest, she gulped down a calming breath.

Moving into the shop, she found Cole waiting anxiously on the other side of the door.

His face lit when he spotted her, though it did nothing to erase the worry etched across his brow.

"Are you all right?"

"I'm fine." It was embarrassing. "Something spooked Butterscotch, and I'm afraid the effect was contagious. It was probably nothing more than the wind."

Concern flickered in his eyes. "There isn't any wind tonight."

She swallowed, ignoring the fear pricking at her. "Then I must have forgotten to lock up."

His expression said he wasn't buying it.

Another knock sounded, and she jumped, her reaction not lost on Cole.

"It's just Landon," he said softly, striding to the door.

She frowned. "You called the sheriff's department?" *Great.* Mortification set in. Now everyone would know she'd freaked out over nothing.

"I called Landon on his cell. He just got back from Washington. Said he was following a lead and had some news to share anyway. Besides, I wasn't taking any chances." He opened the door.

Landon stepped in and tipped his hat in her direction. "Bailey."

Piper followed, wearing an oversized UAF sweatshirt, and was that mud streaked through her hair?

Cole's gaze narrowed on his sister. "What happened to you, and why are you wearing Landon's sweatshirt?"

Piper brushed her mud-streaked hair back from her face and stifled a yawn.

Landon sighed. "It's a long story. But first things first." He turned to Bailey, his tired eyes filled with concern. "Cole said there was an intruder?"

"It was nothing. Butterscotch was just being skittish, and—"

"The front door was open," Cole cut in, worry thick in his voice. It was sweet. Unnecessary, but sweet.

"Are you sure you locked up for the night?" Landon asked, checking the windows.

"Yes, but . . ." What could she say? She knew in her heart she'd locked the front door. It was the first thing she did every night. Besides, she'd already suggested that explanation to Cole and he wasn't buying it. Something told her Landon wouldn't either. "Gus has a key. Maybe he stopped by to drop something off."

"And didn't say anything to you?" Cole said.

"Maybe he didn't realize I was home." It sounded farfetched even to her, but she was running out of explanations, and there had to be a logical one. She wouldn't stop grasping until she found one.

Piper wrapped a comforting arm around her shoulders.

"I'm afraid that doesn't explain why the door was left ajar.

Gus would have locked up after himself. Do you see anything new or different in the room, anything missing?" Landon asked.

Simply to appease him, she took a cursory glance around and was ready to shake her head when something silver caught her eye at the base of the worktable. It would have been easy to overlook—small and slender, the width of a toothpick, only longer.

Landon followed her gaze. He bent and retrieved it with a handkerchief. "You recognize this?" He examined the slender object and his jaw tightened.

The worry in Cole's eyes deepened.

A chill crept up her arms, and she crossed them, refusing to give in to panic. "Who knows how long that's been there. I'm sure it has nothing to do with tonight."

Landon carefully slid it into his pocket. "Mind if I take a look around, just to be safe?"

"Sure. Help yourself."

Piper's gaze shifted between Bailey and Cole. "I think I'll help Landon."

For once Landon didn't protest.

Bailey took a seat beside Cole on the couch as Landon and Piper made the rounds, inspecting first the interior and then the exterior of the building.

"This is silly. I'm sure it was nothing." If she repeated it enough, maybe they'd all start to believe it.

"We just want to make sure you're safe." Cole squeezed her hand.

How could she argue with that?

Landon and Piper returned, and Cole scrambled to his feet. "Well?"

"Everything looks secure."

Relief swept over her.

"What now?" Cole asked.

"Lock up tight. I'll run Piper home and then drive back by and make sure everything looks okay." He handed Bailey his card. "Anything else happens—you hear a sound, the cat gets spooked—you give me a call."

She took the card, knowing she didn't have a choice. "Thanks."

"I mean it. Many crimes could have been forestalled if people listened to their instincts. God gave us an innate reaction to danger. Sometimes listening can make all the difference."

"Thanks."

Piper hugged her. "You want me to stay the night?"

"That's really sweet of you, but I'm fine, really." She couldn't give in to fear.

"You sure?" Piper asked.

"Definitely."

"All right, but if you change your mind, you give me a call. Doesn't matter what time it is."

"Thanks."

"I'll walk them out and be right back," Cole said.

She nodded and tucked Landon's card in her pocket. It was nice being looked after for a change, even if it was overkill.

Landon pulled an evidence bag from the kit in his trunk and slid the pick in. "I'll run it for prints as soon as I get back to the station."

Cole leaned against the patrol car, adrenaline surging through his body. "Is that what I think it is?"

"If you're thinking it's a lock pick, then you're right."

Piper rubbed her arms, looking up and down the dark street.

Fear gnawed at Cole's gut. "I was afraid of that. So someone did try to break in. If I hadn't been on the phone with her at the time, who knows what could have happened."

"Can't be positive."

"How else can you explain the pick?" Piper asked.

"Like Bailey said, we don't know how long it's been there. Maybe Miss Agnes used it to open old jewelry boxes that were missing their key or something. We can't jump to conclusions."

Cole raked a hand through his hair. "I don't like it."

"Neither do I, but there's nothing else we can do at this point. She didn't actually see anyone enter and as far as she can tell nothing's missing. Other than this pick—which may or may not have had any other uses—there's no sign of a break-in."

"I heard the cat screech. He saw something or someone."

"Probably made whoever was using this drop it." Landon sealed the evidence bag. "Hopefully, we'll be lucky and get some prints."

"And if there are none?" Working emergency services, Cole had been privy to enough crime scenes to know that prints were a luxury.

"We'll cross that bridge when we come to it. I'll let you get back to Bailey, and I'll get this pick into evidence."

"Wait, what did you want to talk to us about?"

Landon glanced at Bailey through the window. "It can wait till morning."

"You sure?"

"Absolutely. She needs your undivided attention right now." Landon helped Piper into his car and then moved around to the driver's side. "Make sure Bailey locks up tight, and I'll drive back by after I take Piper home."

Cole tapped the roof. "Thanks, man."

"Anytime."

The door creaked as Cole came back inside. He paused to lock it before sitting down on the couch beside her. "You doing all right?"

Bailey rubbed her arms, trying to chase the lingering chill away. "Yeah, I'm fine."

Butterscotch lumbered in from the kitchen, licking his lips. Stretching, he flopped down contentedly at Bailey's feet.

Cole chuckled. "That was a quick recovery."

She smiled, rubbing Butterscotch's full belly. "A saucer of milk works wonders."

"What about you? Can I get you a cup of tea, a milkshake?"

Her brows knit together. "A milkshake? It's almost midnight." But it sounded good. She hadn't had one in years.

Cole tilted his head at the street outside. "The diner lights are still on. I'm sure I could get Gus to rustle us up a couple of milkshakes."

"I'd forgotten how good Gus's shakes are."

Cole got to his feet. "What's your flavor?"

"You don't have to go to any more trouble."

"No trouble. All this talk about milkshakes, now I'm craving one."

"If you're sure . . ."

"Positive."

"Okay, then, chocolate. But if Gus is leaving for the night, don't keep him."

"You got it. One chocolate, one moose tracks, coming right up." He jiggled the doorknob. "Lock this behind me."

"You're going to be right back."

"And I'll knock like a gentleman."

Now her heart was pounding for an entirely different reason. Different, but no less frightening.

She needed to tread carefully. She was letting Cole slip past her radar, and for what? Nothing could happen between them. Nothing long-range, anyway. He knew her past. He was part of it. He'd never view her as wife material. How could he? To him, no matter what he may say otherwise, she'd always be *that* girl, never *the* girl.

25

Thirty minutes and one fantastic milkshake later, Cole watched the fright fade from Bailey's eyes. Though she insisted it had been nothing, he wasn't convinced. While he couldn't outright dismiss Landon's suggestion that the pick may have belonged to Agnes for some other purpose, that didn't explain Butterscotch's screech, or the open front door.

He closed his eyes, lifting a quick prayer of thanks to God that he'd been on the phone with Bailey when it happened.

The last breaking and entering had been done by Jesse Ryan and his old crowd that wandered down from Kodiak Island on the weekends. But they tended to be way less subtle, using a credit card to slip an easy lock or a rock to bust a window. He'd check with Jesse, see if he'd heard any news concerning his old crowd, if they were back to their old tricks, but the pick seemed a bit sophisticated for a bunch of troubled youth.

A few times over the years, the sheriff's department had caught a tourist trying to make a heist and disappear back onto the cruise ship and into the sunset. More likely they were dealing with a drifter who assumed the shop was unoccupied. It was a natural assumption, as the majority of stores on Main Street were after nightfall, though the Post was the only one that housed items of substantial worth.

Hearing Bailey probably startled the perpetrator and he'd fled, dropping his pick in the process.

It was the most logical scenario, but it brought Cole little peace. What if the thief returned? Tried again while Bailey was sleeping? What if she interrupted him a second time? Would he still flee so easily?

"Thanks for the shake." Bailey fiddled with her straw. "And thanks for coming over."

Her shyness warmed him. She was not the bold girl he remembered, but she was a world stronger. "You're welcome. I'm glad I could be here."

She smiled, her eyes somehow testing him. "It's getting late."

His cue to leave.

"Yeah. I should be going." He got to his feet and stretched. "You sure you're okay?"

"I'm good."

He wished he could say the same. He didn't want to leave her, not with a thief on the loose. "I could bunk out on your couch for the night." At least then he'd know she was safe and he'd sleep a whole lot easier.

"No." The word was clipped, curt.

"Strictly platonic. I'm just worried about you." Didn't she know she could trust him?

The angles of her face softened slightly. "I appreciate your concern, but that's impossible."

His brow furrowed. Interesting choice of words. *Impossible*.

She rubbed her temples. "Everyone would think . . ."

He stepped closer. "What?"

"Never mind." She rubbed her arms. "I better get some sleep."

He contemplated pursuing the conversation, but she needed her rest, not something else to tax her. "I'll see you in the morning."

"Okay." She shut the door, and through the window Cole watched her walk to the stairs and flip out the light.

Cole sighed. He knew exactly what she was going to say. Everyone would think they'd been intimate, that she was back to her old ways.

But that wasn't her anymore. She was a new creation. It was time she started realizing it.

He climbed in his truck as the upstairs light switched on.

Father, I see Bailey struggling and I hate it. She's a new creation, but she's letting the past weigh her down. She's running. She's hiding. I want to see her settled, at peace. I want . . .

I want . . . her back in my life so badly it hurts. The thought of never being with her again . . . it's like a chokehold. How did I let this happen? This can't happen. Change my heart, Lord. Please, change my heart.

The air left his lungs in a whoosh. *Can't go there. Erase the possibility from your mind. Be her friend. That's enough. Enough.*

The upstairs light clicked off and he slouched back into his seat.

One by one the few remaining lights along Main Street followed suit, until the entire street lay shrouded in darkness.

He'd stay and keep watch awhile. He needed the time to think.

He was pacing the wooden floor when Kiril returned, a ski mask clasped tightly in hand.

Something had gone wrong.

Kiril shuffled his feet, his boots making that horrid scuffing sound against the floorboards. How many times had he asked him not to do that?

"What happened?"

"The girl"—Kiril cleared his throat—"she was awake."

"I told you to make sure she was in bed before you went in."

Kiril paled. "The lights were off . . . mostly. I . . . I made a mistake."

A mistake? The imbecile could have cost him everything. "Did she see you?"

"No, but . . ."

"But?" he asked through clenched jaw.

"She called the cops."

Anger pulsated through him.

"That boyfriend of hers, his friend is the deputy. He came over and walked around and . . ."

He narrowed his eyes. What was Kiril holding back? "And?"

"He left."

"Simply left?"

Kiril nodded, perspiration beading on his thick brow. "I'm sorry, boss."

"You're sorry." He stalked to the window. He gazed out over the barren wasteland he was forced to endure until his plan was complete.

"She didn't see me," Kiril repeated, his voice cracking.

Must I do everything myself? "Please tell me you at least found the paper work."

"No, but she found something."

He turned. "Oh?"

"I heard her say something about a sunken island."

"So she's getting closer." He exhaled, trying to vent the rage from his body to keep from killing Kiril. Another dead body was the last thing he needed.

"You want me to take her out?"

"No. I told you. It would draw too much attention." It was the only reason Kiril was still breathing. Back home murder happened; few inquiries were made and then the matter simply vanished. But in this pathetic place every measly crime was earth-shattering.

"But what if she figures it out? What if she finds it?"

He let the gamut of possibilities run through his mind and then smiled. "Maybe that wouldn't be so bad."

"Huh?"

It would save him the effort of hiring another team. He couldn't hire just anyone. He needed qualified divers with experience in retrieving artifacts, needed people with loyalty. He thought he'd had that with Nik, but he'd been dead wrong.

Perhaps waiting was the prudent thing. Give the girl time to figure it out, let her do the work, and then he could sweep in and reap the rewards.

"Boss?" Kiril asked hesitantly.

"Never mind." This was obviously beyond the scope of Kiril's understanding. He'd stick with the simplest of instructions from now on. "Continue to watch the girl. From a *distance*."

"Just watch?"

"Yes." He steepled his fingers. Perhaps Kiril's blunder could play to his advantage. "Let's see where she goes with this new-found information."

26

Butterscotch wove in between Bailey's feet as she made her way downstairs. She'd slept later than usual, and her growling belly was staging a protest. Sun poured through the front shop windows, reminding her she needed to dust.

At least they were in for another gorgeous day. Her gaze fell to the pickup out front and recognition dawned. *Cole. What is he doing here?*

Butterscotch meowed for breakfast.

"Just a minute. If my coffee can wait, so can your milk."

She strode to the door, expecting to let Cole in, but he wasn't there. *That's odd.* She looked up and down the street, and across at Gus's diner, which was still bustling with the breakfast crowd.

As she approached the pickup, there was no doubt—it was definitely Cole's truck, dented bumper and all. She peered inside and jumped.

Cole was crunched up in the tiny cab, his face smashed against the steering wheel, one leg pressed against the gear shift, the other elevated on the passenger seat back. He looked adorable. Had he spent all night there? To make sure she was safe?

Her heart squeezed. *Stubborn man.*

Sunlight streaked across his face, and he shifted restlessly.

She took one more glance up and down the street, found no one watching, and rapped on the window.

It took a moment, but Cole opened his eyes—the haze of

sleep still heavy in them. He sat up, his mouth open, clearly disoriented. Seeing her, he smiled and leaned over, unlocking the passenger door.

She rested against it. "Morning, sleepyhead."

The fog gone, a pair of gorgeous green eyes stared back at her. "Morning." He adjusted his misaligned clothes and ran a hand through his hair. "Sleep well?"

"Very, though I doubt you can say the same."

"It wasn't so bad." He stretched and something popped.

She winced. "That didn't sound good."

"Ah, it's nothing." He stretched his neck side to side, revealing a large steering-wheel imprint.

She laughed.

He narrowed his eyes. "What?"

She indicated his cheek. "The steering wheel left its mark."

"Oh." He grinned sheepishly and rubbed his skin.

"Why don't you come in for a cup of coffee? It looks like you could use one."

"All right. Don't mind if I do." He climbed from the truck, moving a bit gingerly at first, and followed her inside.

"You didn't have to stay," she said over her shoulder, making her way to the kitchen.

"I know."

She pulled two mugs from the cupboard and poured them each a cup. "I was planning on making some pancakes. Mabel got another shipment of fresh blueberries in yesterday. Wanna stay for breakfast?"

"I'd love to."

Cole set his napkin on the table. "That was delicious."

Bailey smiled at his appreciation for something as simple as homemade pancakes. "Glad you enjoyed it." She lifted her plate and reached for his.

"No." He shook his head. "I got this. McKenna rule—he who cooks doesn't do dishes."

"Is that so?" She handed him her plate and watched as he set about clearing the rest of the table.

"Yes, ma'am." He spun a plate on the tip of his finger before sliding it atop the pile already effortlessly balanced in his other hand, whistling as he worked.

"And how often do you provide this entertaining service?"

He grinned, twirling the butter knife in the air before catching it. "More often than I'd like to admit, but it's better than eating my cooking."

She chuckled. "I'll have to remember that."

The kitchen door creaked, and Cole turned.

Much to Bailey's surprise, he managed to keep the towering stack of plates in perfect order.

With a smile, she looked to see who entered and her breath caught.

"Sorry to interrupt," Tom said, looping a finger in his waistband. His gaze raked over her, and her stomach turned sour. There was nothing indecent about her sleeping attire—a pair of flannel pajama bottoms and an oversized T-shirt, but somehow he made her feel dirty with a single glance.

"You weren't interrupting. We were just having breakfast." She fought the urge to explain. Tom wouldn't believe her anyway. He'd already made up his mind about her—to him she'd always be Easy Lay Bay. She cringed at the horrid nickname.

"Looks like a nice hearty breakfast." Tom sauntered forward. "Always good after a lot of activity."

Cole lowered the stack of dishes to the table. "Like the lady said, we were just finishing breakfast."

"Right." Tom took pains to draw the word out.

Cole stepped between her and Tom. "Was there something you needed?"

Tom tilted his head, gazing at Bailey over Cole's shoulder. "Sheriff needs to see Miss Craig."

"Is something wrong?"

"I'm not at liberty to discuss it in detail, but suffice it to say, the sheriff has some news about your aunt's crash."

"Agnes?" What news could there be?

"He'd like you to drop by the station"—Tom's gaze raked over her once more—"after you're properly dressed, of course."

She swallowed the bile burning up her throat. "I'll be over shortly."

Tom didn't move, just stood staring at her, taunting her.

"Anything else?" Cole took another step forward, quickly diminishing the space between him and Tom.

What was he doing? Trying to make things worse by starting a fight? That'd be the flame that would ignite the already tentatively explosive situation into a grand spectacle for all to see. By lunchtime everyone in town would hear of how Tom had caught her and Cole red-handed, trying to play off a night of sex as an innocent breakfast. A fight between Tom and her supposed lover would only add fuel to the fire that would tear her apart all over again.

Her heart physically ached—her chest tightened, strangling the breath from her. At least before she'd deserved the criticism, the harsh words, the cruel nickname, but this time she'd only tried to be nice. She should have known better. She'd let her guard down, and now she was going to pay.

"I asked if there was anything else," Cole said, the words clipped and precise.

Tom seemed to be truly reveling in the moment. "Not a thing." With a tip of his hat, he swaggered to the door and with one last grin was gone.

Biting back tears, Bailey stood and grabbed the stack of dishes.

Cole turned. "Let me get that."

"I've got it."

He reached for them.

She clutched them tighter. "It's fine." To her mortification, her hands shook, rattling the silverware atop the pile. She spun toward the kitchen and the silverware tumbled with a clang to the floor. She bent, scrambling to pick them up. If she just kept moving . . .

Cole knelt beside her and stilled her hand with his. "Hey."

She pulled away, grabbing the forks and springing to her feet. "Look, I've got to get ready and go see Slidell."

"I'll go with you."

"And give Tom more ammo? No thanks." She carried the dishes to the kitchen and flung them in the sink.

"Don't let Tom make you feel guilty about something that *didn't* happen."

"That's not the point." She dumped in dish soap and turned the water on.

Cole stepped closer. "It's precisely the point."

Keep your distance. I'm not strong enough for this. Not now. Not with all that's happening.

She braced her hands on the counter. "Look, I appreciate your concern, but I'm fine. I've got to get ready, so if you could please leave."

"Bay?" The tenderness of his tone nearly unleashed her tears.

"Please." She shut off the water and started scrubbing the first dish she grabbed.

"All right." He stepped back. "Maybe we can talk later."

"We'll see." She kept scrubbing, knowing there wouldn't be a later.

27

Cole strode across Main Street with one thing on his mind—finding Tom and trying, most likely futilely, to make him see the truth of the situation.

The last thing Bailey needed was Tom Murphy spreading ugly rumors about her around town, rumors that would only compound her pain.

Cole's muscles gripped like a vise down his neck, spreading across his shoulders in a triangle of pain.

Why was it guys slept around and got praised for it? A girl did and she was branded for life. Not that he approved of Bailey's past behavior—it had flat-out broken his heart—but it was simply that, in the past. It had no bearing on the present. Bailey was beating herself up every day for things she'd done a decade ago. She was a new creation in Christ, yet she was letting the past suffocate her.

He pushed through the station door, the noxious odor of alcohol and body waste nearly bowling him over.

He looked to the holding tank. Samuel Hancock lay sprawled across the floor snoring, his clothes doused in liquor and vomit.

Cole lifted a hand to his face and strode to the front desk. "Come on, Earl. At least give the man some clean clothes to wear, wash him off . . . something." *Give him a little dignity; show a grain of compassion.*

Deputy Earl Hansen glanced up from his paper. "I'm not touching that mess. Besides, maybe it'll make him think twice before boozing so hard again."

Cole moved toward the bull pen, where the deputies had their desks. He needed to catch Tom before . . .

Raucous laughter echoed down the hall.

. . . it was too late.

Cole rubbed the back of his neck. "Let me guess—Tom's back there?"

Earl grinned, his silver-plated tooth gleaming in the fluorescent beams.

He strode the rest of the way down the hall and into the rear office hub, frustration barely tamped beneath the surface.

Tom sat perched on the corner of Thoreau's desk, a wide grin in place.

Great. Cole grimaced. Now he had two to reason with.

"Well, speak of the devil," Tom said. "Ready to spill the nitty-gritty?"

"That's what I wanted to talk to you about."

"Well, all right." Tom hopped down from the desk. "I knew you weren't the pansy you pretended to be, that deep down you're just like us."

Cole recoiled at the thought.

"So . . ." Tom nudged him in the ribs. "She learn any new tricks over the years?"

"Like I said, nothing happened." He worked to keep his voice firm and even, not to give in to the urge to ream Tom out.

Tom's pleasure faded. "We're back to that story."

"It's not a story. It's the truth. Nothing happened." Maybe if he repeated it enough, it would finally sink in.

Tom folded his arms. "Let me see if I got this right. You just happened to be at her place having breakfast, wearing the same clothes you had on yesterday, while she's in her pj's." Tom glanced over his shoulder at Thoreau with brows raised, then back at Cole. "Is that what you expect us to believe?"

Cole balled his fists, his knuckles cracking. Flashbacks of Tom and Thoreau in the high-school locker room carrying on about their exploits with Bailey raced through his mind. Disgust flooded over him, now as it had back then. Only now he'd be man enough to say something. Their days of talking about Bailey as if she were trash were over.

Back then his pride had been wounded, his heart crushed by what she'd done, at who she'd become. He'd washed his hands of her, written her off as a messed-up girl, and moved on—leaving Bailey among the wolves to be devoured or self-destruct, whichever came first.

Two years later she reentered his world, cornering him at Tag Newton's graduation party wasted, as usual, and trying her best to seduce him. How far she'd fallen from the beautiful, bright-eyed girl he'd known and loved.

He'd rejected her, of course, and done it kindly. Well, what seemed kind to an eighteen-year-old with a chip on his shoulder. He'd told her to go home or sober up, or something to that effect—his tone and distance making it clear he didn't dally with girls like her.

Like her. His own words made him cringe, the hurt in her eyes coming back to haunt him.

If he hadn't been so self-absorbed, if he'd have forgiven her for what she'd done to him two years earlier, if he'd been at all decent . . . he'd have gotten her a cup of coffee and seen her safely home, instead of passing her off to the next guy she'd hit up.

She never spoke to him after that night, never looked him in the eye again. Not until he'd strode into Agnes's shop last week asking for help.

No wonder she hadn't looked happy to see him.

He raked a hand through his hair and looked up to find Tom and Thoreau staring at him.

"Reliving the moment?" Tom chuckled.

Cole exhaled. "Last night Bailey heard a noise. I was on the phone with her at the time discussing the case and insisted on coming over to check it out."

Thoreau rolled his eyes. "Sure she heard a noise."

The muscle in Cole's jaw flickered. How immature could they be? "You can ask Landon if you don't believe me. He was there too."

"Really?" Tom's smile widened.

Focus on the words. For Bailey. "Everything checked out all right except—"

Tom and Thoreau exchanged a knowing glance.

"What?" Cole practically seethed.

"It was a ploy to get you over there," Tom said. "She may act and look like she's Miss Goody Two-Shoes now, but we know better."

His self-control slipping, Cole pressed on. "Landon left to take Piper home. I climbed in my truck and decided to stay awhile just to be certain she was safe."

"Right . . ." Tom drawled out the word.

"I must have fallen asleep. Next thing I knew it was morning and Bailey invited me in for a cup of coffee. That's when you showed up."

"Uh-huh."

"It's the truth." How many times did he have to say it?

Tom lifted his chin. "Here's Landon. Let's see what he has to say."

"What I have to say about what?" Landon asked, striding into the office.

"About last night," Cole began.

"Yeah," Tom interrupted, "Cole was just telling us about it. What I want to know is why Cole called you in. He need some help pleasing the whore?"

That's it. Cole lunged forward, heat seething through his limbs.

Terror flashed in Tom's eyes.

"Whoa!" Landon jumped between them.

Tom spewed out a string of expletives.

"He's not worth it, man." Landon struggled to restrain Cole. "He may wholly deserve it, but as long as he's wearing that uniform, you're looking at assaulting a police officer."

Cole lowered his arms. Taking a deep breath, he took a step back. "You're right."

"If you ladies are done bickering," Slidell barked from the doorway, "we've got more murders on our hands."

Landon turned, his brows raised. "More murders?"

"In my office. Now." Slidell turned heel and strode down the hall.

Tom and Thoreau moved first, followed by Landon and lastly Cole.

"What's this about another murder?" Landon's tone echoed everyone's concern.

Slidell grabbed a sheet of paper from the fax machine and sat down. "NTSB has ruled sabotage as the cause of Henry Reid's crash. I've spoken with Ginny, and Bailey is . . ." His gaze shifted to the door.

Bailey entered, looking all business. The no-nonsense suit was back, her hair tight in a bun. No trace of makeup or color tinged her face, not even the soft peach that naturally brushed her cheeks. No color at all except her blue eyes—pink rimmed and puffy.

Cole's heart lurched. If either one of the twiddle twins said so much as one word to belittle her or that made her the least bit uncomfortable, no one would be able to stop him from silencing them.

"Bailey," Landon said.

She gave a curt nod—no smile touching her lips—careful not to meet anyone's eyes.

Slidell pinned a stern warning glare on Tom and Thoreau before standing to greet her. "Thanks for coming down so quick."

"Your deputy said it was about Agnes?"

He pulled out a chair for her. "Please, have a seat."

She was trying so hard not to look vulnerable that it broke Cole's heart.

"Tom, Thoreau, I can catch you two up to speed later." Slidell settled back into his chair. "Go get Samuel cleaned up and dropped off at home."

Tom hesitated.

Slidell narrowed his eyes.

Tom turned heel and strode from the room. Thoreau followed.

Bailey's rigid posture relaxed slightly once they were gone.

Slidell leaned forward, resting his burly weight on his forearms. "As I was just telling Cole and Landon here, NTSB, the National Transportation Safety Board, has ruled the cause of the plane crash was sabotage."

Shock swept over Bailey's beautiful face. "Are you certain?"

Slidell lifted the fax, his eyes skimming the text. "Quite."

"Why? Why would someone want to . . . ?" Her question trailed off.

Landon cleared his throat. "Do they have any suspects or leads?"

Slidell shook his head. "The NTSB report says that according to commercial airline records three of Gus's passengers flew in early that afternoon from Petropavlovsk-Kamchatsky, Russia."

"Mark Olsen and the mystery passengers," Bailey murmured.

"Actually, no. Mark Olsen is from Anchorage. His wife said he was heading down here for a fishing retreat."

Bailey's brows pinched together. "So . . . Agnes was in Russia?"

"According to Alaska Airlines, yes."

"Why?"

"That's what we were hoping you could tell us."

"I have no idea. I talked to her a few days before the acc—" She swallowed. "Before the crash, and she said nothing about taking a trip." She rubbed her forehead. "I don't understand. This doesn't make any sense."

Slidell's gaze was as grim as his tone. "Murder rarely does."

"Murder?" Bailey choked out.

Slidell nodded. "Afraid so."

Bailey rubbed her temples. "I can't believe this."

Cole rested his hand on her shoulder, and she flinched.

"Sorry." He pulled his hand back. Could he offer her no comfort?

"It's fine." She brushed him off. "I'm just a little shaken."

"Can you think of anyone who would want to harm your aunt?" Slidell asked.

Bailey's eyes widened. "You think . . . you think it was because of Agnes . . . that someone was trying to kill her?"

"We don't know. We have to consider all of the victims equally as the intended target at this point."

Bailey blanched.

"Can I get you some water?" Landon offered.

"Please."

Cole ached to comfort her, to let her know she wasn't alone. Why did she insist on keeping him at arm's length?

"Who else was on the plane?" he asked, trying to focus on the facts rather than his frustration. "There were three passengers my team didn't recognize when we went in. Mark Olsen was—"

Bailey turned, her eyes widening. "You were on the . . . plane?"

He nodded. "I was part of the rescue crew sent in."

She reached out and covered his hand with hers. He tried not to notice how good her touch felt.

"And Agnes . . . Did you see her?"

He nodded again, his throat tightening as Agnes's terror-stricken face flashed through his mind.

"Was she already . . . ?" Bailey's voice cracked, and her hand gripped his.

He shook his head.

Bailey bit her bottom lip, tears glistening in her eyes.

He knelt beside her, his throat like a vise, the staggering weight of that night crushing back down on him. "I thought I had her. I carried her to the surface."

Hope flared in Bailey's eyes. Hope in him, as if somehow

he could defy time and go back, change the outcome of the events. He swallowed. If only he could, to save her the pain. "Her heart gave out before we reached shore." His voice was weak, his words strangled. He watched in anguish as sorrow washed afresh over Bailey's face.

She hung her head as tears fell, splashing off their joined hands.

Landon cleared his throat. "Your water."

She took the cup, along with a tissue. "Thanks."

Slidell shifted uncomfortably. "If this is too difficult a time, we can—"

"No." She held up a hand, the tissue scrunched between her fingers. "I'm fine."

"You can't think of anyone who would want to hurt Agnes?" Slidell asked.

"No."

Slidell added the fax to the file. "Well, I'm sure it will turn out to have nothing to do with her and everything to do with one of the other passengers, but I have to ask."

"I understand."

"The passengers?" Cole asked, bringing the question back to the table.

"Right." Slidell glanced at the file. "The NTSB lists Henry Reid, Agnes Grey, Mark Olsen . . . and the two other passengers have been identified as Fedyna and Iryna Alexandrovich, both residents of Petropavlovsk-Kamchatsky, Russia. We believe they were husband and wife."

"Russian." Landon's eyes lit. "That's very interesting."

Slidell's brows rose. "How's that?"

Landon smiled. "I'll be right back." He returned a moment later with a blue duffel in hand. He set it on Slidell's desk and slipped on a pair of latex gloves. "Piper and I found this in a locker at the Seattle airport. It belonged to our mystery man. Cole, it's what I was planning on telling you guys about last night before the break-in."

Cole stepped forward as Landon emptied the contents—a handful of passports—most Russian, each with a similar photo but different name, a leather pouch holding a bevy of credit cards in a variety of names, a couple of driver's licenses, an obscene amount of cash, and a pair of cell phones.

Cole shook his head. "Who was this guy, and what was he doing on our island?"

"Hopefully there's something in here that will help us find out." Landon bagged each item as he pulled it from the duffel. "I imagine all of these identities will turn out to be aliases, but at least we finally have a photograph to work with, and if we're really lucky, a set of prints."

28

"What do two Russians, a guy from Anchorage, our mystery man—who Landon believes is Russian—a grad student from Cali, and my aunt have to do with each other?" Bailey asked as they made their way back to the Post.

"You think they are connected?" Cole asked.

"I know it sounds absurd, but I have this feeling that somehow it's all intertwined."

"Why and to what purpose? And how would Agnes fit into it all?"

"I have no idea. It doesn't make any sense." She shrugged. "Maybe it really is a series of weird coincidences, but it doesn't explain why Agnes didn't mention anything about the trip to me."

"Maybe it was a last-minute trip."

"Why? What could have been so urgent? And why would she go to Petropavlovsk-Kamchatsky, Russia?"

"Maybe research . . . or a buying trip. She ran a Russian-American shop."

"True, but Agnes mostly did her research and purchasing via the Internet and local resources. She went to Russia more often before I came to live with her, though I can remember at least two trips she made after I left. She loved Russia. Went for the first time with her great-aunt Mildred. My mom was so mad she wasn't the sister chosen to go."

"That's when Agnes got into Russian history?" he asked.

She nodded. "She came back and followed her great-aunt's love for Russian-American history. After Mildred passed, she took over the shop." Now Bailey risked ending that legacy. By selling, she could never ensure it would remain the Post. But she couldn't think about that. What happened at breakfast would happen over and over again, and her heart couldn't take it.

Sure Cole stepped up to defend her, or more likely himself, from Tom's accusation. Sure he was being kind and attentive now, but what happened when the rumor spread? By nightfall the entire town would hear Tom's version of events, and how would Cole react then? It'd be easier for them both if she simply left and never looked back.

"So you can't think of any reason Agnes would go to Russia?"

She exhaled. "I have no idea." It seemed so out of Agnes's temperament.

"Maybe there's something back at the shop that would give us some idea of why she went. Something scribbled on her calendar, an e-mail about her trip," he suggested.

"Good idea. I'll take a look before I leave."

Cole stopped. "Leave?"

"I'm heading back to Oregon tomorrow." It was time.

"Tomorrow?" The word came out strangled.

She nodded, avoiding his gaze. Afraid of what she might find there—relief, disappointment. Not sure which would be worse.

"Is this because of Tom, because of what happened this morning?"

"Yes and no. If it wasn't Tom this morning, it would have been someone else some other time. I owed it to Agnes to come back. To take care of the shop, and now that I have, it's time for me to get back to Oregon."

"Where it's safe?"

She increased her pace. She didn't have to explain to him. He didn't have to agree with her decision.

"Sooner or later you're going to have to face your past or you'll spend the rest of your life running from it."

Her shoulders slumped. He was right, but it was her past they were talking about, her mistakes. Her choice how she dealt with them. Or ran from them. "It was nice seeing you again, Cole. You take care."

She slid the key in the lock, hoping he couldn't see how hard her hands were shaking.

"And the case?"

"I'm sure you all can handle it."

He braced his hand on the doorframe. "We need your help. You know Alaskan history. You know Agnes."

She didn't look up. "I can't." *I can't stay here.* Not long enough for him to change his mind, decide she wasn't worth the fight. Once the rumors were in full swing, he'd pull away. They always did. The cold shoulder and indifferent gaze returning until she was nothing but an unwanted memory. She couldn't face that again. Not with Cole. Not with somebody she truly cared about. It was better to leave before what remained of her heart got pummeled.

"You could be the key to solving this. We need you." He stepped between her and the door, forcing her to look at him, intensity burning in his eyes. He took a deep, shaky breath. "Agnes needs you. Liz Johnson needs you."

Disappointment rumbled through her. Of course not him. Why would he ever need someone like her? She was fooling herself even entertaining the idea there could be something there, that he could ever feel that way about her again. She'd burned that bridge, and there was no way to put the ashes together again. How stupid could she be?

"You're not playing fair." What was he trying to do? Get her to stay? Force her to endure the rumors, the cruel nickname, all over again? "You don't need me."

He never had. Sooner or later he would have realized it. That's why she'd taken the proactive route so many years ago and given him no choice. At least it'd been on her terms. She'd forced him away before he could leave. Before he found someone better and left her in the dust. Tom and the bevy of guys that followed never really cared about her. They only wanted what she provided them, but that too had been her choice. Never giving enough of herself to get hurt. Never showing who she really was, and therefore never truly being rejected.

"I'm sorry." His voice lowered. "But was what happened to Liz Johnson fair? Or what happened to Agnes and everyone else on that flight?"

Her bottom lip quivered.

"You may be the only one who has the key to righting that wrong. Without you we run the risk of never catching this guy."

She exhaled, fighting the almost primal urge to flee. "Fine. I'll give you one more week, but then I'm out of here. Killer or not."

Bailey sat at the desk and switched on Agnes's computer.

It hummed to life and twanged once the dial-up service finally connected them to the Internet. "Here goes nothing." She exhaled. "And everything . . ."

Cole rested his hands on the back of the chair, studying the screen over her shoulder, trying not to think of what had just passed between them. He'd practically begged her to stay. He'd laid it on about the case, but though what he'd said was true, there was a much deeper truth—he wasn't ready to have her walk out of his life. Wasn't ready to let go.

He raked a shaky hand through his hair. He had a week to get ready, because it was clear she wasn't staying. She either didn't trust him enough to be honest and vulnerable with him or she flat out didn't care. Either way she was leaving, and he, once again, had no recourse. She was making a call that would affect both their lives, and he had no say.

"Username and password . . . Let's pray Agnes truly was a creature of habit." She tilted the keyboard up.

Cole leaned farther over her shoulder and read, "Odette and Siegfried?"

"*Swan Lake*," she said, typing it in. "Bingo!" Her eyes narrowed. "That's strange. The in-box is empty."

"Did Agnes get much e-mail?"

"I don't know, but I e-mailed her fairly often, and everyone gets at least a few a day. There should be something here."

"Check her sent mail."

Bailey clicked on the folder. "Empty too." She clicked on each folder in turn and all produced the same result—empty. "It's like it's been wiped clean."

"Maybe Agnes emptied it out before her trip."

Bailey shook her head. "That still doesn't explain why there are no new e-mails."

"Maybe everyone knew about the crash."

"She had to be in Russia for some period of time. I'm not certain when she left, but I spoke with her on the twenty-ninth, and her plane went down on the seventh. That leaves over a week she could have been in Russia. Why are there no e-mails during that time?"

Cole sighed, frustration, hurt, and anger reeling through him. "I don't know."

"Great." She blew a loose strand of hair from her face. "Another dead end. What do we do now?"

"We find out for certain when she left for Russia."

"How? Not to sound crass, but the pilot is dead. . . . I suppose we could call the airport and see if we can track down Agnes's reservation."

"Got that covered."

Her brows pinched together. "How?"

He sank against the desk. "Don't know why I didn't think of this before, but Agnes probably flew *to* Anchorage on Henry's plane too—and it was a family-run operation."

Hope filled her eyes. "And you know the family?"

"Beauty of a small town. I'll give Ginny a call."

29

"Come on, Piper, just pick something," Gage grumbled as Sandy waited to take their order.

Gus's diner was still bustling with the lingering dinner crowd. Kids with ice-cream moustaches and syrupy smiles rustled in their seats as their parents chatted and picked at what remained of their oversized desserts.

Piper's eyes darted over the menu she'd read a thousand times. "I can't decide between the meatloaf and a cheeseburger. Both sound good."

"How about I get the meatloaf, you get the cheeseburger, and we share?" Cole suggested.

Piper smiled. "That sounds perfect."

"Finally," Kayden huffed. "I was getting tired of listening to Gage's stomach growl."

"I can't help it if I'm hungry."

Kayden rolled her eyes. "You're always hungry."

"So . . ." Piper popped a straw in her soda. "How is the case going?"

Cole had wondered how long it would take her to ask. "Slower than any of us like, but Bailey and I may have found a lead."

Piper's brows shot up in anticipation. "Really?"

"Settle down, Nancy Drew." Gage squeezed her shoulder. "He said *may have*."

"Ignore the pessimists." Piper leaned forward. "Tell me about this lead."

Cole lowered his voice. "Well, Bailey and I are going to talk to Ginny Reid tomorrow about—"

Gage cleared his throat. "Speaking of Bailey . . ."

Cole turned to find her standing at the front counter. Her hair in a loose ponytail, she wore a long-sleeve T-shirt and a pair of knit capris. She shifted from foot to foot, clearly anxious to be on her way.

"I'll be right back." He slid out of his family's booth and headed for the counter. "Bailey."

She turned at his voice and a soft smile crossed her lips.

"Why don't you come join us?" He gestured toward his family.

She looked across the crowded restaurant and waved to Piper, who was watching them with clear interest. "Thanks, but I've got a lot of work to do." She slipped a loose strand of hair behind her ear. "I just came in for a milkshake."

"Got a hankering for them?"

"Yeah." She smiled. "You got me hooked."

"Here's your shake, hon." Sandy slid it across the counter.

"Thanks." Bailey grabbed it. "Well, I better . . ."

"Why don't you at least sit and enjoy your shake with us."

She looked back to his family, and he followed her gaze. Piper smiled sweetly, her eyes still fastened on them.

"I've really got a ton of work." She shifted around him, and he could feel her slipping through his fingers all over again. "But thanks for the offer."

"Yep." He waved as the door shut behind her.

"Terrible news about her aunt," Sandy said behind him. "About the plane crash not being an accident."

He turned with a start. How on earth did she know about that? "Where did you hear that?"

She leaned in and lowered her voice. "You know I'm not one to snitch, but what I will say is that we're all shook up about

188

it. First that dead diver and now this. Stuff like that happens in the big cities, not in Yancey."

"Sandy, order's up," Gus called from the kitchen.

"I better go." Sandy slipped her order pad back in her pocket. "Gus doesn't like us talking about this. Says it's police business. But when there's a murderer on the loose, I say it's the entire town's business."

Cole followed Gage out of Gus's diner.

"Want to grab a cup of coffee?" Gage asked.

Cole looked at the light on in Bailey's place. He toyed with the idea of stopping by. . . .

"Cole?"

"Yeah." He shook off the idea. She clearly wanted her space. "Sure. I could go for a cup."

"Polar Espresso or Grizzly Bean?"

"The Bean sounds good." They headed away from the Post toward the coffee shop.

"So . . ." Gage rubbed the back of his neck. "I saw the way you looked at Bailey."

Cole exhaled. He hadn't seen that coming. "And how was that?"

"Like you're falling for her all over again."

He shoved his hands in his jeans pockets. "I know it can't go anywhere."

"Do you?" Gage held him in an appraising gaze.

"Yes." He'd have to be a fool not to. As soon as the case was solved, she was gone. She'd made that painfully clear.

"Look," Gage said, holding the coffee shop door open for him. "I just don't want to see you go down that road again. I remember the devastation."

"That was a long time ago." He approached the counter.

Gage halted him with a hand on his shoulder. "That may be, but it still stings, doesn't it?"

Cole swallowed. Seeing Bailey again had resurrected a flood

of memories—both the good and the excruciating. She was the only woman who'd ever broken his heart, and from the looks of things, he was about to let it happen all over again.

Cole left his cabin in the distance, let the moon light his path. He quickened his stride, the sand shifting beneath his feet, tiny granules slipping between his toes. He just needed to move, to release everything pent up inside of him. Waves slapped rhythmically against the shore, sloshing water on his sweats. His heart thudded in his chest and sweat broke on his brow. *Faster. Leave it all behind.*

Bailey. His feelings. There was no future there. He wouldn't allow his heart to be at the mercy of her whims ever again. He increased his pace, his breath coming in short spurts. *Pound it all out on the sand and let the waves wash away any trace.*

"Carrie." Bailey's heart filled with joy at finally reaching her.

"I was wondering when we'd finally catch each other. You've been busy."

Bailey sank on the couch, twirling the phone cord around her finger. "I suppose so."

"What's going on?"

"What do you mean?"

"You said you're extending your stay another week."

"Oh, right." She supposed the message had been rather vague.

"So . . ."

Bailey explained the situation.

"That's terrible."

"I know. It seems so unreal."

"Poor Agnes."

"Poor all of them." It was enough to break her heart.

"And . . . Cole?"

She sat up. "What about him?"

"I'm assuming this is *the* Cole?"

190

"What do you mean *the* Cole?" She knew exactly what Carrie meant.

"As in the guy in the photograph you keep buried in your dresser, which you nearly ripped out of my hand."

"I didn't rip it out of your hand. I was just startled to see you holding it—that's all."

"You said I could borrow a scarf."

"We both know the box you found the picture in was entirely too small to hold a scarf."

"Okay," Carrie sighed. "I'm sorry. My curiosity got the better of me."

A smile tugged at Bailey's lips. Carrie's curiosity always got the better of her. "It's fine." It was over and done with.

"So is it him?"

"Yeah."

"And?"

"And what?"

"What's it like being around him again? Is he still to-die-for handsome?"

"See, there you go again—curiosity raging out of control."

"You're not going to leave me hanging, are you?"

Bailey weighed her desire to actually share what she was feeling with the one person she felt she could trust against her need for self-preservation. "There's not much to tell."

30

The next morning Bailey opened the Post door before Cole could knock.

"Hey."

She grabbed her keys off the hook, impatient to get going. "Shall we?" She'd spent the night tossing and turning, thoughts of Cole plaguing her. Anticipation of what answers Ginny Reid may hold dancing alongside.

"There's something I want to talk to you about first."

Her hand went slack on the door. "Oh?" Her breath hitched. Is this where he told her he could handle the case on his own? That their spending time together wasn't such a good idea? Had the night's rest brought him to his senses? She'd been expecting as much, even anticipating it, but that did little to lessen the pain and humiliation swelling over her.

"Would you mind if I have someone take a look at Agnes's computer?"

Her brow creased. Where had that come from? "What for?"

"Jesse is Yancey's resident computer whiz. With a little luck he may be able to retrieve the missing e-mails. Or at the very least, tell us when they were wiped out."

Cole waved to Jesse and then held the car door open for Bailey. "He seems like a nice kid," she said, climbing inside, her heart

192

still a jumble of emotions. It was weighing on her—Agnes's death, her past, everything that had happened since she'd set foot in Yancey.

"He's a great kid." Cole shut her door and climbed in the driver's side. "I think he's finally out of danger."

She swallowed the sip of soda she'd been taking. "Danger?" She wiped the drops of soda from her lip. "What danger?"

"Jesse and his stepdad don't get along. Most people don't with Sam. It's not a good situation."

"I'm sorry to hear that." Thankfully, Sam hadn't been home during their visit.

"Unfortunately, to compound matters or as a result of what was going on at home, Jesse fell in with the wrong crowd."

She knew all about that, though she could hardly blame her downward spiral on the "in" crowd. She'd chosen—check that—she'd striven to be part of that crowd, to manipulate her way in. And it had only brought heartache. "Jesse's not still mixed up with that crowd, is he?"

Cole pulled onto the main road, leaving the dirt drive behind. "He says he's not, and I pray that's the truth."

It was hard to break free once you were entrenched in the popularity game. It was no different than any of Satan's lies—the more you gave up, the less you gained. She'd sold her soul for fleeting affection and never realized she'd bought in to the lie. If God, in His goodness, hadn't reached out to her . . . if He'd given up on her as she had on herself . . . She couldn't bear to think what a mess she'd be now . . . couldn't bear to imagine eternal separation from her Savior. Tears welled in her eyes.

"Hey." Cole's fingers barely brushed her jaw. "What's wrong?"

She started to say "nothing," but she couldn't do it. Couldn't blow him off. It was the blasted conversation with Carrie. She'd blown Carrie off, not trusting her enough, not willing to give voice to her feelings, to acknowledge how deeply she cared for Cole. Everything was compounding, reaching a threshold. If she didn't do something, say something—anything to relieve the pressure—it would smother her.

Jesse sounded so much like her, like she used to be. Maybe if she talked with him she could help him in some way. His story, no doubt, was different from hers, but the emptiness that gnawed at him in the dark—the anger, hurt, and rebellion that drove kids into those crowds, into that type of behavior—was eerily the same. Maybe she could tell him about the only way to truly fill that void. Maybe she could introduce him to Jesus as her college roommate had, dragging her to a dorm Bible study and turning her world right side up for the first time in her life.

"Bay?" Cole's voice tugged at her heart.

"I was just thinking about Jesse. Does he know Jesus?"

"He knows about Him, but he hasn't accepted Him as his Savior yet. He comes to church and youth group each week. Landon and I are both trying to build a relationship with him. Letting him know there are some safe people in his life, a safe place he can go. I pray one day soon, he'll open his heart to Jesus."

"It's a difficult thing to do . . . to swallow your pride." She knew that better than anyone, and the sin still plagued her.

"I wrestle with that every day."

"Yeah, right. You hardly seem the type to struggle with pride." He was kind, loving . . . an amazing man. Surely he didn't struggle with the same sins she did.

"Pride wears a lot of different masks. Some are easier to see than others."

Were hers that obvious?

"To be completely honest . . ." He looked at her, then back at the road. "Pride's probably the toughest sin for a man to overcome."

"How so?"

"We're supposed to be tough, resilient, have everything under control . . ." He tapped the wheel. "Truth is we don't have all the answers, we make more than our share of mistakes, and . . ."

He sighed. "Sometimes we encounter a problem we can't fix, can't control. Talk about humbling."

His honesty floored her.

"Now . . ." He inclined his head playfully. "If you tell any other men I've exposed our secret, I'll have to deny everything."

She nibbled her bottom lip. "Thanks."

"For what?" He gave a halfhearted chuckle. "Exposing my flaws?"

"Yes. For exactly that." She leaned across the seat and kissed his cheek.

Cole's cheek still tingled from Bailey's kiss. What was the woman doing to him? He'd determined to be her friend and nothing more, to keep his emotions in check, to not fall for her again, and here he was falling harder than ever. Where was his self-control?

He kicked a stone littering their path.

How'd she get under his skin and into his heart so easily? He was a fool—wanting something he couldn't have, loving someone who didn't love him back.

Please, Lord, strengthen my resolve. I feel like I'm hanging off the side of a cliff, and the harder I struggle to reach the top, the farther down I slip. I know you can't possibly want me to let go.

Bailey tugged his arm before they reached Ginny's stoop. "I didn't think about it until just now . . . I've been so wrapped up with Agnes that I never stopped to consider Ginny. She lost her husband in the same crash. Maybe asking her questions about it isn't such a good idea."

"I wondered the same thing, but Ginny said it'd make her happy if she can be of help. Besides, she can't wait to meet you."

"Me?" Bailey paled. "I thought everyone in town already knew all about me."

"Not everyone in town is as immature as Tom and Thoreau. They're the minority, not the majority. Remember that. As for Ginny, she and Henry relocated here from Kodiak about a year after you left. Ginny says Agnes spoke about you all the time, and she can't wait to meet the apple of Agnes's eye."

The front door swung open. "You must be Bailey." Ginny rushed out, wrapping her arms around Bailey. "I can't tell you how pleased I am to finally get to meet you. Agnes spoke so highly of you."

"I'm afraid she was more than a little biased." Bailey stood ramrod straight in the embrace, almost uneasy with affection.

Maybe he wasn't the only one who made her flinch; maybe it was intimacy that unsettled her.

Ginny chuckled. "Nonsense. I don't believe that for a second." She opened the storm door. "Come on in and make yourselves at home. I hear my kettle whistling."

Bailey sat, plastic crinkling beneath her, the covered furniture a stark reminder of her sterile childhood. Everything in its perfect place. Nothing to be touched. All an elaborate show to hide the dirt inside.

"Oh, don't mind that nasty cover," Ginny called from the kitchen. "Henry and I finally had those sofas cleaned after twenty-five years and three kids. It's amazing they look as clean as they do. Anyhoo, they arrived all plastic covered the evening Henry was due back, so I'd left them for him." She returned from the kitchen, a tea tray in hand. "I guess I really should see to it myself."

"I can take care of it, if you like," Cole offered.

"Oh, you sweet boy." She planted a kiss on his cheek. "Maybe I'll take you up on that after our visit." She set the tray on the coffee table and rested her hands on her hips. "I know it sounds like a crazy lady talking, but I almost hate to make new memories on them without Henry. Ya know?" She swiped at her eyes. "How silly am I? Thinking dog hair or a stain on the couch equals memories."

Bailey's heart went out to her. They shouldn't have come, stirring up memories best left forgotten.

Ginny shook her head with a sigh. "Don't mind me. The crying spells come on swift but seem to leave the same way." She lifted the teakettle and looked at Bailey. "Tea, dear?"

Bailey nodded, bereft of words. Sorrow was etched on every line of Ginny's dear, round face. She longed to pull the woman into her arms and give her a comforting hug. But instinct, drilled in her from youth, overpowered the urge.

"Piper sent over some cookies." Cole handed Ginny the container.

"Oh, the sweet darling. She's been running something up here nearly every day since my Henry . . ." Ginny's eyes welled with tears. "I'll just go put these on a plate. They'll go lovely with the tea."

Cole moved beside Bailey, the plastic scrunching beneath him. He squeezed her hand. "You're doing fine."

How could he be so in tune with her emotions? Know what she needed when she hadn't said a word. He'd always possessed that ability, and it terrified her. She swallowed. "I feel so bad for Ginny. How long were she and Henry married?"

"About thirty-five years, I'd say."

"Wow. I didn't know people stayed married that long."

"My folks were married close to thirty years before Dad died."

"You're lucky."

"Here we go." Ginny sailed back into the room, Piper's cookies arranged in a circular pattern on the plate. "So . . . how can I be of help?"

Bailey cranked down the window as they wove their way down Ginny's flower-lined drive. "Ginny is wonderful. I still feel rotten, though, asking her about Henry's last flights."

"I think it made her happy to help. To feel she could be useful in such a bad situation."

Bailey clutched the copied itinerary, scanning the data. "Agnes's flight left Yancey for Anchorage at 11:05 on the morning of August first. Henry noted on the books that she was headed to

Russia from there—but he didn't include any flight or destination information. And he picked Agnes up in Anchorage at four thirty in the afternoon on August the seventh. So we can assume she was in Russia for approximately five days. Now we just need to figure out what she was doing there. Maybe Landon or Slidell can pull her credit card slips."

"Good idea. I'll give Landon a call." Cole pulled the truck into a scenic overlook off the highway. "I've seen too many accidents caused by talking on the cell when driving. Safer just to stop and take in the scenery." He yanked the phone from his pocket and it rang. "Good timing," he said, flipping it open. "McKenna here . . . Oh hey, Jesse. What's up? . . . Uh-huh." He reached across the dash and grabbed a pad and pen from the glove compartment. "Great, eight thirty on the first. Hang on a sec." He covered the mouthpiece. "Looks like Agnes may have wiped them out before her trip after all."

"Really?" Disappointment flooded Bailey. Why? What had she been hoping for? Confirmation Agnes was the reason for the crash? Like that would somehow make it better.

"Jesse says the last date the system was touched was 8:30 a.m. on the—" Cole slid his hand away. "Yeah, Jesse, I'm here. What did you say?" His jaw tensed as he listened. "You're sure? Okay. Thanks. Yeah. Keep me posted." He shut the phone.

"What?"

"Jesse said before we logged on yesterday the computer hadn't been touched since 8:30 *p.m.* on the first."

"Agnes was already gone." Color drained from her face. "Someone was in the Post after she left, erasing her e-mails."

"There's more. According to Jesse, it looks like Agnes's e-mails are being rerouted to an alternate e-mail account."

"What account?"

"He doesn't know yet. He needs more time."

"We better tell Slidell."

"My thoughts exactly."

31

Cole held the sheriff's station door open for Bailey.

Before she could enter, Slidell strode out, a stark expression fixed on his face. "McKenna, good timing. Follow me." He waggled two fingers in the direction of his vehicle.

"We found something interesting," Cole said, striding across the parking lot to keep up.

"Yeah?" Slidell opened his truck door. "So did Piper."

"Huh?" What was his little sister up to now? And why was Slidell in such a hurry?

"She was walking Aurora out by the point, tossed the dog a ball, and it came back with a femur."

Landon gathered Piper's hair in his hand, pulling it back from her face while she retched, her slight frame convulsing from the force.

He didn't know what to say, what to do, how to make things right. He patted her back, his hand feeling awkward and clumsy. He sucked at consolation. Lecturing, protecting—those he could handle. Jesting and teasing—he excelled at them. But comforting? Not up his alley.

He checked his watch again. Where was Cole? He should have been there by now. He'd have the right words, the right touch.

Piper straightened, swiping the back of her hand across her face.

"Here." Landon offered her a handkerchief.

"Thanks." She dabbed her mouth and sniffed. "Some detective I'd make." Despite the tearstains, her cheeks still held the telltale blush of embarrassment.

"We all do it," he said, trying to offer some modicum of reassurance. The last thing she ought to be embarrassed about was tossing her cookies like a rookie.

She blew her nose in the hanky. "Do what?"

"Lose our lunch, at one time or another. It happens to everyone."

She narrowed her puffy eyes. "Even you?"

He shifted his weight. "Well . . . not everyone reacts the same."

"So in other words, no." She shrugged. "It figures." A hiccup racked her slender body.

"What does?"

"That stuff—" another hiccup jolted her—"like this, wouldn't bother you."

"Not bother me?" He'd have to be heartless not to be upset at finding a man's remains strewn across a half-mile patch of beach. "Where'd you get an idea like that?"

"Piper," Cole called. He raced across the open stretch of beach, kicking sand up in his wake. Bailey and Slidell followed.

Rushes swayed in the breeze as the wind shifted, sweeping the putrid odor of decay over them anew.

Piper grabbed her stomach, her eyes filling with humiliation before she doubled over and lost what was left of her lunch.

Cole cradled her in his arms as soon as she was upright. "Thank God you're okay. When Slidell said you'd found remains, my heart dropped." He pressed a fierce kiss to her brow, then slackened his hold only enough to study her face. "You all right, kid?"

She nodded and buried her head into his chest, her body heaving with sobs.

Landon moved to stand beside Bailey at the edge of the police tape, giving them their space.

"I better talk to Booth," Slidell said, striding toward the town's medical examiner.

"What happened?" Bailey asked, lifting her chin toward Slidell's retreating back. "He didn't say much."

"It's too early to be positive, but I think Piper may have just found our mystery man." The breeze shifted and Landon grimaced. "Or what's left of him."

Piper woke in a cold sweat, the odor of death still rancid in her mind.

Landon leapt from the armchair. "You okay?"

"Aside from finding someone in pieces?" She wriggled to a seated position, ignoring the light-headedness. "Any word from Slidell?"

"Not yet. These things take time." Landon sat on the couch by her feet, a bag of potato chips in his hand.

"How will they even be able to tell, there was so little left of—" She stopped. On site Booth had been unable to even determine if the limbs and torso belonged to a man or a woman. What if it wasn't the mystery man as they all seemed to believe? What if it was someone they knew?

"You'd be amazed what Booth can do with practically nothing."

She bit her bottom lip and nodded, afraid if she spoke she'd break down in tears, again. Landon must think her the biggest baby.

"Are you thirsty? Hungry?" he asked. "I can fix you something."

"Water would be nice." She propped herself against the couch cushions. "I don't think I'll be eating for a while."

"Right." Landon shoved the chips behind his back. "One water coming up."

She brushed the damp hair from her brow and noticed the throw spread across her. The house was dim, quiet. How long had she been asleep? "Where is everybody?" Cole and Bailey had been there. Sheriff Slidell for a time. Gage, Kayden, and Jake had all dropped by. It was like she'd broken her collarbone all over again—everyone fussing over her. But this was worse, much worse. This would haunt her for years to come.

Landon returned with the water and a plate of saltine crackers. "Slidell's back at the station. Gage, Jake, and Kayden are up on Kodiak, leading that survival camping excursion. They offered to cancel, but Cole insisted you'd want them to go."

"Of course." But why was Landon here? Why did he have to be the one to see her fall apart?

"Cole dropped Bailey off at Agnes's and went into the shop."

"Ahh," she grunted. "It was my night to close up." She scrambled to her feet, only to be knocked back by a wave of dizziness.

"Easy now." Landon lowered her back down. "You're in no shape to go anywhere."

"I'm fine." Minus the wooziness swarming her brain.

"You haven't eaten in hours. What you had this morning is long gone. And it only makes sense, given what you saw, that you're experiencing at least a mild degree of shock." He covered her with the blanket, tucking her in. "Which means you're staying put."

She opened her mouth to argue and he shoved a cracker inside.

Cole walked Bailey to her door, not willing to leave until he saw her safely inside. She'd witnessed only a fraction of what Piper had, but it'd been enough to rattle anyone. She needed comfort too. Whether she was willing to admit it or not.

Bailey turned, key in hand. "Is she going to be all right?"

"Piper's tenderhearted, but she's strong. It'll take some time, but she'll eventually get past this."

"Landon's very brotherly towards her."

"Yeah. Landon and I have been friends since Piper was born. He's watched her grow from her terrible twos, to her knock-kneed, gangly teen years, on till now." Cole shook his head with a grin. "Those two fight and jab like they really are siblings."

Bailey rubbed her arms as if a chill had just washed over her. "It's nice she has so many people looking out for her."

His heart squeezed at the deep ache in her words. He stepped closer, and to his amazement, she didn't move back. "You need someone like that in your life, Bailey." He tipped her chin up, staring into her fierce blue eyes.

Her jaw set as if ready for a fight. "I can take care of myself."

Air jolted from his lungs as if he'd been hit. "Of that I have no doubt." She didn't have room for him in her life. There'd always be a wall there, a distance she wouldn't let him breach, and the realization left him starved.

32

Cole stacked the last of the flippers on the rack and glanced at the clock. Five of nine. The day had flown by—running a handful of excursions followed by a steady flow of customers. He was thankful business was booming, but equally thankful it was just about closing time. He pulled to his feet as "Wipe Out!" sounded behind him.

A man entered. Early forties, tall, athletic. Definitely not local.

"How's it going?" he said.

The man gazed about the shop before cracking a smile. "Oh, can't complain."

"Can I help you find something?"

The man closed the distance between them. "I surely hope so."

"What are you in the market for?"

"Oil," the man said with a smile and a hint of a southern accent.

"As in suntan?" Cole pointed to the small display. They didn't get much call for it in Yancey.

The man laughed. "No, as in crude oil, son." He yanked a business card from his shirt pocket and handed it to Cole. "I'm with Pentrinium Oil."

Cole studied the card. "Greg Stevens."

Greg extended a hand. "Nice to meet you."

"Same here. My name is Cole. What can I do for you, Greg?"

"Well, I'm in need of a diver to map a grid of underwater caves. We just secured the drilling rights and believe there's oil just waiting for us, but before I can send my boys in, I need to know what we're looking at terrain-wise."

Cole studied the man as he spoke, noticing for the first time the uncertainty filling him. All this talk of murder was apparently getting to him. "Why come to me?" he asked, feeling the strange need to test the man. To make sure Greg and Pentrinium Oil were aboveboard.

"I'm not the sort of man who enjoys wasting time. I asked around, learned you were the best, so here I am."

"Who do I have to thank for recommending me?"

"Sheldon Graves over at P and R. Mike Thornton at Burnett."

Greg's answers fit, but something still didn't feel right. Cole couldn't put a finger on it. Just felt it in his gut. "Well, my family and I have done a number of exploration and mapping dives." He stepped behind the counter and retrieved the date and log book. "How large a grid are we talking about?"

Greg removed a schematic from his briefcase and spread it out on the counter between them.

Cole studied the area boxed in with red marker. It included Herring Cove, where Cleary's missing boat had been found, the vicinity where Liz Johnson's body had been recovered, and encompassed the area offshore of Chirikof Island. The preliminary grid he'd made for Slidell was eerily identical. He leaned against the counter, his arms crossed. "What makes you think there's oil there?"

"Based on preliminaries. So when can you start?"

"I'm afraid not for a while. We're swamped right now."

"Oh?" Greg's pleasantness faded.

Cole flipped through his book. "Looks like next month would be the earliest we could commit to that chunk of time."

"Even if the price was right?"

"Sorry. My hands are tied."

"I see." Greg rolled up the schematic and tapped the counter with it. "You have my card. Give me a call if anything opens up. I don't have a month to waste."

"Will do." Cole looked back at the card, finding only a 1-800 number. "Say . . . where are you staying in town?"

The only answer he got was "Wipe Out!" playing as the door shut behind the man.

Cole picked up the phone and called Landon.

"Grainger."

"Hey, man, it's me. How's Piper?"

"Quickly getting back to her spitfire self."

"That's great."

"If you say so . . ." The tension had slipped from Landon's voice, replaced with a hint of his teasing manner. Piper really must be doing better.

"A guy just tried to hire me for a cave-mapping expedition."

"Okay?"

"It's in the same region we've been spending a lot of our time."

"Is that right? He didn't resemble our mystery man, did he?"

"No. Too old. Besides, aren't we assuming Piper already found our mystery man?"

"I pray that's the case. Otherwise we're looking at yet another victim. I tell you, Booth can't make his report fast enough for me."

"Or me." The possibility of another victim seemed ludicrous, but Cole had learned from experience, when it rained it poured.

"So tell me about this guy. Did you get a name?"

"Yeah. Greg Stevens of Pentrinium Oil. Left his business card with me. I'll drop it by your place on my way home."

"Actually, I was thinking since Kayden's away tonight, maybe I should bunk out on the girls' couch."

"Probably not a bad idea, but I can do that."

"It's no bother. Besides, you had your turn guarding Bailey. I'll take this round."

"All right. Thanks, man. Call if you need anything."

"No problem. You should stop by the station after you close

up, though. See what kind of sketch you can give Earl. Who knows . . . might come in handy."

"Will do."

A smile crept over his face as he strolled away from Last Frontier Adventures and into the night. Cole McKenna's reaction to the proposed schematic was everything he'd hoped for. He'd targeted his best guess and the man responded beautifully, albeit with evasion rather than acceptance of his offer, but it mattered not.

Clearly he'd roused Cole's suspicion, and his curiosity along with it. It wouldn't be long before he and the girl were in the water. Both were bright and experienced. He chuckled at the promising turn of fate—he couldn't have fashioned a better team for his purposes if he'd tried. They'd find what he needed—and when they did, he'd take it from them. Simple as that.

It wasn't how he'd planned it, but the result would be the same. And that was the mark of greatness—what separated natural-born leaders like himself from mere pawns—the ability to fashion everything to suit one's needs, one's desire. He'd done just that and they had no clue.

33

"How's Piper doing?" Bailey asked the following afternoon as they made what was quickly becoming their daily walk over to the sheriff's station. She wore a knee-length copper sundress and a pair of flip-flops. It was as casual as Cole had seen her, and it made him smile.

"Better. Though Landon said she suffered a few nightmares." Not that he'd slept much better. All the time spent with Bailey was only confirming how much he was going to miss her when she was gone, and it frustrated him to no end. He prayed God would answer his plea and change his heart. He was falling fast, and if something didn't shift soon, he was in for one painful landing.

Cole sidestepped a string of jubilant kids skipping with their newly won prizes—stuffed animals ranging in size from small husky dogs that little hands could easily curl around all the way up to an oversized moose that was nearly double the size of the preschooler insisting he could carry it.

Today kicked off the Summer Festival, and tourists and locals alike crammed the town square to take part in the action. A bevy of booths lined the space, offering everything from the ring toss to native crafts. The scent of cotton candy danced in the air, bringing to mind the Summer Festivals of his childhood.

"Looks like they're having fun," he commented as they passed an elderly couple feeding each other funnel cake.

Bailey blushed. "Yeah, it does."

"Are you planning to go?"

"To the festival?" She fidgeted with the hemp bracelet on her slender wrist. "I don't think so."

"Well, if you change your mind, I'm pretty good at the ring toss."

She smiled. "I'll keep that in mind."

"I saw the way you were eyeing that moose. It could be yours."

She chuckled. "Very tempting, but I've got—"

He held up a hand. "Let me guess—a lot of work?"

She nodded and they continued their stroll, an unbearable silence enveloping them. Why couldn't she stop pushing so hard to leave? Why couldn't she let her guard down just a little? Why couldn't she enjoy what time they had together?

"I made it over to the historical society this morning," she said, finally breaking the silence.

"Oh?" He'd forgotten all about that. "Anything helpful in the letters?"

"Actually, it turns out it was a diary, not letters."

"Huh. I guess Agnes made a mistake in her notation."

"Actually she didn't."

"But you just said . . ."

"Mrs. Anderson said the princess used the diary as a sort of first draft for all her correspondence. As a way to get her thoughts down and also to keep track of who she told what."

Cole misstepped. "Princess?"

"The diary belonged to Princess Ma—"

"Maksutov," he finished.

She halted, her brow furrowed. "How did you know that?"

"Piper told me about her."

"Piper?" Bailey squinted as the sun lit her eyes the deep blue of Tariuk Island's waters. "Did she also tell you the diary was stolen?"

"The night of Agnes's crash."

"What?"

He raked a hand through his hair, his mind scrambling to put all the pieces together into something that made sense. "I'd forgotten all about it until you mentioned the princess's name. Who would have thought a hundred-year-old diary would cause such commotion? What do you think it contains that's of so much interest?"

"Perhaps information on which artifacts were kept in the church. The icon may be just the tip of the iceberg."

"I guess we'll never know."

"That might not be entirely true."

"What do you mean?"

"Mrs. Anderson gave me the name of the diary's owner. Usually when an item of that worth is donated, the benefactor has copies made. That way if the item is ever damaged or destroyed, the historical information still remains."

"Great thinking. So who donated it?"

"Agnes."

"How'd the diary come to be in her possession?"

"Mrs. Anderson said Agnes told her that it had been passed down for generations in her family. She'd inherited it from her great-aunt, and since it represented such an integral part of Yancey history, Agnes wanted it to be available for all to see. So she donated it to the historical society, at least for the time being. One day, she said she'd pass it on to her niece."

Cole smiled as he held the station door open for her. "You."

Bailey nodded as she stepped inside. "I've been racking my brain, trying to go back through all the conversations we had, all the history and stories she overloaded me with, to see if anything could be of help."

"And?" Cole waved to Earl as the deputy juggled phone calls.

"And . . ." Bailey sighed. "I just get more frustrated. Maybe if I'd paid better attention."

"You were a teenager."

"I know. I just keep thinking there's something in the Post she wanted me to find. Something for me to discover."

"Go on back," Earl said, his hand clapped over the receiver. "Slidell's expecting you."

"Maybe if you find the copy of the diary, you'll find some answers."

"That's what I keep hoping."

Slidell stood as they entered his office. "Thanks for coming down."

"You said it was important."

"It's quickly becoming so." Slidell lifted the receiver and pressed the intercom exchange. "Grainger, get in here."

"Be right there, Chief."

He rested the phone back in the cradle and indicated for them to sit.

Slidell's office was his home away from home. Still single and with no family in the area, he apparently didn't have much to go home for.

Cole glanced at the tweed sofa that looked like it would be more at home in a hunting cabin than an office. The coatrack held a variety of shirts and a worn pair of jeans, and a handful of empty Ramen containers littered the trash can beside it.

Landon skidded into the office. "I got our mystery man."

Slidell arched two bushy brows.

"When I didn't get a hit on the US database, I sent the info to a friend at Interpol." Landon dropped the booking photo on Slidell's desk. "Nikolai Sokolov. Previously from St. Petersburg, Russia, but it looks like he's been in the States for at least a year. Primarily in California."

"Where Liz is from," Bailey said.

"Exactly. Nikolai Sokolov is Liz's boyfriend, Nick."

Slidell scanned the printout. "He's got quite the rap sheet. Petty theft, grand larceny, aggravated assault. Good work, Landon."

"There's more. I did a little searching on the man who tried to hire Cole."

"Greg Stevens?"

Landon perched on the edge of Slidell's desk, his arms

crossed. "He doesn't exist. Neither does Pentrinium Oil. And here comes the strange part, the 1-800 number he left Cole . . . I can't find any records on it. No one seems to know where the number originated or who carries the service. But I do know it's the last number Nikolai texted."

"What?"

"Nikolai texted the icon image and the *let's talk* message to Pentrinium Oil's 1-800 number."

"We can assume the talk did not go well." Slidell slid a folder to Landon. "Booth's report is in. The remains Piper found on the beach belong to whoever's blood was on that boat—with one exception."

"Exception?" Cole's heart lurched.

"There was an extra ear. By the cartilage structure and piercing . . . Booth says it's female."

"But Liz Johnson's ears were both intact."

"Right. Which means we have another victim. If not dead, wounded."

"What now?"

"Now, thanks to Landon's thorough work, we can give Booth a name and hopefully enough information to make a positive ID on the body parts recovered."

"But we're no closer to finding the killer," Bailey said.

"Exactly." Slidell refilled his mug. "The body count is rising, and other than a fake name and business, we have no leads. I hate to say it, but Mayor Cox is right. Townsfolk are getting worried, and if word of this leaks to the cruise ships . . ." He faced the window, his shoulders rigid. "Shop owners depend on the tourist traffic to keep them going the rest of the year. We need answers and we need them now."

Landon stood. "We find what Liz Johnson and Nikolai were looking for, what the man who tried to hire Cole is still searching for, and you'll have your answers."

"You really think finding some trinket under the sea will actually solve anything?" Tom said from the doorway.

"The icon is the only thing we have tying the murders together," Landon insisted. "My gut tells me it's at the heart of this case."

Tom strutted into the office. "How do we know this isn't all some wild-goose chase? That they haven't already found what they are looking for?"

Cole felt Bailey stiffen as Tom approached.

Landon continued, "Because they wouldn't still be hanging around, trying to hire another diver if they had what they wanted." He shifted his focus from Tom to Slidell. "Chief, I'm telling you, retrieving that icon is the key. Who knows how many more lives will be in jeopardy until it's found."

Slidell set his mug on the desk. "What are we talking?"

"We take the grid you had Cole draw up and we go down. Locate the ruins, the icon, and stop this in its tracks before anyone else gets hurt."

Slidell inhaled, then released the breath slowly, his stomach rising and lowering with a motion like that of a slumbering dog. "All right. Cole, you gather a team. Get started as soon as you're able." He pinned his gaze on Landon. "I expect to be kept in the loop."

"Absolutely."

Slidell picked up his mug. "Well, get going. This case isn't going to solve itself."

"I'd like to be part of the team," Bailey said, her voice so low, Cole doubted he'd heard her right.

She was asking to be part of the team, his team? "Really?"

"Less civilians involved, the better." Tom cocked his head in Bailey's direction. "We don't need anyone clouding the team's judgment, now do we?"

Cole looked at Bailey, fearing she'd cower.

She took a steadying breath and squared her shoulders. "I'm the only expert on Russian artifacts you've got. You need me down there to identify whatever you find."

Cole's heart swelled with pride. "She's right. She'd be an asset to the team. It's just a matter of safety." He turned to Bailey. "I know you still dive, but what level of certification do you hold?"

"I'm cave-and-cavern certified."

"Well, all right." He prayed Slidell wouldn't shoot down her offer, not in front of Tom. Not when she'd finally taken a stand.

Tom shifted his weight. "Sheriff?"

Slidell exhaled. "Like Cole said, the lady will make a valuable addition to his team." He leaned forward, resting his weight on his forearms. "Who else will you be taking?"

"Two teams of two should be good. I'll partner with Bailey."

Tom snorted, and Cole flashed him a warning glare.

"Landon can pair with Piper, as long as she's up to it," he continued. "Kayden and Gage can run topside."

"How long until you're in the water?"

"I just need to ready the equipment and finalize the grid, so a day."

"Good. I don't need to remind you the clock is ticking."

34

Bailey followed Cole outside the station, her heart roaring in her chest. She'd finally held her own with Tom. Now she just needed the queasiness to subside.

"Hey, man," Landon called, striding out after them. "I wanted you to take another look at this."

Cole's brows dipped. "The sketch of Greg Stevens?"

"Now that a day has passed, I thought you could recheck it. Anything you'd add or change?"

He studied it. "Sorry, man. Still looks the same to me."

"Don't be sorry. That's good. I'm going to fax it over to my friend at Interpol, see if it pulls up anything."

"Mind if I take a look?" Bailey asked. If the man had anything to do with Agnes's death, she wanted to see his face.

"Sure." Landon nodded, and Cole handed her the image.

She nearly dropped it.

"You've seen him?" Landon said.

She nodded, suddenly feeling very cold despite the sunshine. "When?"

She held her trembling hand to her mouth. "The day of Agnes's funeral, but he looked different."

"Different, how?"

"Older."

Landon frowned. "How much older?"

"I don't know. . . . A good fifteen, twenty years."

"Are you sure it's the same man?"

"Positive. I remember the eyes."

"Could you come back inside the station and let Earl do another sketch of how he appeared to you? If he's wearing disguises, it would be helpful for us to know all his looks."

Bailey slammed the cupboard door. She'd looked everywhere and still couldn't find Agnes's copy of the diary. Had she purposely hidden it, and if so, why? Did she know someone was after it? If so, who?

With a sigh, she stalked over to the steps and sank down. Why was she letting herself get pulled in so deep? When was it going to end? When the murderer was caught? When the icon was found? She was only fooling herself. She didn't want to leave Yancey, and that scared her more than anything.

This is ridiculous. You are being ridiculous.

She tapped her irritation out on the bottom step, her foot moving in rapid melody.

A hollow echo answered back.

She tapped again and the same echo replied.

The bottom step. It'd always sounded different. *Hollow.*

She'd written it off as another of the old building's quirks. Just one of many creaks, but now she wasn't so sure.

Getting down on her hands and knees she moved in for a closer look.

"Where did you find it?" Cole asked as soon as the door opened.

Bailey tugged him inside and locked the door. "Beneath the bottom step," she said in a rushed whisper, excitement alight in her eyes.

"What?" Why on earth had she thought to look there?

"I was getting desperate. Never mind, it's a long story." She knelt at the base of the stairs. "This is what's important." She grabbed hold of the bottom step and slid the top piece toward her, revealing a cubbyhole within.

He chuckled. "Agnes was quite the secret-keeper."

Bailey pulled out the slim, soft-sided binder. "Makes me wonder what other secrets she and this old building are hiding."

Cole settled on the couch beside Bailey. She smelled like a meadow after a spring rain. Tendrils of her amber hair slipped from the loose clip she'd bunched it into, grazing her supple neck and collarbone. . . .

"I'd divide up the pages so we could read twice as fast, but I'm afraid we'd lose context."

"So . . ." He cleared the gravel from his throat, feeling like a sixteen-year-old in the throes of first love. Funny . . . it was with the same girl. Funny and equally sad. Falling in love with someone who didn't love you back was bad enough the first time around; doing it a second time was downright pathetic. "So"—he tried again, this time finding his voice—"let's start from the beginning."

"All right." Bailey flipped open the binder and began with the first copied page.

June 15, 1864

My dearest Ekaterina,

Life here isn't so bad. In fact, the village is coming more and more to resemble home. Dimitri says the company is doing well. The local people are kind, and I'm finding my way. I think I have finally located them— well, the few that remain. They ask me much about the homeland, those alive never seeing it firsthand. It appears it has lived on in their hearts through the tales of their elders. I hope my humble words do it justice.

Please write again soon. I do look so forward to your letters. Give my love to Auntie.

With love,

Sofia

The air was soothingly warm, the sun shining in a crystal blue sky, and the waters calm. It was a perfect day to be at sea.

A gull circled overhead, and Cole let his hand dangle over the side of the boat, feeling the spray of the sea on his fingertips. "So how late did you read after I left?"

Bailey shrugged. "Not long."

He wasn't buying it. He'd barely pulled himself away at midnight. He narrowed his gaze. "How come I don't believe you?"

Her full lips cracked into a gorgeous smile. "It was addicting. Sofia paints such a vivid account of life in nineteenth-century Russian Alaska and of life on Tariuk, in particular."

Cole reclined beside her. "So bring me up to speed."

"She discusses each building erected in town and notes which were present upon her arrival. I think the Post was one of the originals. She refers to it as the caretaker's house, whatever that means, but its description matches perfectly, right down to the upper dormer windows."

"Could be, but you've got to remember a number of buildings have come and gone since that time."

"I know, but wouldn't it be cool if it turned out to be the Post? It was built in that general time period. Agnes even filed paper work to get it put on the historic registry at one time."

"It's cool, but I still don't see the connection between the diary and the icon."

"We still have a lot to read. Maybe that comes later."

"I hope so. It'd be nice if some of the pieces would start falling into place."

"It'd make my job a whole lot easier," Landon remarked from the bow.

"Any news on Greg Stevens?" Cole asked.

Landon shook his head. "Not yet."

"You think he killed Nikolai and Liz to keep the find quiet?" Gage asked while running a final inspection on everyone's tanks.

"I think he hired them to find the icon, and Nikolai tried to up the price," Landon said.

"And Liz?" Bailey asked.

"Either Nikolai didn't want to share the reward, or Greg was tying up loose ends. My gut says the former."

Kayden slowed the engine. "We're over grid one," she called from the wheelhouse, the boat rocking on the waves.

"That's our cue." Cole pulled his dry suit up the remainder of the way and zipped it.

"So is there anything Kayden can't drive?" Bailey asked, yanking her flippers on. "Floatplanes, boats . . ."

"Helicopters, motorcycles," Gage continued the list.

"Dune buggies," Kayden poked her head out of the wheelhouse with a grin.

"Dune buggies?" Bailey's brows rose.

"To let loose we like to race dune buggies on our beach," Cole explained.

"And who's the reigning champion?" Kayden strode across deck, her step and tone both light and lyrical for a change.

Piper grunted out a strangled sigh. "It's not all about winning."

"That's what losers always say."

Piper stuck out her tongue.

"Real mature, Piper."

"I thought you'd cornered the market on mature."

"Time's a-wasting," Cole cut in before Kayden could counter. "We've got a job to do. Besides, we've got company. Let's not show her all our flaws right off the bat."

"Bailey's not company." Piper wrapped an arm around

Bailey's shoulder, giving her a squeeze. "She's been around long enough. She's family."

Family? Bailey fought the scourge of tears pricking her eyes. They viewed her as family? Outside Agnes, family had never really existed for her.

Jake's admonition replayed in her ears, *"You hang around here much longer and you'll be part of the family, whether you like it or not."*

"Bay"—Cole nudged her—"you all right?"

"Oh yeah, fine." She zipped her suit. "So how's this going to work?"

"We'll go in two teams. You and me. Piper and Landon. Gage and Kayden run topside. We'll start with grid one. Piper and Landon are on grid two. First one to find something signals the others."

"Sounds good."

She readied the last of her gear, marveling at how the McKennas had turned their family boat into a diver's dream. A platform at the stern made entry and exit a breeze, while the heated interior cabin made for cozy quarters after a dip in fifty-degree water.

Within minutes, Cole flipped off the side of the boat, and Bailey quickly followed—both deciding to exit the boat the old-fashioned way, for memories' sake. The rush of water as she righted herself brought back the peaceful surge that always filled her when diving.

It'd only been a matter of months since she'd last been diving, but it had been a decade since she'd been beneath Alaskan waters. She'd forgotten how abundant the algae could be in the summer, the hefty phytoplankton blooms keeping visibility to a mere five feet.

Fortunately, the farther they descended, the greater their visibility grew.

Vast kelp forests blanketed the sea floor, and myriads of fish wove between the tall green stems. The ocean was alive around her.

She couldn't believe she was here, diving again with Cole. How much had changed since that first dive lesson. Her heart thudded in her ears. If she could just go back and undo all the damage she'd done.

"We've got two at five o'clock," Cole said over the headset, and Bailey immediately shifted her gaze in that direction.

A pair of stellar sea lions frolicked not twenty feet from their party. Their graceful, gliding movements mimicked birds in flight.

"There's a sight you never tire of," Cole said.

"Unbelievable," she murmured, wondering what other incredible sights she might encounter.

35

Cole lugged the remainder of the equipment off the boat, frustration teeming beneath the surface. Three days and not a thing to show for it. It would be a lot less frustrating if their bottom time wasn't so limited or if their bodies didn't require such long surface intervals between dives. But nitrogen narcosis was nothing to fool around with. They'd adhere to standard dive table times or they wouldn't dive at all.

Tonight they needed to relax, reassess, and refresh their supplies before heading back in the morning.

Piper sighed as she set the last of the tanks on the pier. "We need to rethink our approach."

"No." Cole smiled. "What we need's a diversion."

Kayden looked up from hosing out the cooler. "What do you have in mind?"

Bailey couldn't stop laughing as she flew over the sand dunes. Her buggy jolting as she sped across the McKennas' property. Kayden led the pack with Cole and Jake in hot pursuit. The rest of them seemed to be having fun in the moment rather than with the hunger to win. Gage skimmed across her path and, with a holler of glee, flew off the dune to her right.

Piper cut in front of him, making a beeline for the water, spraying him in the deluge off her rear tire.

Gage whistled. "Game on, little one."

Piper bubbled with laughter as she sped away.

Cole closed in on Kayden, he and Jake racing each other more than her. If one of them didn't back off, they'd be racing for second rather than beating Kayden.

Cole signaled for Jake to take her. Jake nodded with a grin and sped forward as Cole fell back. If Jake managed to win, Kayden would be fit to be tied.

Jake pulled into the lead with a hundred yards to go, fifty, forty, thirty.

He was actually going to beat her.

Twenty.

Ten.

They were nose to nose.

And . . .

Kayden won?

She took her usual celebratory donut spin before rocking to a halt.

Cole pulled to Jake's side as he climbed from the buggy. "I thought you had her, man."

Jake slipped off his helmet. "Me too."

Cole narrowed his gaze. Jake didn't look overly disappointed. "You didn't let her win, did you?"

Jake chuckled. "Now, why on earth would I go and do something like that?"

Cole studied him more closely, wondering the very same thing.

Gage rocked to a stop beside them. "Let's get the fire going. I'm famished."

"When aren't you?" Kayden asked with cooler in hand.

"I hope the meal didn't get smashed to bits." Piper bent, examining the contents.

Bailey removed her helmet, her cheeks rosy with activity.

Cole smiled at the flush on her face. "How'd you like it?"

"That was a blast!"

Bailey buried her toes deeper in the sand. The fire crackled beside her, casting a warm glow on her skin as a cool breeze wafted off the ocean. *I'm in paradise.* Not a soul around but the seven of them. The sea at their fingertips, the starlit sky dazzling overhead.

Cole lounged beside her, a contented glow on his handsome face, the peach flames dancing along his toned muscles. "This is the life," he sighed.

She rolled onto her side to face him better. "You can say that again." And, for the moment, she let herself imagine a life spent with Cole, futile as it was.

"You think we'll have any luck tomorrow?" Landon asked over the crackle of flames.

Cole tossed a piece of driftwood in the fire. "I hope so. We're running out of grids."

"You think we're off?" Piper asked. "You miss by an inch . . ."

"You miss by a mile," Cole said. It was a truth every wreck diver knew. In the ocean if you missed the mark by an inch, you might as well have missed by a mile.

"Maybe we should look at extending the grid," Gage said.

"We don't have far to go. South, we run into Chirikof. North, the canyon system . . ." Cole sat up.

"What?" Landon's eyes narrowed.

"The canyons." Cole shook his head. "I don't know why I didn't think of it before."

"Surely, you don't think the ruins . . ." Bailey's eyes widened. "I suppose that could be possible."

"More than possible." Cole clambered to his feet. "Logical. Think about it. . . . The island is swallowed whole in the quake. The ruins could have settled into the canyons. Over time it becomes part of the system. That would explain the damage to Liz's tank and the calcite under her nails."

"So what do we need to expand our search there?" Bailey asked.

"We're talking a drop of thirty feet in depth, mountainlike terrain, and unpredictable currents within the canyon system— so strong they can disorient a diver in seconds. Basically, the danger level just skyrocketed."

36

Cole moved through the still, silent water, Bailey at his side. He loved having her there, sharing his work and his passion for diving. It made thoughts of her imminent departure all the more painful. Like rubbing alcohol on an open wound.

She was everything he wanted in a wife—strong and determined, yet loving and gentle. She possessed an amazing sense of enthusiasm, a genuine love for the outdoors, and most importantly, a deep and abiding love for Christ.

And she stirred his soul. Always had.

He allowed his mind to drift back to the summer they first met. He sixteen, she fifteen—young and gorgeous, with a hearty chip on her shoulder and a reckless spirit that both enthralled and terrified him.

He'd hoped their friendship would be an anchor for her, and for a while it was. But looking back, he could see she'd always had one foot out the door, always looking for bigger and better. Unfortunately her idea of bigger and better equaled finding fulfillment in empty things—partying and popularity.

As soon as summer ended and the school term began, she'd drifted away. New friends, new crowd. Skipping class to go island-hopping, neglecting her studies for parties and booze. He'd tried holding on, not wanting to lose her, but that night she'd left him no choice.

Against his voiced concerns, she'd drunk way too much at David's party. Something that was quickly becoming a habit.

His heart sank as the gut-wrenching loss of that night knotted inside him.

She'd disappeared, and he'd foolishly spent a half hour searching for her, only to find her in bed with Tom Murphy.

Humiliation washed over him anew.

She'd given her virginity to a guy who cared nothing about her. When she reappeared, disheveled and drunk, she hadn't even had the decency to look him in the eye. She slurred something about being sorry but having to move on.

Her "relationship" with Tom didn't last the week, only the occasional tumble he was forced to hear about in lurid detail during gym.

Her partying increased until Monday-morning homeroom became a regular chronicle of her drunken escapades the weekend before.

Demeaning nicknames and locker-room jargon—he'd tried to ignore it all. Ignore the amazing girl he'd known and loved self-destructing before his eyes.

The pain it inflicted lingered, the experience branding him to a deeper degree than he'd realized. But Bailey . . .

He looked over at her descending the depths of the canyon, darkness enfolding her. He hated to imagine the scar it had seared into her.

For most who had gone through what she had, there'd be no healing, no freedom. But Bailey had found the answer. She'd found Jesus and, in Him, redemption and rebirth. It was time she started embracing the life He had for her, rather than drowning in regret over the sins of her past. Sins Jesus had already nailed to the cross.

Please, Lord, help her to release it all to you. Only you can make the broken whole. I know that only too well.

"Cole." Kayden's voice crackled in his headset.

"Yeah?"

"We've got a storm moving our way. This is going to be your only descent today."

Storms weren't uncommon on the Alaskan Peninsula—sunny days were. "How long?"

"An hour and a half tops."

"All right, crew. You heard the lady. We've got fifty-five minutes down here before we push the narcosis limit. Let's use all of it. Looks like this will be our only dive of the day."

"You got it," Landon said.

Piper and Bailey both gave the okay signal.

"Landon, why don't you and Piper finish up grid six. Bailey and I can at least get a start on seven."

"You got it."

He waited until Landon and Piper faded into the darkness before heading with Bailey to grid seven. So far they'd cleared five grids with no signs of the ruins. A few alcoves, a small canyon, and the remnants of a ship he hoped to return to and explore when they had the time. But not now. Every day, every hour they lost gave the killer more opportunity to swoop in and find the ruins before them.

Fifty-five minutes didn't give them much time, but at least they could take a look.

The sea wall narrowed as they progressed farther into the belly of the canyon. Coral encased both sides of the passageway, anemone moving in rhythmic sway with the water as fish darted in and out of their sea home.

Cole panned his light at an opening before them. "Looks like we may have found the entrance to a cave system. Hang back while I check it out."

Bailey signaled in the affirmative.

Cole secured the guide rope around his waist and Bailey double-checked it.

"Be careful, Cole."

"Always. Careful's my middle name."

"No it's not." Laughter danced in her voice. "I remember your middle name—Huckleberry."

Why did his mother have to love Mark Twain so? "I'll be back as soon as I can."

She nodded again, and he entered the hole, assessing the path before him. Two feet wide and not much higher. Slipping his tanks from his back, he pushed them in first, then wriggled in behind.

"What do you see?" she asked after a few moments of silence.

"Not a lot. It's pretty cramped." The tanks scraped across the rocks as he pressed forward, wriggling on his belly like a fish. Silt plumed up, clouding what limited sight he had.

"Maybe you should turn back."

"I'll give it a few more feet. Looks like there might be an opening ahead." His torch bounced off the tunnel wall.

A few more feet and the cramped dimensions slowly widened until it opened up into an air-filled cavity.

Cold and damp, the scent of water lingered. He lit his secondary light and fanned it. A lake filled the center of the chamber, ripples reflecting off the domed rock ceiling. A myriad of tunnels branched off in various directions. *Too many to search now.* He checked his watch. Thirty-five minutes before they needed to start making their ascent. He checked his gauge. Plenty of air. He could explore one, maybe two, depending on how deep they ran.

But where to start?

He shone his light across the opening of each in turn, and his breath hitched when he hit the one directly across from him. Was that a marker flagging the tunnel entrance?

He moved toward it, across the lake, water rising over his ankles, creeping up his legs.

"Cole," Kayden's voice garbled over the radio, faint and distant.

"Kayd?"

More garble.

Bailey's voice cut in. "Cole's exploring a cave."

More garble.

"Roger that. I'll tell him," Bailey replied.

A spurt of garble.

"Cole?"

"Yeah, Bay?"

"Kayden says the storm is picking up speed. She recommends we start heading up in fifteen."

"Roger that. I just need ten to check something out."

He descended into the depths of the lake, knowing straight across would be the fastest route to the marker, though he didn't exactly want to think about what creatures might be sharing the dark water with him.

Reaching the other side, he climbed from the water onto the dry patch of land and grabbed hold of the flag. "I've got a marker flagging one of the tunnel entrances down here."

"You think Liz and Nikolai left it?"

"That'd be my guess."

"Great. Leave it and we can check it out after the storm passes."

He shone his light down the tunnel. "It doesn't look long. I'm going to take a cursory glance."

"Time's running short, Cole."

"Give me five. If I don't see anything, I'll turn back." No sense coming this far and not see what they were dealing with.

"Don't push it."

"Five and I turn back."

He crept forward, once again sliding his tanks through the cramped space before him. Twenty feet in, the tunnel split, and a second marker flagged the right branch entrance.

He took it to its sudden end. Lowering his tanks until he felt solid ground, he released them and wriggled out. He panned his torch and his eyes widened in awe.

Leaving the markers in place, Cole retraced his path to the first entrance, where he found Bailey waiting on the other end of the guide rope.

Landon and Piper had joined her.

"You took long enough," Landon said.

"I found it."

"What?" Bailey's eyes grew wide inside her mask.

"The church, just as Elma described, in the heart of the system." In theory it had sounded remotely plausible, but seeing it intact and frozen in time . . . it'd been awe-inspiring.

"And the icon?" Bailey asked.

"No time."

"Speaking of time." Landon tapped his dive watch. "Kayden said the storm's pressing in fast."

37

Cole breached the surface of the water to gale-force winds.

The *North Star* rocked, tossed by the burgeoning waves cresting over the sides, sloshing water across their path.

He yanked off his mask and handed Gage his equipment. "Thanks, man."

Going below, he changed into dry clothes and headed for the galley, the boat rocking as he trekked the narrow corridor.

He slid into the bench beside Bailey, who had also changed into dry attire.

"Don't keep us waiting, man," Landon said.

Cole exhaled. "Where to start?" He'd seen his share of amazing things, but . . . a church preserved through time a hundred feet beneath the sea. "It was literally like the canyon swallowed the church whole. Debris from the island must have settled on top, encapsulating it, if you will. Then the sea and its creatures went to work incorporating it into their world. The outer shell is covered with coral and anemone in a reef-like structure. The church itself is filled with air, as is the entry chamber where I located the first marker. The church's contents appear untouched. The only water inside the system is a large underground lake in the primary chamber and it's held in check by a series of tunnels, limiting it to the outer rim."

Bailey angled to face him better. "I know you didn't have long, but did you see anything? Can you describe any of the interior?"

Piper handed him a cup of coffee. "Thanks." He took a sip, letting it warm him as the storm raged on outside.

"I didn't see much, but there was a long, narrow table, tilted a bit to one side. I think one of the legs was broken."

"Most likely the altar," Bailey said, leaning in closer, her attention riveted.

He couldn't wait to see her reaction when she saw it firsthand, to watch the wonder dance in her eyes and spread across her lovely face.

"Anything else?" she asked.

It was hard to focus with her so close and her attention so fixed on him. It almost inspired hope to rise within him, but he knew better. She'd already made up her mind and he didn't factor in the decision. "A structure, sort of like a long wooden wall toppled on its side. I only had a moment, but it held a series of images and carvings, some appearing to have jarred loose. Very intricate work."

"Images like icons?"

"Possibly."

"It might have been an iconostasis."

"A what?"

"An iconostasis. It's a wall of icons and religious paintings, separating the nave, or inner arcade, from the sanctuary or it can be a portable icon stand that can be placed anywhere within a church. This is unbelievable. Do you realize what an amazing cultural find this is? A nineteenth-century Russian-Orthodox church, for all intents and purposes, untouched by time. Thank goodness we found it before Greg Stevens or other treasure hunters; otherwise, the only people to enjoy it would be black-market dealers and their rich clientele. How soon can we get back down there?"

"As soon as this storm passes." Cole set down his mug, the rubber bottom keeping it still despite the rocking of the waves. "Hopefully first thing tomorrow."

"I wouldn't bank on it," Gage said, entering the galley.

"Weather station's reporting a massive storm." He sat on the bench and opened his soda. "Looks like we could be grounded several days."

Cole sank back as disappointment spread over everyone's faces. *Wonderful.* They'd finally found what they'd been searching for and they couldn't touch it.

But, on the bright side, Bailey would be sticking around a little while longer. He recognized the hunger in her eyes. She was hooked. No way she'd leave without seeing the ruins.

Question was, was that a good thing?

Two rocky hours later, Tariuk Island's rugged mountains appeared in the distance, the peaks breaching the heavy cloud cover. As they discussed the protocol they'd follow once in the ruins, Bailey marveled at how quickly she had been drawn into the adventure—into this place and its people.

"I've got a friend who's an antiquities theft investigator," she said. "She deals with this sort of thing every day. I'll give her a call and find out the best way to retrieve the artifacts in the most expedient manner, while still preserving their integrity, of course. We obviously don't have time to go through the typical laborious documentation process, not with a killer on the loose."

Cole poured a refill of coffee for him and Bailey. "I imagine we'll utilize methods similar to those we use for salvaging wrecks."

Bailey swallowed a sip. "You salvage ships?"

"Now and then an underwater archaeologist shows up with a theory about where a particular ship may be resting, but they need up-front divers who know the area. We only work with trained archaeologists, never treasure hunters out to make a quick buck." He retook his seat beside her. "Once we locate the ship, we typically help them with artifact retrieval. A couple of years ago we assisted with the salvage of the *Dorian*. The contents are on display at the University of Anchorage. It's always exciting work."

"Wow, you really are a man of many talents."

Cole shrugged with a sexy smile. "I try."

Landon entered the station, feeling hope for the first time since the case began. An end looked within reach. Whatever secrets the church held would surely provide the answers they sought and lead them to the killer, or the killer to them.

"Grainger." Slidell lifted his chin in greeting. "Any luck?"

Landon dropped his duffel on the chair. "Would you believe we found the intact ruins of the church in an undersea canyon?"

"Seriously?"

"I kid you not."

Slidell rocked forward, the front legs of his chair hitting the linoleum floor with a thud. "That's great news. Did you find the icon?"

Landon shook his head. "Cole discovered the entrance to the ruins just as the storm blew in. We had to note the location and haul out. Soon as this storm's gone, we're back down there."

"Well, looks like this is our lucky day."

"What do you mean?"

"Someone recognized Greg Stevens's sketch—the older version Bailey gave us, that is."

"Who?"

"Peg Wilson said she's been renting him her hunting cabin for about two months."

"Two months?" What had he been doing in Yancey all that time? "That's a month before Liz and Nikolai's arrival and nearly six weeks before Agnes's crash."

"You think he and Agnes had any contact?"

"At this rate, it wouldn't surprise me. Definitely gives us cause to pull her phone records."

"Good. Get on that."

"Will do. Peg say anything else about him?"

Slidell thumbed through his notes. "Only that he paid the first month's rent up front and in cash."

"He mention how long he was planning to stay?"

Slidell shook his head. "Said he hadn't decided, so he and Peg have been working on a month-to-month basis. Peg didn't seem to mind. Said he was a great tenant. Quiet. Kept to himself."

"I'll bet. Did he tell her what he was doing out here?"

"Said he was looking for some peace and quiet."

"Probably shouldn't have started killing people, then, should he have?" At least they had him now. "When are we going in?"

"Already done. Right after I spoke with Peg."

"And?" No one was in the holding cell.

"Gone."

"Gone?" Surely he wouldn't leave town without the icon. "How long?"

"Not long. Probably out for the day and got wind we were on to him. Earl's watching the place. He hasn't returned, and I don't expect him to. He's too smart."

"You check the hotels in town? See if they got any new patrons?"

Slidell nodded. "Nada."

"Cole said he'd have needed a boat to meet up with Nick on Cleary's. Maybe he's bunked down on it somewhere."

"I'll have Tom check the marina."

"It's worth a shot, but I doubt you'll find him there. If he knows we're on to him, I'm sure he's well out of sight."

"One positive. He left some stuff behind."

Landon arched a brow as anticipation surged through him.

"Not much, mind you. Some clothes, a few personal items. Nothing overly useful, but we sent it all to the lab. Maybe they'll be able to get a full print this time."

"We can hope." But he doubted it. The guy was too good at covering his tracks.

38

Bailey stared out the Trading Post window at the sheets of rain blanketing Yancey and groaned. "Weather says it'll be another day before it lets up." The find at their fingertips and a storm blocking their path.

"With this case, it seems par for the course." Cole sank down on the couch. "Should we get back to the diary?"

She stretched. "I suppose so." Settling back in her chair, she opened the diary. "Either I'm getting old or the lighting in here is dimming." She reached to turn on the end-table lamp, only to find it gone. "That's strange."

"What's that?" Cole asked, popping a tortilla chip in his mouth.

"Agnes had a Tiffany lamp here. She read by it every night."

"Maybe it broke."

"Maybe. I'll see what else I can find." She stood and strode the length of the store looking for a lamp she could use. She was ready to head upstairs when the Tiffany lamp caught her eye, settled on a small accent table in the crook of the wall. *That's a weird place for it. Nothing to illuminate there.* She bent, unplugged it, and carried it back to the end table. "No idea why she put it over there." She plugged it in. "Much more useful here." She reached for the switch, and something cold jiggled against her palm. "That's odd."

Cole arched a brow.

"There's something attached to the string." Shifting, she ducked to look under the antique lampshade. "Huh."

"What is it?"

"A key."

"A key?" Curiosity piqued in Cole's husky voice.

"Yeah." It took a moment, but she tugged it free. Forgetting her original purpose, she left the light off and sank back into place, holding the key in front of her.

Cole moved beside her, examining it over her shoulder. "It's not a house key. Too small. Looks more like a key to a . . . a . . . safety deposit box."

A *safety deposit box*. Bailey smiled. *Oh, Agnes, you sneaky, wonderful woman. . . .*

"Safety deposit box, you say?" Gus asked over the crackling phone line. "Don't recall Agnes having one. But that don't mean much." He chuckled. "Agnes had her secrets. A woman of intrigue, I used to tease her."

Bailey shook her head. She'd learned more about Agnes in the past few weeks than she had in the three years living with her. "If she did have a box, which bank do you think it'd be at?"

Gus whistled. "Far as I know, she did all her banking at Morton's. She and Phil went way back. If I was a betting man, I'd check there first."

Thunder rocked the building, and the lights dimmed. They brightened for a brief moment before returning to normal.

"Thanks, Gus."

"No problem." He paused. "Say, if you don't mind me asking, what's this all about?"

Bailey huddled against the building in the onslaught of the storm, her windbreaker wrapped fast about her. Rain poured off the rim of her hood.

"Sorry to drag you out here after closing, Phil. And in such weather," Cole said.

Phil Morton slipped his key in the lock and turned it. "Gus said it was important. That's good enough for me."

Yanking the door open, he ushered them inside. An alarm trilled in the background, and Phil shuffled to the keypad, punching in a code. The ringing stopped and a series of recessed lights flickered on.

Bailey slipped the hood from her head and ran a hand through her damp hair. "Thank you again for meeting us tonight." She'd have never slept if they'd had to wait until morning.

"No worries." The elderly man smiled, his wrinkled face creasing with the motion. "Vault's back here." He signaled them to follow. "Watch your step," he cautioned as they filed down a series of steps at the rear of the building.

"How long ago did you say Agnes rented the box?" Bailey asked.

"Let's see now. It was Ida's birthday that day. I remember because I was fixing to close up shop a little early. I had tickets to a show to surprise her with and we had to catch the five-o'clock ferry to make it in time."

At the base of the stairwell, Phil unlocked another door and ushered them into a second hallway, leading them by flashlight until he reached the switch plate on the wall. "There now, that's better." He smiled. "Where was I?"

"You were closing early," Cole said.

"Oh yes. It's not that Marilyn and Tess aren't competent enough. Those ladies keep me on the straight and narrow and could probably run the place better than I, but it's a Morton tradition that goes back to my great-grandpappy and the founding of Morton's Depository in 1898. We Mortons are here from open to close, Monday through Friday. When tradition stands, banks don't crumble. I don't understand high-falutin' banks where the owners are never on the premises. Why, I bet they don't even know who their employees are." He shook his head. "No way to run a business, if you ask me."

The hallway, which looked more like a subterranean tunnel, banked right and ended at the vault door—solid and imposing in stature.

"They don't make safes like they used to." Phil sighed. "Now, if you kind folks would turn around for a moment."

"Of course." Cole turned, and Bailey followed suit.

A creaking signaled the opening of the vault, and Cole moved to help Phil with the door.

"Thank you, son. That door keeps getting heavier and heavier. Now to business." He straightened his coat and turned to Bailey. "Gus informs me that you are Agnes's heir and are in possession of the box key. Is that correct?"

"Yes, sir."

"Well, then the contents of box twenty-two belong to you." He pulled a master key from his breast pocket, led her to the box, inserted his key, and signaled her to do the same.

Excitement coursed through her. What would they find? Would it be of any help with the case? What new thing would she learn about the aunt she'd thought she'd known so well?

On Phil's instruction, Bailey turned her key simultaneously with his. The door opened and Phil retracted his key. He stepped back. "I'll give you folks some privacy. Just holler when you're done."

"Thanks." Bailey pulled the key from the lock and slid it into her jeans pocket. "I'm sorry, when did you say Agnes purchased the box?"

"I guess I never did finish that story." Phil's cheeks flushed a mottled pink. "My mind seems to do that these days, wandering from one point to another without finishing the first." He gave a weak smile. "The glories of getting old. On the good side, the shorter you realize your time is on this earth, the more important things that truly matter become to you. Faith. Family. You don't waste time on senseless pursuits. . . ."

He shook his head resignedly. "I've gone and done it again. Off on a tangent. The answer to your question, my dear, is that Agnes opened the box on July thirty-first. I was just about to leave when she came in. She seemed quite urgent about it, so I took the time to rent her the box." He chuckled. "Fastest I ever processed one. But it all worked out in the end. Agnes got her box, and Ida and I made the play with time to spare."

"Did Agnes say why it was so urgent, or what she needed the box for?" Cole asked.

"No, sir. She didn't say and I didn't ask. A security box . . ." He lifted onto his toes, then rocked back, sliding his hands in his pockets. "Now, that's a person's private business. And on that note, I'll leave you to your privacy."

With a breath of anticipation, Bailey slid the box from its slot and set it on the long table running the length of the compact room. "July thirty-first. That's the evening before Agnes flew to Russia."

"Makes me wonder what she was trying to keep safe."

"One way to find out." Biting her bottom lip, Bailey lifted the lid and stared inside. *Not another diary.* She lifted the brown leather book from the box, its cover worn and aged with time. She flipped through the crude parchment pages, trying not to let disappointment consume her. She didn't know what she'd been expecting—she just knew this wasn't it. "It looks like a story of some sort, or perhaps a journal."

"Another one?"

Her sentiments exactly. What was it going to hold that the other didn't? Was this all some wild-goose chase? Did the murders have nothing to do with Agnes or the stolen diary? Were they forcing connections where there were none?

"Wait." His hand stilled hers. "There's something else." He pointed to the envelope wedged in the back of the box.

Bailey fished it out. "Agnes's handwriting." With trembling hands, she flipped it over. "It's addressed to me." She scanned the note scrawled across the seal and exhaled.

"What?"

"It says not to open the letter until I've read the book."

39

Bailey flipped another page as the lights flickered, the storm raging on outside. "Unbelievable."

Cole wiggled her foot. "What does it say?"

"Sorry." She gave a sheepish grin. It was just too captivating. "It chronicles Tsar Ivan VI's escape from Shlisselburg Fortress. According to the history books Ivan was murdered during the attempt, but this says the escape was successful."

Cole scooted forward. "Go on."

Bailey flipped to the next page, and everything went dark.

"Looks like the electrical lines finally gave out. Good thing Yancey only gets a handful of thunderstorms a year." He clicked the flashlight on. "You got any candles?"

"Guess we'll find out."

The candles aglow, Bailey settled in once more beside Cole on the couch. The flames flickered and danced in shadows along the walls—the russet glow shimmering along Cole's tanned face and arms, highlighting the golden streaks in his hair.

He smiled at her lingering gaze, and heat shot through her.

She stared at the page, willing her eyes to focus on the words.

"Okay." He reclined. "Russian history's not really my area of expertise. . . . Who was Ivan the VI and why was he imprisoned?"

"Ivan VI was the grandson of Ivan V, who was co-tsar with his half brother Peter the Great."

"I didn't realize Peter the Great had a co-tsar."

"Most people don't, and for all intents and purposes, he didn't. Ivan V was the true heir to the Romanov throne, the eldest living son of Alexis I by his first marriage. So, by law, he was next in line for the throne upon his father's death. Unfortunately Ivan V was mentally handicapped. So, to avoid a coup, or a power struggle for the throne, they came to the best agreement they could to keep the monarchy strong and unified. They named Peter Ivan's co-tsar. Peter was the son of Alexis I by his second wife, and he ushered Russia into the modern age."

"And Ivan VI?"

"Right. When he ascended the throne after the deaths of Ivan V and Peter, Peter the Great's daughter Elizabeth staged a coup. She seized the throne and had Ivan and his entire family imprisoned."

"And no one objected?"

"I'm sure some did. Elizabeth's claim on the throne was shaky at best, and she feared an uprising, so she kept Ivan completely isolated from the rest of his family. Since he was so young and had only been tsar for a matter of months, she hoped to wipe any memory of him from the people's minds. So she set about erasing every trace of him from all documents and anything else mentioning his name. She even sent out a decree directing the public to turn in any coins depicting Ivan for an exchange of new coins at full value.

"When Elizabeth's nephew, Peter III, ascended the throne upon her death, he visited Ivan and sympathized with him. Some believed Peter might even release Ivan, but the hope was short-lived. Peter III died unexpectedly.

"Historians are quite confident his murder was orchestrated by his wife, who took over the throne as Catherine the Great. She—a German princess suspected of murdering her husband, with her son known in court circles to be the illegitimate child of her lover, Serge Saltykov—feared Ivan all the more."

"So Ivan languished in prison?"

"In Shlisselburg Fortress, where he was kept in solitary confinement and, under Catherine's orders, only referred to as the Nameless One."

"But he escaped?"

"According to the history books, no. He died during the attempt. But, according to this"—she tapped the book—"the attempt was successful."

"And then what?"

"According to this, they traveled to Alaska."

"Why Alaska?" Cole asked, stretching.

Bailey glanced at the clock—a quarter of eleven. She blinked, trying to jar the sleepiness from her eyes. "Apparently they believed they needed to leave Russia to keep Ivan safe until a large enough force could be organized to stage an effective coup."

"But that never happened."

She shook her head.

"What went wrong?"

"The lieutenant who rescued Ivan died on the journey. Ivan was left to travel with a Russian Orthodoxy missionary priest and the lieutenant's wife, Olga."

"The one who wrote this diary?" he asked.

Bailey ran her hand reverently over the leather-bound journal. "Yes."

She turned to the last page, skimming the faded parchment.

My dearest Natalia,

I fear my time is fading and there is much to say before I go to your father's arms. We have been entrusted with a great charge, an honorable duty bestowed upon me by your father with his dying breath while you were still in my belly. I became Ivan's caretaker in this rugged, foreign land. The keeper of the truth and the protector of the items of proof.

*Ivan chose to remain in this land, to turn from his past,
to marry and make a new life. To protect his new bride
and his children from the horrors he suffered as a result
of his birthright.*

*He made the choice, but we must continue to bear the
secret, to protect the treasures, to keep the truth alive in
the hearts of his children and grandchildren in whatever
way we can. We must honor your father's charge as well
as Ivan's wish. This is your duty now. To keep the legacy,
passing it on to your daughter, and she on to hers. We must
never allow the legacy to die, even if it remains forever
hidden, tucked in the truth of a bedtime story.*

All my love,

Mother

Cole sat with his back against the couch, his legs stretched
out in front of him, his head a mere inch from her knee. "He
chose not to go back. To give up his throne . . ."

"It makes me think of Edward VIII of England, who gave up
the throne in 1936 to marry American divorcée Wallis Simpson.
He did it for love, just as it says Ivan did."

"To protect his family. If he'd attempted a coup and it failed . . ."
Cole began.

"They'd all have been executed or imprisoned. Ivan spent
twenty-two years of his life in prison. He watched his family be ripped apart. Spent years in solitary confinement. It's a
wonder it didn't destroy him. He wanted to avoid that fate for
his children at all cost."

"So he started a new life. Brave man."

She wished she could be brave like that. Brave enough to
face her past. Brave enough to sacrifice for love, lay her pride
on the altar and tell Cole how she really felt about him. That
she loved him. That she'd been a fool. And that if he'd let her,

she wanted to spend the rest of her life making it up to him. If only she were that brave. "I wonder what he did here? What name he took? How he spent his years?"

"It'd be fun to find out. Maybe we could track it down together." He wiggled her knee.

"Maybe, but let's focus on one puzzle at a time." One step at a time. It was all her heart could take.

"Time to read Agnes's letter." He handed her the envelope. With shaking hands, she took it.

"It'll be all right."

She nodded with a weak smile. He thought she was trembling because of the letter. If only he knew it was because of him. She unfolded the sheet.

My dearest Bailey,

This diary has been passed down to the women in our family from generation to generation since our ancestor Olga traveled with Ivan VI from Russia to Alaska. First to the St. Stephen settlement, and then to the location that is now Yancey. Where, you may find it interesting to note, she took up residence in the very building I call home. I never could resist an added bit of history.

My great-aunt Mildred bestowed this calling onto me and when my time is near, I shall pass it on to you along with all the responsibilities inherent with it.

We are caretakers, each one of us, since Olga's daughter, Natalia, pledged to keep the secret safe, to keep the legacy alive. The location of the items of proof has seemingly faded with time, but the legacy and our job remain. We must preserve the truth and the lineage. I pass this charge into your capable hands with utmost confidence.

Of particular importance to all of this is a diary written by one of Ivan's relatives, Princess Sofia Maksutov. She was the wife of the last governor of Russian Alaska and a direct descendant of Ivan's sister Elizaveta.

In 1780 Catherine the Great, believing Ivan dead and her hold on the throne secure, released Ivan's remaining siblings from prison and allowed them to live in exile in Denmark. It appears Princess Maksutov had some knowledge of Ivan's escape, and when she moved to Alaska with her husband, she hoped to seek out Ivan's descendants. It's a fascinating chronicle that I know you will enjoy. I've lent it to the historical society for the time being, so others may enjoy her vivid description of daily life in Russian Alaska, but they have agreed that you may retrieve it any time you wish.

I hope to be sharing all of this with you in person, but as Great Aunt Mildred insisted, "Always be prepared for the unexpected," so I draft this in case the unexpected occurs. Fortunately nothing is unexpected with God, and so if I am not with you, know I am with Him and I will see you again one day.

Be blessed, my dear Bailey. Be loved. Be open to all God has in store for you. And don't be afraid to enjoy His gifts.

Agnes

Bailey sank back, tears streaming down her face. "No wonder Agnes strove so hard to teach me about Russian history, why she was so passionate about it. It wasn't history to her." Sniffing, she pulled out the first of two folded papers and laid it open. "It's the Romanov family tree." She examined it, Cole looking on as she traced the line from Michael to Ivan V to Ivan VI, below which sat the names of two children—Peter and Anna, and off to the side was scribbled the notation—*orb in the image.*

"What do you think that means?" he asked.

"I have no idea." She turned back to the lineage, to Peter's and Anna's children, and on to their children's children, and then it ended at the next generation.

"What happened then?"

She flipped it over and started at the blank back. "It just stops." She spread it across her lap and scanned the lineage with a more critical eye. "The information begins to fade with Ivan's grandkids. See, up until then everyone's birth and death dates are recorded, along with marriages. With Ivan's grandkids, only the birth dates and locations are recorded. By the great-grandkids, it's only the year of birth."

"I wonder why?"

"Maybe the caretaker lost track of his descendants. Perhaps the family started to spread out, as families do, and the caretaker lost touch, or neglected to keep the information up to date."

Bailey reached for the second document, noting the difference. The first was parchment, tanned with age, the second, modern. She unfolded it and could barely believe her eyes. "This is what Agnes must have been working on when she died. She's completed the Romanov line from Ivan's great-grandchildren until now."

"Now?" Cole's brows shot up as he leaned in to read the document. "Are you saying there are living heirs?"

"According to this, there are at least three."

Bailey moved to the computer and typed in the first heir's name, Vasilli Alexandrovich, and hit Enter, her heart racing while Google searched. It was almost too amazing to believe. History being revealed before their eyes.

She clicked on the first link that popped up—a news article from July.

Her breath caught. "He was murdered. A week before Agnes flew to Russia."

Cole rested his hands on the back of her chair. "Check heir number two."

She typed in his name, Feodor Alexandrovich, and waited. Her heart nearly fainting as she scanned the page. "He was injured in a horse-riding accident but is recuperating at his home in Petropavlovsk-Kamchatsky, Russia. Wait." She dragged the mouse down. "There's an updated story." She clicked on the link and felt the blood drain from her face. "He was dead a week later."

"As a result of his injuries?"

"No. In a plane crash." She swallowed. "Agnes's crash."

"What?"

"Fedyna is a variant of Feodor."

"The Russian couple on the plane?"

Bailey nodded somberly.

"Somebody is killing off heirs."

She swiveled to face him. "Question is . . . does the killer know they're heirs?"

Cole exhaled. "If I were a betting man . . ."

"I'm right there with you."

"But why?"

"I have no idea."

"We better warn whoever is next on the list."

"According to this, there's only one heir left, Grigor Ivanov." She turned and Googled his name, sighing with relief when nothing turned up. "We need to find him and warn him."

"Let's go see Slidell."

Cole hung his slicker on the coatrack beside Bailey's. The station was quiet, the stark overhead lighting giving way to the muted glow of desk lamps.

"Slidell in?" Cole asked.

Earl thumbed over his shoulder. "Back in his office."

Nearly midnight. The man really didn't have a life outside work.

Cole knocked on the closed door.

"Yeah, come in."

Dressed in a pair of faded jeans and white undershirt, Slidell reclined on the couch, his socked feet stretched out over the sofa's edge. A slice of pizza in hand, his attention was fixed on the twenty-inch TV in the corner. "What's up?"

"Sorry to interrupt your game," Cole said.

Slidell paused the recording. "Panners are losing anyway." He shifted to a seated position and dropped his slice back in the box. "What can I do for you?"

Cole looked at Bailey. "Go ahead. It's your discovery."

"Our discovery." She smiled, and his heart warmed.

Slidell cleared his throat. "One of you want to let me in on it?"

"Right." Bailey's cheeks flushed. "Where to start? I guess Agnes's safety deposit box . . ."

She proceeded to bring him up to speed.

"So you see, we've got to find—"

Landon bolted through the door. "I got him!"

Slidell straightened. "Got who?"

"Greg Stevens. I finally got a hit on Interpol. Apparently it's only one of a number of aliases this guy uses—Greg Stevens, Stephen Gregory, Greg Stanford . . . You get the idea."

"You get his real name?" Slidell asked with arched brow.

Landon smiled. "Yep. Grigor Ivanov."

40

Slidell rocked forward in his chair, his fingers steepled. "So you're saying this Grigor Ivanov and Greg Stevens are one and the same?"

Landon slipped into a chair. "Yep."

"And he's our killer?"

"The best and only suspect we've got."

Slidell sat back with an exhale. "Motive?"

Landon shrugged. "Not a clue."

"Tell them what we found in the diary, in the letters," Cole said.

"Right." Bailey began relaying all they'd discovered, and when she was finished, she sighed. "Of course . . . " *It's all so clear.* "I can't believe I didn't think of it before."

Cole's brows dipped. "Think of what?"

"Grigor's motive." Before she and Cole discovered Agnes's safety deposit box and its contents, they'd had no idea they were dealing with a living Romanov heir. Up to that point they'd assumed the search and resulting killings had been about treasure, and in a way it still was, just treasure of a different kind. "Whoever's head of the Romanov Trust controls the Trust's vast holdings."

"What is the Romanov Trust?"

"The Trust's stated purpose is to strengthen the links between the Romanov family and protect it from impostors. Its not so public function is to maintain its immense holdings."

Landon angled his head in her direction. "What kind of holdings?"

"I'm not positive. No one is. It's all based on the supposition that large amounts of the Romanov treasure were smuggled out of Russia during the Bolshevik revolt and protected by Nicholas I's various relatives that escaped. Whoever is head of the Trust controls the treasure, along with anything added to it over the years."

"Who is currently in charge of the Trust?"

"Prince Nicholas Romanovich."

"Then wouldn't Grigor have to get rid of him too?"

"Not necessarily. If Grigor is in fact a direct descendant of Ivan VI, he would have a much stronger claim for headship than Prince Nicholas."

"Why?"

"Because all known Romanovs alive today trace their ancestry through Paul I. It was believed in court circles that Paul was the illegitimate son of Catherine the Great, a German princess, and her lover, Serge Saltykov—which means no true Romanov blood. Grigor, on the other hand, is directly descended from Nicholas I, the founder of the Romanov dynasty."

"So if Grigor is who you think he is, he'd have claim to the headship of the Romanov family?" Landon said.

"Absolutely."

Slidell rubbed his forehead. "Crazy as it sounds, I think you're on the right track. Grigor links to all our victims. He was the last person Nikolai texted before he died. Grigor also links to the two heirs as they were what he believed stood between him and his inheritance. Now that we know what we're looking for, I bet we'll find that Grigor was in Denmark when Vasilli was killed. And, of course, he links to Agnes."

"Agnes?" Bailey blanched. "How?"

Slidell reached in his drawer, pulled out a file, and slid it to her. "Your aunt's phone records. The highlighted calls are to, or from, the 1-800 number for the bogus Pentrinium Oil."

Bailey scanned the page. They went as far back as the end of June, and stopped the day Agnes left for Russia. She swallowed. "He knew she wasn't coming back."

Cole squeezed her shoulder.

"What if Greg or Grigor, whatever his name is"—she scrambled to put the pieces in place—"is the one who hired Agnes to trace the family line in the first place?"

"Maybe Agnes found out he killed Vasilli and flew to Russia to warn Feodor," Cole said. "Maybe his riding accident was no accident."

"Grigor must have figured out what she was up to and sabotaged Henry's plane."

"Killing two birds with one stone." Landon sat back with a solemn expression. "Both the heir in his way and the one person who could expose him."

Oh, Agnes. Bailey squeezed her eyes shut.

"So, what . . . Now he's after the proof he thinks he needs to claim his inheritance?" Slidell said.

"Exactly," Bailey said.

"So the icon's the proof?" Landon asked.

"One of them." Bailey nodded. "According to the diaries, both Princess Maksutov's and Olga's, there are two items of proof. The second isn't mentioned. . . ." She stood, pacing the length of the crowded room as she thought. "There has to be a clue in one of the diaries. . . ." She turned to Cole. "The notation."

Landon arched a brow. "What?"

"The notation on the bottom of the family tree. Cole, remember . . . it said 'orb in the image.' "

He leaned forward, a smile gracing his lips. "The second item is an orb."

Slidell frowned. "What does 'orb in the image' mean?"

"I don't know." Bailey retook her seat, her heart pounding.

They were so close. "I am sure it was written by Agnes. Maybe she wanted me to find an orb that is pictured in the icon painting."

"But there wasn't an orb in the painting," Cole said, rubbing Bailey's tense shoulders.

"We've only seen a small portion of the painting—just their faces. Perhaps one of them is holding an orb. If so, then we'll know what the orb looks like."

"Okay, but how does that help us?" Slidell asked.

"It's a lot easier to find something if we know what it looks like," Bailey continued. "It seems logical that the orb would have been in the church with the painting, but it's possible it was kept somewhere else."

"Maybe Grigor already has it. Either way, we need to get back down to the church," Landon said. "If he reaches the icon before we do and flees the country, we'll have no recourse."

"How can you say that? We've tied him to all the murders." They couldn't let her aunt's killer go free.

"Unfortunately, it's all circumstantial evidence. We've got no fingerprints or DNA on the victims, or at the scenes of the crimes. No eyewitnesses . . ."

"So we've got to keep him here until we either build our case, or get a confession from him. We have to charge him with the murders before he claims his inheritance. Russia is not just going to hand over the long-lost heir of the Romanov dynasty to stand trial for murder when all the evidence is circumstantial."

Slidell cleared his throat. "While we're on the subject of evidence . . . We know who the female ear belonged to. Police pulled the body of Nikolai Sokolov's sister out of the Santa Ynez River, minus an ear."

"Santa Ynez? That's in Southern California," Bailey said.

Slidell nodded. "Santa Barbara area."

"Where Liz Johnson is from."

"Exactly."

"So, if the sister was killed there, how did her ear end up on the beach with Nikolai's remains?"

Landon inhaled. "I imagine Grigor used it as a bargaining chip to get Nikolai to hand over the location of the items."

Cole shook his head sadly. "But Nikolai held out?"

Landon nodded. "He must have known Grigor would have already killed his sister. So he went to his death protecting the location."

Cole handed Bailey a cup of tea, thankful she'd agreed to spend the night at his sisters' place. The thought of her alone at the Post with Grigor on the loose nearly suffocated him. Particularly after the call he'd just received. "That was Jesse."

She looked up at him—fear and optimism dueling for purchase. "And?"

"He's retrieved a dozen e-mails between Agnes and Greg Stevens of Pentrinium Oil."

"Grigor."

Every trail led back to him. "There's more. . . ."

"I'm afraid to ask."

"Agnes's e-mails are being forwarded to an account registered to Pentrinium Oil."

"What does he want with them?"

"I guess he's hoping something will come through, some information he can use to find the items of proof."

"But she's gone."

Cole sighed. "He's probably banking on the fact that not everybody she was in contact with knows that."

41

Tension and excitement pulsed through Cole—the rush of riding the big one combined with the threat of imminent danger pushed it to the extreme.

Focus was key. They had an objective—retrieve the icon and the orb, if it was in the church, and get everyone safely back on board the *North Star.*

He caught sight of the cavern entrance and motioned to his party. "I go in first, then Bailey, and then Piper. Landon, you close up the rear. Ninety seconds between each for the sediment to settle. We don't want anyone going in blind. There are some pretty tight spots, so go slow."

He entered the passageway and worked his way through as he had three days ago. Climbing free into the first cavern, he sighed with relief at the sight of the first marker.

Nothing appeared disturbed.

He waited for the rest of his team before traversing the lake; then he led them the remainder of the way to the ruins.

As they made the final bend, he heard Bailey's sharp intake of breath.

"I don't believe it," she murmured.

Landon helped him set up a perimeter of lights while Piper tested the air.

"All clean," she reported.

Cole removed his mask and inhaled the musty air. "Let's get to work."

Bailey reverently touched the edge of the portrait. "Over here."

Everyone came rushing over.

"That's not a religious icon," Landon said with pensive brow.

Piper rolled her eyes. "Thank you, Captain Obvious."

"What I meant was we were all under the impression it was an icon, a religious painting, but this looks more like a portrait."

"It is a portrait," Bailey said in awe. "A royal portrait."

Piper sighed. "I'm confused."

"You see, in the cell image it looked remarkably like an icon. Nikolai only captured the face. The hair, here"—Bailey pointed—"reflected like a golden halo, which is typical of Russian iconic paintings of that particular time period."

"Does the fact that it's a royal portrait rather than a religious icon change our situation? Is it still an item of proof?" Cole asked.

"Absolutely and it makes even more sense now."

"How so?" Landon asked.

"This royal portrait of young Ivan sitting on his mother's lap, holding the dynastic orb, with a regal red robe proves he was the tsar. If Grigor were to present this painting along with the actual orb, they could not contest that it belonged to Ivan VI."

"It's dated . . ." Piper squinted to read it better. "Seventeen forty-one."

"It must have been painted just prior to his imprisonment. Hand me a pair of gloves." She slid them on and carefully removed the portrait from the frame, as Cole and Landon readied the water-safe transport bag.

"Wait." Piper's eyes widened. "There's another painting on the back."

"What?" Bailey shifted it to find another portrait—this time of a man, somewhere in his mid-to-late thirties, handsome and regal, and holding the same orb.

Piper pointed. "It's dated too."

Bailey's gaze shifted down. " 'Ivan VI Antonovich, July 1778. Russian Alaska.' It's Ivan as an adult. Here in Alaska." *Unbelievable.*

"It's proof he escaped and made it safely to Alaska," Cole said with admiration.

"And the orb?" Landon asked.

Bailey shook her head as her history lessons came back in full swing. "When Catherine the Great ascended the throne she had new coronation regalia made. I never understood why, but if one piece was missing, it would draw suspicion. . . ."

"So she had it remade," Cole said, totally in tune with what she was thinking.

"Right. Ivan had the orb, and Catherine, to not draw attention to that fact, commissioned a new crown as well."

"So where's the orb now?" Landon asked.

"It's got to be here somewhere." Bailey slid the portrait into the container and rested her hands on her hips. It just had to be.

"It isn't here," Cole said, laying a hand on Bailey's shoulder.

She shifted to rest her weary weight against him, teetering on the brink of discouragement as cold exhaustion spread through her limbs. "I had hoped . . . "

"Maybe someone removed it from the church before the earthquake. I mean there's no way anyone took it and left all this."

"What about Nikolai and Liz?" Landon said.

"They only took photos of the portrait. If they'd found the orb, why not photograph it as well? Unless . . ." Bailey said.

Cole's brow furrowed. "Unless?"

"Unless they retrieved the orb. Sort of as a show of faith that they had in fact found the ruins."

"Then why bother photographing the portrait?" Cole asked. "Why not just show them the orb?"

"Maybe Grigor required more than a photo," Landon said.

Bailey exhaled. "If that's true, then Grigor may already have the orb."

Cole tapped the case. "Which makes protecting this all the more critical."

Piper's flippers disappeared over the boat's edge. Bailey swam the remaining feet between her and the dive platform and grabbed the hand extended to her. The fingers tightened around her wrist and a warning shot pinged through her. The touch was unfamiliar and . . . *wrong.*

Gripping her tighter, the man yanked her upward, propelling her at a dizzying rate onto the metal platform. She lifted her head, her heart racing as she came face-to-face with Grigor. He was younger than the last time they'd met, but those eyes—gray and unyielding—she'd never forget.

"She doesn't have the bag either," he nearly growled. "Kiril, put her over with the others."

Her gaze flashed in the direction he pointed and her heart stopped. Gage unconscious. Kayden, bound and gagged. Piper in the process of being so.

"I said move!" He shoved her, and she lost her balance, flailing forward and falling face-first into Kiril's boot. Her jaw slammed against the heel, and blood swelled in her mouth.

"Let's go." Kiril hauled her to her feet. He ripped the mask from her face and bound her hands with startling efficiency.

Landon surfaced and climbed onto the platform, his eyes widening in horror. He lunged at Grigor, knocking him from his feet, only to be clobbered over the head by a third man.

Piper screamed, the thick gag muffling the sound. Tears welled in her eyes.

Grigor got to his feet. "Thanks, Anton."

Anton nodded, taking position over Landon, his gun cocked.

Bailey struggled against the blood-saturated rag shoved in her mouth, the overwhelming metallic taste churning her already queasy stomach. If only there was some way to warn Cole.

Cole climbed onto the dive platform to a gun barrel leveled between his eyes. Blinking, he looked past the weapon at Gage unconscious, then to Bailey and his sisters bound and gagged, and finally to Landon sprawled on the floor. He lifted his hands in surrender.

"Finally, a wise one. The bag, please?" Grigor held out his hand.

Cole heaved it over.

Grigor peered inside. "Kiril, cover him and call the boat over." Kiril moved into position and relayed the radio call.

Grigor reached inside, drawing the portrait out. "Beautiful." He handed it to Anton as an inflatable boat approached.

Grigor reached back in the bag, his smile fading. He reached deeper still, then pulled the bag inside out and flung it at Cole's feet. "Where is it? Where is the orb?"

Cole swallowed. Apparently Grigor didn't have the orb. . . . Which made matters all the more precarious. "It wasn't down there."

Grigor studied him a moment, then turned and strode to Bailey. He squatted in front of her, his pistol dangling in his left hand. He pulled her gag down.

Blood stained the white rag. Cole clenched his fists. What had he done to her?

"Where is the orb?"

"It wasn't down there." Her panic-stricken gaze flashed from Grigor to him.

If Grigor didn't have the orb, who did? And how did they convince him of the truth?

Grigor straightened, glancing from one of them to the next.

Cole's fear swelled. What was going through his mind?

Landon came to, and Kiril pressed a firm boot into the small of his back, cocking his gun. "Uh-uh."

Landon held his hands out, fingers spread, palms down.

"Not so cocky now, are we?" Kiril chuckled.

Grigor smirked and strode to Piper.

Cole's heart lodged in his throat.

Standing behind her, Grigor yanked Piper to her feet. Wrapping one arm around her waist, he pulled her tight against him, smirking at Landon's discomfort. "There's one way to discover the truth. A round of Russian roulette ought to take care of it." He slid a bullet out of the chamber and let it clang to the floor. Closing the chamber, he spun the cylinder, then pressed the butt of the muzzle against Piper's left temple.

"I'll ask one more time," he said, his voice calm, even, cold.

"It wasn't down there," Cole and Bailey hollered in unison.

Landon strained under Kiril's weight, his face bulging purple.

"Take me." Cole stepped forward. "Kill me."

"No!" Bailey yelled, tears streaming down her cheeks.

"That's far enough," Grigor said, the hunger in his eyes deepening.

Anton pulled Cole into a choke hold.

Dear Lord, please. Please don't let him do this. Not Piper.

For the first time in his life he felt utterly helpless.

Please, Lord. I'm on my knees, begging.

Piper whimpered.

Kayden lunged forward, but Grigor quickly knocked her back, his boot colliding with her already bruised and bloodied face.

"There will be no substitutes," he roared. "You want to save her, then simply tell the truth."

"We are. I swear." Cole held up his hands. "Search us. We aren't hiding anything. The orb wasn't there."

"I don't believe you." Grigor pulled the trigger.

Cole reared against Anton's choke hold, his body shaking with agony.

Grigor laughed as Piper nearly fainted. "I guess fate was kind to you today."

Cole squeezed his eyes shut. *Thank you, Lord.*

"Now I believe you." Grigor released Piper.

She puddled to the deck in a heap, crying.

Cole burned to run to her, to sweep her up in his arms, but Anton's gun remained fixed on him. He couldn't afford to do anything stupid—not when lives were at stake.

Grigor moved back to Bailey. "So where is it?"

"I don't know."

"Don't try my patience. It's clear you're the brains of this operation." He clasped her jaw. "Tell me where the orb is."

She shook her head, tears streaking down her cheeks.

Grigor pressed the gun to her head. "I assure you the rest of the chambers are full. Now, I will ask you one more time. Think very carefully how you answer. It may be your last. Where is the orb?"

Cole lurched forward. "We don't know."

Anton cocked his gun. "Don't bother. You'll be dead before you reach her. I guarantee it."

Then he'd go right along with her.

Fear squeezed Bailey's voice. "We really don't know. It wasn't down there."

Grigor's gaze hardened as his finger itched the trigger. "Then you're of no further use to me."

"Wait!" Cole shouted.

Grigor turned, a sadistic smile creeping on his lips. "I'm listening."

"Maybe . . ." Fear glazing her eyes, Bailey took a deep breath. "Maybe I missed something in the diary."

"The diary?" He angled his head back toward her. "The one I took from the historical society?"

"Yes."

His eyes narrowed. "How do you know what's in it?"

"Agnes made a copy."

He scowled. "Of course she did."

Tears streamed down Bailey's face. "Maybe I missed a clue that tells where the orb is. If I read it again with what I now know in mind . . ."

"All right." Grigor seized her arm. "We'll try it that way." He hauled her to the port side.

Cole shot his elbow straight back, and it cracked as it collided with Anton's jaw. He sprang forward, reeling toward Bailey.

He only made it a few feet before Kiril clotheslined him, knocking the air from his lungs. He toppled to the deck.

Grigor lifted his chin to Kiril. "Kill them."

Kiril readied his gun. "With pleasure."

"No!" Bailey screamed, struggling in his hold. "I won't help you if you do."

"*You* are in no position to be giving me orders," he barked.

"You need me to find what you seek. You kill them and you might as well kill me, because I won't help you."

His jaw tightened, and after a minute he exhaled. "Very well." He turned to Kiril. "Leave them. Just make sure they can't follow."

"You don't have to do this," Cole said, struggling to his feet, struggling to reach her.

"Shut him up," Grigor hollered.

Kiril smiled.

A crack sounded.

Everything went black.

42

Cole woke, his head spinning. "Bailey." He staggered to his feet.

Landon steadied him. "She's gone, man."

He seized Landon by the arms. "How could you just let him take her?"

"He would have killed us all."

"So we just sacrifice Bailey? Let him kill her?"

"It's not like that, man. She said to tell you it'd all be okay. To trust her."

Cole wiped the blood seeping down his brow. "What does that mean?"

"It means she's buying us all some time," Gage said, rubbing the welt on his head.

"Time for what?" Grigor had Bailey. How could he have let him take her?

"To figure out where the orb is."

"What? I don't care about the stupid orb. All I care about is getting Bailey back safe."

"Don't you see?" Piper rested her hand on his. "We figure out where the orb is by the time Bailey figures it out, we'll know where Grigor is going to be. We beat him there and rescue Bailey."

Cole exhaled, squeezing his eyes shut.

Please tell me that's not what she had in mind, that she didn't risk her life to spare ours.

"There is one obstacle we have to overcome first."

"What's that?"

"Before leaving," Kayden began with irritation, "Grigor had his thugs disable our rudder, shoot up our radio, and slice our intake hose. Cabin's already a foot deep with water. He said since we all loved the ocean so much, he'd give it the privilege of slowly killing us."

"How long do we got?"

"Couple hours tops."

"All right, Landon, come with me. Let's see what we can do to stop the flooding. Gage, see if there's any way to repair the radio. Piper, you start sending up flares. Kayden, you're on alternative means out of here."

"Great." She sighed. "Give me the easy one."

The water cresting his knees, Cole finally managed to seal off the intake hose. He swallowed the blood still seeping from his cracked lip and fought the dizziness swimming in his head from the blow Kiril had given him. He couldn't stop, couldn't rest—not until he had Bailey safely back in his arms.

"No flares," Piper said, panic lacing her voice. "Grigor's men must have taken them."

Gage entered the cabin. "Control system is shot." He chucked the wrench he'd been using, and it glanced off the metal toolbox with a clang. "I'm sorry, man. There's no way to repair the radio or the rudder controls. Not with what we have at our disposal."

"I'll grab a tank and go down," Landon offered. "Maybe there's something I can do to manually repair the rudder."

"I'll go with you." Piper moved to his side.

"No. You've been through enough. I can take care of it."

"But I want to help."

"I know, but I'll work faster if I'm not worried about you."

"Fine." She sighed. "At least let me help you get suited."

"Deal."

Kayden hurried down the few steps separating the cabin from topside. "The life raft has been knifed to shreds. It's beyond repair."

Cole had suspected as much. For being in a hurry, Grigor's men had certainly been thorough.

"We've got auxiliary tanks and the rest of our gear. We could swim for shore," she suggested.

Cole shook his head. "It'd take way too long." Grigor would have the orb and be long gone. "We need to find a way to get a signal out." He scoured the cabin for possibilities.

Everyone spread out, searching through cabinets and inside berths.

Gage yanked cleaning supplies out from under the sink. "An explosion should do it."

Kayden paused. "Explosion?"

"A small concentrated one." He loaded his arms with bottles. "Think of it as our very own fireworks display."

Cole held the tube they'd fashioned out of the grappling hook handle steady as Gage funneled the concoction into it. "You sure about this?"

"We're about to find out."

"Everyone secure back there?" he hollered. They'd pulled Landon out of the water, and he and Cole's sisters were huddled behind the wheelhouse at the ship's bow.

"We're ready," Piper called.

"Heaven help us," Kayden added.

Cole and Gage lifted the crudely constructed raft and moved gingerly to the stern. Kneeling on the dive platform, they cautiously lowered it into the water.

Cole held it level while Gage flicked the lighter.

"On three?" Gage said.

Cole nodded, holding his breath.

"One, two, three." Gage lit the fuse.

They gave a steady, concerted shove, then turned and raced for the bow.

The bomb ignited, spurting twenty feet in the air as he and Gage dove behind the wheelhouse.

"I'm not even going to ask how you knew to do that," Kayden said. She covered her ears as the makeshift bomb exploded into a fiery mass of flames and smoke.

An hour passed agonizingly slow, with no sign that anyone had seen their signal. Panic bit at Cole as time slipped away. He couldn't let Bailey down.

Please, God. I can't let her down, can't fail.

He paced the length of the deck, his mind scrambling for something, anything that might work.

Piper sat up. "Do you hear that?"

Cole halted, straining to hear over the blood roaring in his ears. Seconds passed, and he feared Piper had been mistaken, but then he heard it—the distinct sound of helicopter blades slicing the air.

"There." Piper leapt to her feet.

Cole followed her outstretched hand, and relief painfully coursed through his veins as he spotted the orange-and-white Coast Guard chopper.

Rain pelted Agnes's front window. Kayden's reflection shone in the glass, and Cole watched her pace back and forth with open file in hand. Her frustration was palpable—just like his. She was a doer, just like he was. Knowing someone he cared about so deeply was in danger, and not being able to reach her, was torture—heartrending torture.

Each minute that passed equaled another thousand-pound weight settled on his chest. Every breath was suffocating, every tick of the second hand excruciating.

Too much was happening. And not nearly enough.

Landon barked out orders on his cell and radio in conjunction, coordinating the manhunt for Grigor with the Trading Post serving as command central.

Search-and-rescue teams were on full alert and deep in the process of combing every waterway and byway accessible by boat between Yancey and the dive site.

While he deeply appreciated their efforts, he knew it was a shot in the dark. If Grigor didn't want to be found, he wouldn't be. He'd already proven that.

Cole jammed his fist into the window frame, feeling no pain. Only numbness. How could he just sit around and do nothing while Grigor had Bailey? He should be out there, searching for her. Doing something.

He loved her—with a fierceness and depth he'd never experienced before. If only he'd been man enough to tell her. Now he might never have the chance.

Landon's hand clamped on his shoulder. "How you holding up?"

"I'm going nuts. I can't just sit here. You and I both know the SAR guys can use my help." With the McKenna clan constituting a third of Tariuk Island's search-and-rescue team, they were beyond shorthanded, even with Kodiak lending a hand.

"I understand the need to be out there. Believe me, I do. But it's more important that you're here. Determining where Grigor's going to be is our best shot at getting Bailey back. You know that."

Cole exhaled and shook out his hands as adrenaline surged relentlessly through him. "You're right. I just wish Jake was with them." Jake was the best tracker he'd ever seen.

"We put an alert out with all the northern patrols. If Jake's survival group comes within ten miles of a station, they'll get the news to him. And knowing Jake, he'll haul back here faster than I can blink. But right now I need you to get back to these questions. I know it's tedious, but you're the only one who can tell us what you and Bailey have already covered, what Bailey's thoughts were. It's often the tiniest nugget of information that cracks a case wide open. It may be a single line that points to the location of the orb."

"You're right." Cole raked a shaky hand through his hair. "Where were we?"

Landon flipped to his notes. "Let's see. Before the last call I was asking you about . . . Bailey's reaction to finding Olga's diary."

"Right." Methodically Cole retraced his and Bailey's steps, trying not to let his mind focus on how her eyes had grown wide with surprise and delight on page four, how her brow furrowed on page eight.

"What about differences in the two accounts? Any contrasts between the two diaries—Princess Maksutov's and Olga's?" Landon asked.

"The focus was on different things. The second one was written by the lieutenant's wife that traveled with Ivan VI from Russia."

"Olga," Piper supplied.

"Correct. And the first one Bailey read—the one Grigor stole from the historical society, was written by a descendant of Ivan's sister. She married Prince Maksutov, who was the last governor of Russian Alaska. Her diary is a series of correspondences between her and a relative back in Denmark."

"Where Ivan's siblings lived in exile," Piper said, looking up from the copy.

"Right."

"So it seems Princess Maksutov was aware of Ivan's escape and his life in Alaska?"

Cole nodded. "Yes. Agnes's letter to Bailey explained that Princess Maksutov appeared to have some knowledge of Ivan's escape. When she came to Alaska with her husband, she tried to seek out Ivan's heirs. I will say that having read Olga's diary, Princess Maksutov's now makes a lot more sense."

Landon's brows arched. "How do you mean?"

"It works on different levels." Cole lifted a sheet of the copy.

"Here, for instance . . . 'I fear our history may be lost for good.' At first we assumed she was talking about Russian heritage. . . ."

"But she was talking about the lost Romanov line," Piper said.

"Exactly."

Kayden's brows furrowed. "How does that help us?"

"It shows we have to consider multiple meanings, hidden truths." Piper sorted the pages. "Almost like a code."

Bailey splashed tepid water from the tiny bathroom sink on her face, then braced her hands on the rim.

She couldn't stall much longer. She was surprised he'd given her the time he had. She'd read the diary Grigor had stolen from the historical society as slowly as possible, tried looking as befuddled and deep in concentration as could be merited, but his patience was bound to wear out. Keeping her features schooled when she'd discovered it—that was harder than she'd expected. It'd been right there in front of her; it simply had to be read in context. Princess Maksutov had tracked down the orb and concealed it in the one place she could rest assured it would remain hidden.

" 'Urry up in there." Kiril rapped on the door.

"Just a minute."

She peered out the porthole, praying she'd spot something, anything, other than ocean to determine her location. Still nothing. Nothing but the faint wisps of dawn breaching the horizon.

Her time was up.

Cracking the door, she found the hall empty. Kiril's scratchy voice echoed down the corridor. He wasn't far. Steeling her courage, she bolted in the opposite direction.

She wouldn't make it off the boat, the deck was highly guarded, but maybe, if she was fast enough, she could get off a signal. She ducked in the first room—a supply closet. Nothing useful—food, batteries, cleaner.

She darted to the next room. Another supply closet. This time filled with emergency equipment. *Perfect.* She grabbed a flare, lighter, and knife, then hightailed it back to the bathroom. She shut the door as Kiril's heavy footfalls sounded outside.

" 'Urry up in there or I'll 'urry you up."

"Just a minute. I'm seasick." She faked a retching noise, and Kiril grumbled.

Moving to the porthole, she struggled to yank it open. "Oh, come on," she muttered in a heated whisper. What remained of her nails splintered beneath the corroded metal casing. She slid the blade under as leverage and pulled, popping the window open.

Kiril jiggled the handle. "What was that?"

She flushed the toilet. "I'll be right out. Just let me rinse my mouth."

She lit the flare and the door crashed in over her. She struggled to release the flare as Kiril's thick hands clamped onto her arm.

Red flashed before her eyes, then everything went black.

43

Bailey woke, her head swimming. Voices bounced back and forth around her—heated and clipped. She pried her eyes open a slit and the nausea swelled. She squeezed them shut and tried again. Movement, hazy and disjointed, passed in and out of her clouded line of sight.

She worked to focus on the object moving. Nausea threatened to overcome her, and she struggled to remain still against the scratchy surface.

Legs. That's what was moving. A pair of legs—in and out of her peripheral vision.

"She'd better wake up or it's your head."

"She was trying to send a signal."

"And how did she get a flare?"

"I don't know."

"You don't know. I told you to take her to the toilet. That was it. I assume we don't keep flares in the bathroom."

"No."

"No." Grigor exhaled. "She's no good to me unconscious."

"I didn't whack her that hard."

"The knot on the back of her head would suggest otherwise."

Bailey fought the urge to feel it and remained still. The longer he thought her unconscious, the more time she bought.

The pungent odor of fish and cigar smoke blanketed the stuffy air.

Her stomach protested as her world bobbed up and down, faster than before. Water smacked against the surface behind her. They were moving. Question was, where to?

The legs out of sight, she took a moment to quickly assess her surroundings—orange-and-brown-patterned cushions, a table, and cupboards. She was in the galley, shoved onto one of the narrow benches that doubled as a bed at night.

Kiril sat at the table, eating tuna from a can with the knife she'd pocketed.

So much for that plan.

Grigor reclined against the counter, popping olives, or was it grapes, into his mouth. He caught her gaze and straightened, spitting out the pit.

Olives.

She squeezed her eyes shut.

He stalked to her. "Hopefully the rest will help you think clearer. You're out of time." He yanked her to a sitting position, and her head swam.

Dots danced in her hazy field of vision. She swallowed the bile burning up her throat. Why was she so warm?

Shafts of sunlight poured in beneath the curtains. It was morning. No wonder his patience had reached an end.

Grigor sat beside her, wedging her between his hard physique and the faux wood paneling.

"I'm losing my patience." He tossed a knife as one tossed a dart, fixing it in the paneling opposite them, quivering. "*Where* is the orb?"

"I don't know." She braced for the impending blow.

He struck, and hot pain seared her cheek.

She scooted back until she was pressed against the wall. With nowhere to run, she pulled her legs in toward her, providing at least a semblance of a barrier, weak as it was.

"You think I'm a fool? I warn you—do not underestimate me. Your aunt did, and look how it ended for her."

Agnes. He'd killed dear Agnes. She'd known it, of course,

but hearing him say it so casually, so indifferently set her blood to boil.

She lashed out at him. "You miserable, heartless . . ."

He pinned her arm back, and pain—electric and throbbing—radiated down it.

"Tough, this one." He chuckled to Kiril. Then he looked her dead set in the eyes. "Shame I'm going to have to kill you."

She struggled to yank her arm from his grip, but he only tightened his hold, stopping the flow of blood. Her arm numbed, blood swelling above his crooked fingers. She bit back a cry of pain, unwilling to give him the satisfaction.

"This is the last time I'll ask. Where is the orb?"

She shook her head, afraid if she parted her lips a cry would escape.

He released her and stood, shoving away from her. "Then you're of no further use to me."

He signaled Kiril with a flick of his head.

Kiril stood and pulled his gun from his holster.

Grigor leaned against the counter. He scooped up a few olives and popped one in his mouth with a grin. "Looks like I'll have to go to your boyfriend for help after all."

"Cole will never help you."

He popped another olive in his mouth, not bothering to chew. His Adam's apple bobbed as he swallowed it whole. She hoped he would choke on it. "I can be very persuasive. I simply require the proper leverage."

Her stomach flipped. *Piper and Kayden.*

She was dispensable. But Cole's sisters . . .

He'd already lost both parents; he couldn't lose them too. And he wouldn't, not if she had anything to say about it.

"You leave me no choice. Unless you help me, I'm forced to go to them. Sweet Piper and . . . Kayden, was it?"

"Never! You have no right!"

He stepped toward her, his taunting countenance gone. "No. I have every right. I'm the heir, the true heir of the Romanov dynasty."

274

"Only because you killed those in your way. Vasilli and Feodor were family. How could you kill your own flesh and blood?"

"It's no different than when Elizabeth attempted to kill my ancestor Ivan. Or when she killed Ivan's mother, letting her bleed out in childbirth in a dank, dark prison. Elizabeth wanted the throne, and unlike her, I deserve it. Vasilli and Feodor, family? Ha! Where were they when my father died, when my mother and I were penniless? They refused to help and she died. That's not family."

"What about Liz Johnson and Nikolai?"

"Nik chose to kill the girl rather than share the find, then sealed his own fate by trying to cheat me out of what was rightfully mine."

"What about the rest of the people on Agnes's flight? The innocent bystanders?"

He shrugged. "Collateral damage."

"You're a monster."

He stalked toward her, his eyes darkening. "Michael did not found our great dynasty by sitting back and letting others less worthy walk all over him. He took action. He seized what was his. I'm doing the same. Claiming what is rightfully mine. I am a Romanov." He thumped his chest. "I deserve my rightful place."

She scooted away from him. He was mad.

He smacked his hands, palms down, on the table before her. "So what's it going to be? You or Cole's lovely sisters?"

44

Landon leaned against the display case watching Piper, the copied sheets of Princess Maksutov's diary spread out around her, Olga's diary in hand. She jotted down notes and nibbled her thumbnail intermittently. He could almost see the wheels spinning.

She was getting close. He recognized that gleam in her eyes. He knew she could do it.

She was an amazing lady.

He swallowed, realizing that was the first he'd thought of Piper as a lady. She'd always been Cole's baby sister. Now . . .

He raked a hand through his hair. He didn't want to think about what he saw when he looked at her now. That train of thought would only get him in trouble, and he had enough trouble on his plate. But until Grigor was caught, he wasn't letting Piper out of his sight.

He shuddered to think of the moment Grigor had held the gun to her head and pulled the trigger. He'd envisioned her shot and out of his life forever. . . .

His stomach lurched, as it had then.

It'd shaken him to the core. He didn't think he'd ever get that image out of his head. *Sweet Piper.* Nearly torn from all their lives.

Piper leapt to her feet, papers splaying everywhere. "I've got it."

Cole raced to her side, nearly knocking Landon over in the process. "Where?"

"It's right here in the last line of Princess Maksutov's diary. I can't believe I didn't see it right off the bat. It's so clear."

"What is?" Anxiety saturated Cole's tone, and Landon couldn't blame him. The woman he loved was in mortal danger.

Piper cleared her throat and read, " 'I will take the secret to my grave.' "

Landon thought for a moment. "The orb is buried with the princess!"

"Exactly, and she's buried in the old Russian cemetery."

Cole grabbed his coat. "Let's go."

Landon clamped a hand on his shoulder. "Not so fast."

Kayden paused at the door, her eyes rimmed with dark circles. "I don't feel right leaving."

Cole squeezed her shoulder. "I know, but Landon's right. We all need some rest or we won't be at our best when Bailey needs us most."

"What if something changes? What if he shows up at the cemetery before nightfall?"

She echoed his own concerns, but he'd chosen to trust Landon. Landon had never let him down before.

His head was so clouded with worry, he couldn't trust his instincts, and that left him floundering. Landon had his back. Even during his downward spirals, he had always been there for Cole.

But if Landon was wrong . . .

If anything happened to Bailey . . .

"He won't show up without the cover of night," Landon said at Cole's silence. "He's too careful. Besides, we've got two undercover deputies staked out over there just in case."

Cole braced his hands on Kayden's shoulders. She was looking to him, as they all had ever since Mom and Dad passed. He was their guardian, their protector, but he felt utterly helpless. Piper nearly shot before his eyes. Bailey kidnapped. He'd never felt more inept. Now he truly understood what it meant to rely solely on Christ. "You get some rest, Kayden. I need you at your best."

A weak smile flickered across her lips.

He leaned down and kissed her forehead.

"I love you, bro."

His knees nearly gave way. Kayden hadn't spoken those words in as long as he could remember. He knew she loved him, loved them all, but to hear her say so touched his soul. "I love you too." He let her step back from the embrace, let her save face as she straightened and cleared her throat to hide the tears threatening to fall. He softly slugged her arm. "Now get out of here."

She nodded, her eyes expressing gratitude at his accepting her loving gesture without making a fuss over it.

Gage clasped Cole in his arms. "We'll be back with the equipment before sundown. Try and get some sleep."

Like that was possible.

He shut the door behind Kayden and Gage and leaned against it, the weariness of it all crushing down on him. "This better work."

"It will." Landon steadfastly held his gaze. "We'll make it work."

Cole nodded. The plan was solid, but it was the woman he loved whose life was at stake.

"You two get some shut-eye," Landon said, "I'll take the first watch."

"No." Cole stepped from the door. "I'll take it. We both know I'll never sleep." Not with Bailey out there.

"It's my shift. I've got to coordinate everything for tonight." Landon grabbed his cell, brooking no argument. "Go. You're no good to Bailey exhausted."

Cole sighed. "Fine." No sense arguing. "I'll see you in a few." He strode to the stairs and paused at the creak of the bottom step, remembering how Bailey's eyes had lit when she discovered Agnes's hollow hiding spot. He had to get her back. He'd be half a man without her. "If any word comes . . ."

"You'll be the first to know."

Cole tapped the banister and looked at Piper still seated on the couch. "You gonna rest?"

"Yeah, I'll be up soon. Just gonna grab a cup of tea first."

"All right, you take Bay's room. I'll bunk on the couch."

Piper gave a sleepy smile. "Gotcha."

He climbed the remainder of the stairs to the living quarters Agnes and Bailey had shared. A galley-style kitchenette ran along the north wall. A simple sink, dorm-size fridge, and a couple cupboards . . . more a wet bar to supplement the full kitchen downstairs than a kitchen in its own right. The table and chairs sat nearby, a half-finished puzzle of Big Ben on top of it. He wondered if Bailey was working it or if it'd been Agnes before her demise.

A brown tweed sofa, seventies in style and softened with age, sat in the center of the room—sheets, blankets, and a pillow piled on it. An older TV on an equally old TV cart sat against the tiny wall separating the two bedrooms.

Agnes's appeared untouched since Bailey's arrival, and he had no desire to disturb that. Bailey's room looked equally untouched, and he wondered why. Why had she opted to sleep on the couch instead?

He kicked off his shoes and lay back on the sofa. He rolled on his side and inhaled the scent of Bailey from the pillow.

Lord, I can't do this. Not without you. I see that so clearly now. But through you I can do all things. Please strengthen me and please protect Bailey. Let her feel your abiding presence. She must be so scared.

I know I'm terrified.

Piper tapped the empty mug in her hand.

"You'd better head up now," Landon said, wondering why she was stalling.

She stood slowly, her hair tousled from leaning against the couch for hours. She looked sleepy, sweet, and sexy.

Piper, sexy? I'm losing my mind.

Maybe he needed some shut-eye after all.

"What about you?" she asked, her voice a soft purr that tickled his ears.

"I . . ." He cleared his throat.

"Hmm?" She glided toward him, her scent of honeysuckle growing tantalizingly stronger, closer. What on earth was wrong with him? This was *Piper*. Annoying, busybody Piper.

Obviously he was overworked, exhausted, and clearly still in shock from seeing her nearly killed. When everything went back to normal, so would he. He just had to ignore the feelings, the extremely unwanted urges to be near her, to pull her close.

"Landon?"

"Sorry. What was the question?" He was behaving like an idiot. Embarrassment and anger mixed through him.

"When are you going to rest?"

He thumbed through the stack of papers nearest him. "I'll grab some later."

She crossed her arms, the stubborn set of her jaw returning. "We both know you won't."

"There's a lot to do. I can sleep tomorrow." He moved for his coffee cup.

She intercepted his path. "You never look after yourself, do you? You're too busy worrying about us." She tilted her head, a lock of her auburn hair sliding across her brow. "You know, you aren't nearly as annoying and gruff as you let on."

He shrugged a shoulder. "I have my moments."

I have my moments? What was he going for . . . cute?

"Yes, you do."

He'd never seen her look at him like that before.

No. His head was playing tricks on him. He was tired, distracted, coming off an adrenaline high. "You . . ." He cleared his throat, the words feeling thick. "You'd better get up there."

She nodded. "Thanks for being such a good friend to Cole." She slipped the loose strand of hair behind her ear, sweeping her gaze down before bringing it back to his eyes. "He really needs you now." She rose on her tiptoes and planted a feather-soft kiss to his cheek.

He stood stock-still as she climbed the stairs, terrified to move . . . his cheek, his entire body, aflame.

45

Rain slithered down Cole's neck, pinging off his forearms and thighs as he and Landon crouched in the deepening mud.

Fog rose in an eerie mist, dancing and weaving between the tombstones—some old, some new. It was hard to believe they'd been standing in the same graveyard less than a month ago burying Agnes. That it had only been a month since Bailey walked back into his life and made it whole.

Footsteps smacked through the mud, and he turned.

Sheriff Slidell crouched between him and Landon. "Perimeter's secure. Earl is by the front gate. Tom and Thoreau have the other two covered. No one is getting in or out of here without being seen."

It brought Cole little reassurance. Until Bailey was safe in his arms, nothing would. Against Slidell and Landon's wishes he had insisted on being at the center of the action so he could be the first one to Bailey when everything went down.

Slidell stood. "I'm going to head to my post. I'll radio first sign of anything."

Landon nodded, and Slidell slinked back into the shadows.

"Everyone in position and ready?" Landon asked, double-checking.

A round of affirmations signaled back over the radio.

Cole clenched his fists. "This has to work. We have to be right." If they'd chosen the wrong location, if their timing was off . . .

He couldn't let his mind wander there.

"We'll get her back."

"Seriously, Landon, if we botch this, if anything happens to Bailey . . ." He couldn't live with himself.

"I know," Landon said, his resolute gaze saying even more.

"We've got movement," Slidell radioed.

Cole's heart lurched, and he scanned the perimeter.

"Four at the east entrance," Slidell continued.

"Can you confirm?" Landon asked.

"Not yet. Hang on . . ."

Cole feared the silence would last forever.

"It's our target."

"Is Bailey there? Is she all right?"

"Her arms are bound, but otherwise she appears to be moving fine."

Not the level of reassurance Cole had been hoping for. If Grigor had hurt her . . . He clenched his fists.

Please, Lord, let her be unharmed. Please let this work. Don't bring her back into my life just to rip her from it.

Kiril's fingers bit into Bailey's flesh. "Keep moving." He shoved her, and she fought to remain upright on the slick ground.

The temperature had dropped with the sun's parting, and the swimsuit she'd been wearing under her dive suit and the oversized T-shirt and men's shorts Grigor had told her to put on provided little warmth. They clung to her as rain battered the saturated fabric. No shoes on the boat had come close to fitting her, so she trudged barefoot, mud oozing between her toes as Kiril pushed her through a maze of tombstones.

"Which way?" Grigor asked.

"It will be somewhere in the older section." She pointed east, her body shivering in the damp cold. The tumultuous sea roared in the background.

Agnes's grave sat on the opposite end of the small cemetery, but Bailey could still see it from her vantage point. She wondered if she too would die at Grigor's hands?

She prayed she was right about the location. Prayed the orb remained untouched and he'd be satisfied with finding it. Prayed he'd take it and leave Tariuk Island without more killing.

As long as Cole and his family were safe . . . that's all that mattered.

Thank you, Lord, for this time you've blessed me with. For the time I've had with Cole.

She just prayed he didn't attempt anything stupid . . . try and rescue her. She prayed he and his entire family were safe and warm in their beds. But she doubted it. Her only hope was that they hadn't discovered the location yet.

Please, Lord, let Cole and his family be safe. Don't let them be hurt. Not on my account. I'm not worth it. Please help him see that.

46

Cole slouched farther behind the gravestone and adjusted his headset as the men and Bailey approached. It took every ounce of self-control not to spring up and rush for her.

Landon signaled for everyone to remain steady.

After searching for a bit, the party stopped in front of Princess Maksutov's grave. Anton dropped an equipment bag on the ground, water splashing in its wake.

Grigor seized Bailey from Kiril, and pressed his gun to her side. "You had better be right. And don't even think about trying to run, or you'll get more than the knock Kiril gave you on that pretty head of yours."

They'd hurt Bailey. Cole fought every instinct tearing at him to race for her, to wrap her in his arms, but Landon was right. They had one shot and he couldn't let his anger get the better of him. Too much was at stake.

"Start digging, boys," Grigor instructed, and the other two set to work as he kept Bailey pinned to his side. She stood stiffly beside him, wearing an oversized white T-shirt, her dark swimsuit showing through the drenched fabric. Shovelfuls of mud flung past them, and Grigor scanned the perimeter intermittently, his right leg shaking as they waited.

Thirty minutes passed, an hour. Cole would have chosen to rush the men sooner, but Slidell and Landon had insisted that they wait until the optimal moment. So . . . they waited.

Kiril and Anton were starting to move slower, each mound of mud appearing heavier and denser than the last, until finally a thump pierced the silence.

"I think we've got something," Kiril said.

"Faster," Grigor urged.

"When they reach down to lift the casket lid, we move in," Landon instructed. "That should leave only Grigor freehanded."

"And what if he shoots Bailey?"

Landon patted his sidearm. "I'll have him in my sights the entire time."

Cole nodded, adrenaline and fear racing through him.

"I can see the casket," Kiril said.

"Clear it off," Grigor clipped.

Landon lifted a hand. "On my mark."

"We've got trouble," Slidell radioed.

Grigor shifted his gaze in their direction.

Landon cut the volume.

Cole slouched down beside him, his heart thudding in his ears, afraid to even breathe.

Seconds passed excruciatingly slow, but finally Grigor shifted his attention back to the dig.

Landon turned the volume back on its lowest setting and whispered, "What?"

"We've got company."

Cole lifted his head and scanned the area. "There." Someone staggered across the cemetery. He was young, clutching a bottle in one hand.

The boy took a large swig and stumbled. "Here's to you, Dad." He lifted the bottle in the air. Grigor's head whipped in that direction, and he stilled Kiril and Anton with his hand.

He waved his gun at Bailey and signaled for her to be quiet.

The boy stumbled closer, mumbling under his breath. He finished the bottle off and smashed it against a tombstone, sending shards of glass flying.

Cole's stomach lurched as he came into view. *Jesse.* It was the anniversary of his dad's death. With everything going on, he'd completely forgotten.

Jesse pulled another beer from his cargo pants pocket and wrestled with the cap.

Grigor signaled to Kiril. "Take care of it."

Kiril nodded and stalked toward Jesse.

Cole's heart lodged in his throat.

"I'm sorry, Cole," Landon said. "We've got to help Jesse."

"I know." He just prayed that Grigor wouldn't react by killing Bailey.

"I'll take care of Kiril," Slidell instructed. "Landon, you neutralize Grigor. Tom and Thoreau have Anton." He exhaled. "On my mark . . ."

Jesse spun around. "Who's there?" His hazy gaze fixed on Kiril. "Who are you?"

"The last person you'll ever see." Kiril raised his gun.

A shot pierced the night.

The bottle dropped from Jesse's hand.

Kiril stumbled back, then slowly slumped to the ground clutching his chest.

Slidell appeared out of the gloom, his gun still leveled on Kiril.

In horror Cole lunged toward Grigor. If he couldn't reach Bailey in time, he could at least give Grigor another target.

Grigor's arm lifted, his weapon shifting toward Cole.

"No!" Bailey screamed, struggling in Grigor's hold.

Grigor's hardened gaze met Cole's, and a smile flickered across his lips.

"Down," Landon roared, barreling at Grigor from behind.

Shoving Bailey to the side as he turned, Grigor fired.

A bolt of heat and pain collided with Cole's arm, jarring the breath from his lungs. He hit the ground, the shot reverberating in his ears.

Bailey raced to his side, tears streaming down her face. "Cole, are you hurt? You shouldn't have come."

Shots rang out in quick succession, like a rifle's report.

Cole rolled over, pulling Bailey to the ground and shielding her with his body.

"Get her out of here," Landon shouted.

Scrambling to his feet, Cole wrapped his arm around Bailey's waist and they ran, heads ducked as bullets sailed overhead. With a lunge, they landed in a heap at the base of a tombstone. "Are you all right, Bay?"

Rain streaked down her face, her eyes wide with horror. She nodded frantically, wincing with each gun report.

He peered over the concrete marker.

Flashlights flooded the cemetery. Backup had arrived.

He slouched back down.

"You're bleeding, Cole."

He followed Bailey's gaze to the blood pooling at the base of his arm.

"You're shot. You should've stayed away."

"How could I? I love you."

"You love me?" Her eyes widened. "No, I'm not worth it. Can't you see that?"

Heat and pain seared down his arm. "Bailey, you are worth it—to me, to us all."

When she reached down to explore his wound, he moved his arm away. "It'll be fine. I'll be fine. What's important is that you're okay."

"Piper, stop." Landon's anguished admonition rent the air.

Cole staggered to his feet, assessing the situation. What was Piper doing? She was supposed to stay at the Post. "Bailey, don't move. I'll be right back."

"No." Tears rolled down her face. "You're hurt."

"I've got to." He stumbled forward, his gaze blurring. "Landon?"

"Over here."

A shot pierced the night.

"Piper, no!" The terror in Landon's voice cut Cole to the quick.

He ran blindly forward.

Another shot and another.

His heart pounding in his throat, he came upon Grigor, dead at the foot of a tombstone, a bullet square between his eyes.

He rounded the stone and his heart lurched.

Landon cradled a body in his arms, tears streaming down his hardened face. He looked up, his hand covered with blood.

Cole dropped to his knees, the breath whooshing from his body. *Piper.*

47

Bailey stood numb as the paramedics loaded Piper into the ambulance.

Cole insisted on riding with his sister, despite the fact that he required treatment as well. "Slidell will take you home," he instructed as he climbed in beside Piper's stretcher.

As the ambulance doors shut, she bit her bottom lip and remained rooted in place, her feet sinking into the sodden earth as the ambulance pulled away, red lights swirling eerily through the dense fog.

Slidell draped a jacket across her shoulders. "Let's get you home."

"I'm not going home. Take me to the hospital."

"You need warm clothes and rest."

"I need to be with Cole and his family."

Everyone moved as if in a dream—doctors meeting the gurney at the sliding emergency-room doors, running with it, shouting orders as they determined what needed to be done.

Cole clasped Piper's hand. "Hang in there, kid."

Her wide brown eyes stared up at him in disbelief. She choked whenever she struggled to speak. An oxygen mask covered her face as tears streamed down her cheeks. Gauze bandages swaddled her head, but blood continued to seep through, turning the once white cloth bright red.

"Is she going to be okay?" Landon asked from somewhere behind him.

The doctor continued barking orders as Cole ran with the gurney into the operating room.

"Is she going to be all right?" Gage asked as a second set of doors swung open.

Two nurses crowded the operating room entrance, and Cole could hear Gage and Landon fighting the blockade.

"Sugar." A hand landed on his shoulder.

Cole looked up into the worried eyes of Peggy Wilson. "I'm going to need you to come with me."

He shook his head, unable to form the words.

"You're hurt. You need medical attention."

He shook his head again.

"I need him out of here," Dr. Graham shouted.

"You can't be in the OR," Peggy said, her voice full of compassion. "Please don't make this any harder on us. She needs surgery. You can't be in here."

Cole blinked, trying to clear his vision. Tears flooded his gaze. He took Peggy's outstretched hand. She led him back through the double doors to find Landon, Gage, and Kayden standing on the other side.

"She needs surgery to remove the bullet. I will keep you posted," Peggy said. "In the meantime, let's get Cole into a room."

"I don't need a room. I need to stay right here."

"You've been shot too. You won't do Piper any good not tending to yourself."

"She's right."

Cole looked past his siblings to Bailey, still barefoot—her legs splattered with mud, her T-shirt still clinging to her. Slidell's coat hung over her shoulders.

He moved to her. "What are you doing here?" He surveyed her for injuries. "Are you hurt?"

She shook her head. "I wanted to be here for Piper, for you."

It meant the world to him, but she was in no condition to be there. "You need a hot shower, dry clothes, food, water, and sleep."

"You need to let them take a look at your arm."

"I will if you will."

"Let them look at your arm first, and then we'll see."

"Bay." He cupped her face with his good arm. "Please. I need to know you are safe and warm in your bed."

"I am safe. I'm here with you."

"She can shower in the nurse's changing room, and I'm sure we've got an extra set of scrubs lying around," Peggy suggested.

"I'm not leaving," Bailey said before he could argue.

"Okay. You go get warm and I'll go have my arm looked at. Deal?"

"Deal."

Cole's jaw clenched as they rooted the bullet out of his arm. He'd refused sedation, wanting to be fully alert for Piper. So they'd given him a nominal local that barely eased the pain.

"You are lucky. Very little tissue damage," Dr. Miller said as he stitched Cole up.

He prayed the same would be true for Piper.

"You should regain full use of your arm. You just have to be diligent with the antibiotics I prescribe and the cleansing I'll explain. We don't want infection setting in."

"We'll make sure he follows orders," Bailey said from the doorway. Her skin radiated a freshly washed glow, and the oversized purple scrubs nearly swallowed her slender frame.

"Hey."

"Hey back," she said, shuffling toward him—blue fuzzy socks peeking out with each step.

"You feel better?"

"Now that I hear you're going to be okay."

"He's going to be fine." Dr. Miller stood and dropped the surgical needle into the metal tray with a clang. "Good as new before you know it." He pulled off his latex gloves, balled them up, and tossed them in the trash. "Peggy will be in with your antibiotics and instruction sheet shortly."

"Any word on Piper?"

He smiled that "It's too soon, but I'll check anyway" smile. "I'll see what I can find out."

"Thank you, Dr. Miller."

"You can thank me by keeping that wound clean. No diving until it's fully healed."

"You got it."

Dr. Miller looked at Bailey.

"I'll hold him to it," she said.

"Does that mean you'll be sticking around?" he asked as Dr. Miller left.

She wound her fingers through his. "For a while."

Not the answer he was hoping for, but he'd take it. The longer she stayed, the longer he had to convince her that she was exactly where she belonged.

Shafts of early dawn's light speared through the blinds in the hospital waiting room. Bailey craned her neck to check the time.

"It's five," Gage said, ripping another piece of Styrofoam off his coffee cup. He had quite the pile built up beside him.

"It can't be much longer," Kayden said, pacing. She hadn't sat for more than five minutes all night, but at least she'd tried a few times. Landon refused to sit, wearing a path down the tile hallway outside of the OR door.

"This is ridiculous," he muttered as he stalked past. "Can't they at least tell us something?"

Gage glanced at his watch. "It's about time for another update."

Peggy Wilson had been faithful to report every half hour since Piper's surgery commenced, but she was beginning to sound like a broken record. *"Still in surgery. Vitals are stable."*

What did that mean? Was Piper going to pull through? Was everything okay? Why was it taking so long?

"Doc," Landon said in a flurry as Dr. Graham finally exited the operating room. "How is she?"

Bailey, Landon, and Jake followed the McKennas into the hall.

Dr. Graham slipped the green surgical cap from his head and clasped it in his hand. He looked exhausted. "She's resting now, and her vitals are stable. Unfortunately the bullet shattered upon impact, causing extensive damage. We stopped the bleeding and removed all the fragments." He exhaled. "Now it's just a waiting game."

"Wh-what do you mean?" Landon asked, horror dulling his eyes. "Could she die?"

"I believe her prognosis is favorable."

Landon gripped him by the shirt, faded green material bunching beneath his knuckles. "What does that mean?"

"It means that I've done all I can do. It's up to Piper now."

"She's a fighter," Kayden said.

"Good." Dr. Graham stepped back as Landon released him. "Then my hope is not unfounded."

Bailey handed Cole a cup of coffee. "You need to drink something, eat something."

He wasn't hungry, wasn't thirsty, wasn't anything but terrified. He rubbed Piper's cold hand.

"Bailey's right," Kayden said. "We're all here. Go get something to eat in the cafeteria. We'll let you know if there's any change."

He wasn't leaving. Not until he knew Piper would be okay. The doctor said it was critical that she regain consciousness in the first twenty-four hours. He looked at the clock. Only an hour to go and no sign of stirring on Piper's part. What would they do without her?

"Cole," Kayden said.

"I'm fine."

"I give up." Kayden shifted, resting her head on Gage's shoulder. "He's impossible."

"There'll be time to eat later," Gage said softly. "Right now Cole needs to be here. We all do."

Cole watched as Kayden's gaze shifted to Jake, huddled against the back wall.

"Any movement?" Peggy asked, shuffling in.

"None." The word alone hurt.

Kayden glanced at the clock and then back to Piper. "She'll pull through; I just know it."

Cole wished he did. He couldn't remember ever praying more than he had in the last thirty-six hours. First Bailey nearly ripped from his life, and now Piper.

Peggy swapped out the IV bag and jotted down the readings blipping across the machine.

Bailey rubbed his shoulder, her presence the only thing holding him together.

Time passed faster than any of them would have wished.

Landon stalked like a madman up and down the hall. He blamed himself, Cole knew it. He could see it in Landon's eyes, in his wild, grief-stricken countenance.

It wasn't Landon's fault. Piper had chosen to enter the fray against their orders. And Grigor had set the whole thing in motion. But Landon would never accept that consolation, even if Piper pulled through. It would haunt him.

"Cole." Bailey squeezed his shoulder. She pointed at Piper.

His eyes roamed over his sister, searching for what had caught Bailey's attention. It took a moment before he saw it—the flicker of her eyelids, the stirring of her hand. He rushed to her side—they all did, swarming around Piper's hospital bed.

"Piper," he said, clasping her hand.

Her eyelids continued to flutter.

"I'm here, kid. We all are."

A moan rose in her chest, and after what seemed an eternity, she opened her eyes. Cole dropped to his knees in gratitude. He'd never seen a more beautiful sight.

48

Bailey climbed the front porch steps of Cole's cabin.

Kayden opened the door before she could knock. "Hey, Bailey. Come on in."

Hewn pine planks covered the walls, the floor, and the ceiling. Recessed lighting brought out the warm honey hues in the wood. "Is Cole awake?" she asked quietly, not wanting to disturb him. Piper wasn't the only one recovering from a bullet wound.

"Yeah, right here on the couch," he called from the rear of the cabin. "Come on in."

She moved down the hallway and into the main living space of the house. The open kitchen, dining area, and family room all had window-to-floor views of the forest. He'd done a nice job decorating the place. Hunter green and deep blues accented the pine beautifully. Photographs of moose and whales, and underwater shots of Alaska's famed coral dotted the walls. The decorating looked so well put together she wondered if his sisters hadn't played a role in it.

Cole angled his head back with a smile. "Hey, gorgeous." Wearing his red-and-white Scuba Cowboy T-shirt and faded cargo shorts, he looked perfectly at ease.

"You look like you're feeling better."

"What can I say—you bring out the best in me."

Heat flushed her cheeks.

Kayden jingled her keys. "I'm gonna head out."

Cole lifted the bowl in his hand. "Thanks for the soup."

"I'll drop by later."

"I'm really okay. You can stop fussing."

"Piper insisted. You think I'm bad, wait until she gets released."

"Have they given her a date?" Bailey asked.

"Doc says if she keeps healing at this rate, she'll be home next week."

"That's wonderful."

"She's a strong kid," Kayden said with pride.

"Takes after her sister." Cole winked.

Kayden smiled. "Catch you guys later."

The door shut, and Cole set the soup bowl down. "I thought she'd never leave."

"Cole!"

"No. It's not how it sounds. I love seeing Kayden, just not her soup. She was hovering over me to make sure I ate it."

"That bad?"

"You have no idea."

Bailey chuckled and reached for the bowl. "I'll pour it out for you."

"Nah. I can do that later. Right now, I want you to sit here." He tugged her onto his lap.

"Cole."

"We need to talk, and I need to be sure you stay put for the length of it."

"I don't think"—she wriggled as if to escape his clutches—"this is necessary."

"Probably not, but I'm not complaining."

She laughed. "You're impossible."

"Determined," he corrected. "Determined to tell you I love you."

"I know you *think* you love me." But he couldn't possibly.

"I don't *think* . . . I *know* I love you. Question is, do you love me too?"

She did with all her heart. "I'm not right for you."

He clasped her hand, intertwining their fingers. "You're perfect for me."

"How can you say that? After all I've done."

"Done. As in the past."

"Don't you know—'The past isn't forgotten. In fact, it isn't even past.' " Faulkner had it right.

"Bailey . . ." He said her name with so much love, her heart nearly broke. "You're a new creation. Your sins are forgiven. Why carry a burden Christ died to relieve you of?"

She exhaled, trying to pull away, but he held her tight. "It's not that simple, Cole."

"Yes it is. Come with me." He clasped her hand and led her to a full-length mirror at the base of the landing. Positioning her in front of him, he rested his hands on her shoulders. "What do you see when you look in the mirror?"

Filthy rags. The woman who deserved to be stoned.

"You need to start seeing yourself through God's eyes."

But what He sees is the same. She was flawed and undeserving.

"When God looks at you He sees His beloved child."

"Not me. You're wrong."

"No. I'm not."

"How can you sound so certain?"

"Because I know He loves you."

"How?"

"Because He died for you."

Her lip quivered. "But I am so unworthy."

"We all are. That's the beauty of God's grace and the depth of Christ's love. God loves you." He swallowed, his Adam's apple bobbing against her cheek. "And so do I."

"But you deserve better." He was respected, looked up to in the community. She couldn't destroy that, couldn't cast a black smudge on his family name, not when they'd all been so kind and selfless toward her.

He tipped her chin up. "There could be nobody better for me than you."

How could he love her after all she'd done, after how she'd treated him? She'd never even apologized. Steeling her courage, she turned to face him. "This is something I should have done years ago, but I was too prideful."

"It's not necessary."

"Yes it is. I need to tell you how sorry I am about how I treated you. It wasn't because you weren't special to me. It was because I was so screwed up. I thought I needed guys like Tom's approval to have value. But even more than that . . ." *Here comes the hard part*. "Truth is I was terrified. Terrified you'd discover I wasn't worthy of your friendship and affection, terrified you'd . . ." *Abandon me like my parents*.

"Bailey." Cole clasped her hands. "I forgive you and I love you."

"But I'm still such a mess."

"We all are. We don't instantly become like Jesus the moment we're saved. It's a journey." He cupped her face. "A journey I'd like to share with you."

"What are you saying?"

"I'm saying I want to spend my life with you."

Her head spun. How could a man—a wonderful, kind man like Cole—forgive her so easily and love her so deeply in spite of her flaws? She studied him a moment, searching his eyes, finding only truth and love. If a human being could love and forgive her like that, then maybe God could too.

The breath left her body in a whoosh as His truth seeped into her soul.

Christ had not only saved her from her sins, but He loved *her*. Not based on how she measured up, but because she was His.

It was unfathomable, but true.

49

Cole dropped by Bailey's on the way to the hospital.

She opened the door with a smile. "Good morning. What are you doing here?"

"Can't a guy visit his gal just to say he loves her?"

Her cheeks tinged pink. "Always."

"I do believe you are blushing, Miss Craig." He wrapped an arm around her waist and pulled her to him. She smelled of sugar and blueberries. "Making pancakes again?"

"Mabel says it's the last batch of the season. You up for some?"

"I wish I could, but I promised Piper I'd be by. I'm bringing Rori as a surprise."

Bailey looked past him at the truck. "They let dogs in the hospital?"

He smiled. "Not usually, but Dr. Graham's making an exception. He delivered Piper, so he's got a soft spot for her."

"She'll love it."

"Doc says she'll be home day after tomorrow."

"That's great."

Cole gripped her tighter. "A lot of great things are happening. Piper's going to be fine, you're staying in Yancey . . ."

"Well, I think it's only right I continue in Agnes's footsteps. I've always loved the shop and it's about time I settled down."

"Anyone in mind for settling down with?"

"I've got a couple ideas." She smirked.

"Very funny." He bunched the tie of her sundress in his hand and brought his lips to hers.

She sighed when he pulled back, resting his forehead against hers.

"Definitely bumps you up on the list."

He kissed her again, long and tantalizingly slow.

From Cole's truck, Aurora howled.

Bailey giggled. "I think someone's getting impatient."

"She's not the only one." He checked his watch. "Only seven hours until our first official date."

"And what do you have planned, Mr. McKenna?"

"That's a surprise, Miss Craig."

She lifted onto her tiptoes. "A good surprise?"

He winked. "The best."

Landon cut the ignition and sat back, exhaling long and low.

Maybe this wasn't such a good idea after all. What was he expecting? He'd waltz into Piper's hospital room all jazzed up in his best—well, his only—blazer, with a bouquet of flowers in one hand and a stuffed moose in the other, and . . . what?

He swatted down the visor. "You're an idiot," he said to his reflection.

What was he doing? This was Piper. Cole's baby sister, and he wanted . . . what?

A relationship? The word alone terrified him. Too much time and energy involved. Too much change. Too much risk.

But what did it matter? He was fooling himself. Piper had made it clear how she felt about him—annoying, gruff, lucky to have any woman put up with him.

Piper was hardly any woman. She was kind and intelligent, mischievous and beautiful.

Enough!

He glanced over at Harvey in the passenger seat. "What do you think, boy? Am I crazy?"

The oversized mutt tilted his head.

"Right." Time to go before the dog started answering him. He grabbed the bouquet off the dash and tucked the goofy moose under his arm. He'd never understand why Piper loved them so.

He'd simply walk in there, say hey as he always did, and let her reaction be his guide.

"Be right back, boy."

At the elevator, he pressed the Up button and paused at his reflection in the doors—his best buttoned-up shirt, his newest pair of jeans, his blazer, and his unbummiest pair of sneakers, the moose peeking at him from under his arm.

The doors opened, and Peggy got off.

Her step faltered. "Landon." She nodded with a grin.

"Peggy."

Great. He not only felt like an idiot, he must look like one too.

He jammed the third-floor button with his thumb and hummed over the elevator tunes.

The doors binged open and out he stepped. Before he could breathe, he was outside Piper's door, his heart racing.

He steeled himself. He could do this. He got shot at for a living.

He lifted his hand to knock when laughter emanated from her room. Piper's sweet laugh, followed by . . . a man's?

"Oh, Denny, you shouldn't have."

Denny. Landon gritted his teeth and peered inside.

Piper held an enormous teddy bear on her lap, white with a bright red bow. His gaze shifted to the enormous vase of roses on her nightstand.

He looked down at the sad little moose in his hand and the pathetic bouquet of wild flowers. Who was he kidding?

"The roses are beautiful, but it's too much," Piper's voice trailed out.

"Nothing's ever too much when it comes to you." Denny kissed her hand.

Landon's stomach lurched. He dropped the moose and flowers on the breakfast cart outside her door and turned heel. Piper deserved someone with so much more to offer her. While he didn't believe that was Denny, it certainly wasn't him. What had he been thinking, anyway?

He yanked off his jacket and climbed into his truck.

Harvey tilted his head.

"Not a word."

He revved the engine.

Cole rapped on the window.

This day just kept getting better and better.

"You just see Piper?" he asked.

"Nah. She's got company."

"So? You're family. Why don't you come back up? I've got bagels." He held up the bag. "And Aurora." He jiggled the leash, and Aurora leapt up, placing two oversized paws on the windowsill.

Harvey whimpered. "Easy, boy." At least he wasn't the only one pining after a McKenna.

"What do you say?"

"Nah. I've got a lot to do. Just tell her I said get well."

"All right." Cole tugged Aurora back to his side. "You okay, man?"

"Yeah, fine. Just a lot to do."

"All right. Have a good one."

"Yep." Landon reversed and shifted into drive. He glanced at Harvey. "Looks like it's just you and me."

Harvey moaned.

That evening, Bailey opened the door to find Cole holding a bouquet of flowers in one hand and a scuba mask in the other.

She laughed. "Well, I can safely say I've never seen that combination before."

"Good. I pride myself on being original."

She smiled as he tugged her into his arms. "You're definitely one of a kind."

"As are you, Miss Craig."

"I'm afraid to ask, but what do you have planned for tonight?"

"That's a surprise. You just need a swimsuit. I've got the rest taken care of."

"Okay. I'll be right back." She put her suit on under her sundress, her heart racing as she pondered exactly what he had in store.

"Ready?" he asked when she crested the stairs.

"I think so."

"You sound nervous."

"Excited," she corrected.

"Good." His gaze traveled to her neck, and his smile faltered.

She instinctively touched the locket he'd given her all those years ago.

"You kept it." Joy gleamed in his eyes.

"It was from you."

"Can I look yet?" Bailey asked as Cole led her by the hand. He'd made her shut her eyes the minute she climbed into his truck. She'd kept up with the turns he'd made as far as Harbor Lane, but then she'd lost all sense of direction. It was almost as if he'd deliberately taken a circuitous route to throw her off.

"Almost." His timbre was music to her ears.

The cool grass beneath her feet grew sparser, coarser until velvety sand replaced it. Her toes sunk into the granules, and Cole steadied her.

"A few more feet," he said, his fingers enveloping hers.

The sun's warmth still lingered in the sand, and its heat was a nice contrast to the cool ocean breeze riffling through her hair.

The fresh scent of saltwater tickled her nose.

"Okay . . ." Cole slowed to a halt. "Now."

She opened her eyes and her breath caught. Blue Paradise—where he'd taught her to dive, where he'd given her the locket she now wore around her neck.

"I thought we'd go for a moonlight dip."

Tears welled in her eyes.

Concern flashed across his handsome face. "If you'd rather do something else . . . I just thought . . ."

She squeezed his hand. "There's nothing else I'd rather do and no one else I'd rather share it with."

Pleasure danced in his eyes. "I love you, Bailey."

"I love you too." It was the first time she'd told him, and her heart had never felt lighter.

Suiting up, they waded out into the ocean.

The moon shone brightly, its reflection shimmering across the dark surface. The sea was calm—nothing more than gentle waves lapping against the shore. Stars twinkled overhead as they slipped beneath the surface into what felt like a world of their own.

It was amazing to think that little more than a month ago she was living in Oregon with no intention of ever setting foot in Yancey again. Now Yancey was home. She was reopening the Post, volunteering with teen girls at church, and enjoying a phenomenal relationship with the man she loved.

If she hadn't before, she certainly believed in miracles now.

Two blissful hours later, she stretched out on the beach blanket beside Cole—the sand tickling her feet, the bonfire warming her back. "Are all our dates going to be this magical?" she asked, staring up at the vast canopy of stars glistening overhead.

Cole intertwined his hand with hers. "This," he said, brushing a kiss across her fingertips, "is just the beginning."

Epilogue

"I can hardly believe it's here," Bailey said, positioning the last of the Russian teapots on the shelf.

"It's going to be the best grand reopening Yancey's ever seen." Cole tugged Bailey into his arms, inhaling the lavender scent of her hair. He'd been waiting patiently for her to finish so they could talk, and now that the moment had finally arrived, his knees were threatening to give way.

"It'll definitely be the best fed." She angled her head in Piper's direction as his sister carried in yet another tray of cookies. "She shouldn't have gone to all that trouble," Bailey whispered, her breath tickling his ear.

"It's no trouble at all," Piper said, squeezing the tray onto the already overly crowded table.

Bailey looked to Cole.

"Ears like an elephant," he whispered back, indulging in the sensation of her skin beneath his lips.

"I'll take that as a compliment," Piper said, practically singing the words as she shuffled back outside.

"Take what as a compliment?" Gage asked, passing Piper as he strolled in.

"Piper's uncanny ability to hear a mouse's whisper."

"That particular ability got me into more than one tight spot as a kid." Gage popped a cookie in his mouth.

"Someone's got to keep you on your toes." Piper placed a stack of plastic cups on the counter. "Now, stop snitching the food and help me carry in the lemonade."

Gage waited until she headed back outside before snagging a second cookie and following after her.

"Finally . . ." Cole slipped a loose strand of Bailey's hair behind her ear. "A moment alone. There's something I've been wanting to—"

"Bailey, girl." Gus hobbled in, dressed in his Sunday best.

Bailey smiled. "Well, don't you look dapper."

Gus straightened his bow tie. "This is a big occasion. And unlike some folks"—his gaze shifted to Gage's attire of jeans and a T-shirt—"I know how to dress properly for a big occasion."

"What?" Gage shrugged after setting the pitchers of lemonade on the counter. "This is one of my best T-shirts."

Gus shook his head. "Youth."

"Speaking of youth . . ." Gage inclined his head toward the door.

Jesse entered, followed by Pastor Braden.

"Hey, guys," Bailey said, moving to greet them. "Thanks so much for coming."

Cole shook Jesse's hand, so happy to see him. Following the shooting, they'd shared a heart-to-heart, and that Sunday Jesse committed his life to Christ. Cole had never seen so much joy in one place, the entire congregation rejoicing with the young man.

"We couldn't wait to see what you've done with the place." Pastor Braden looked around. "It looks—"

"Incredible," Kayden said, entering the fray.

"Thanks." Bailey greeted her with a hug. "I couldn't have done it without all of your help."

"That's what family's for." Piper smiled. "Oh, that reminds me, weren't you supposed to hear from the genetics lab today?"

"They called this morning. I was just getting ready to tell Cole, but stuff kept happening."

"You mean people keep showing up," he muttered under his breath. Everyone except Landon—he'd been strangely absent lately. Last time that happened had been years ago, and Landon had been in a very bad place. Cole prayed that wasn't happening again. Surely after all these good years Landon wasn't slipping back into destructive patterns.

"Well?" Piper asked Bailey, impatiently.

"DNA confirmed Grigor was a direct descendant of Michael Romanov."

"Amazing," Piper breathed. "And was he the last of the line, or are there other lost heirs we don't know about?"

"That's up to me to find out. But I've got to believe there are more. Three seems like such a small number."

"What will happen to the portrait and orb?" Kayden asked.

Slidell had ordered Princess Maksutov's casket exhumed the day after the shooting, and they'd found the orb safely secured inside.

"We're hoping to keep them in Yancey's historical society, but the Romanovs may petition to have them returned."

"That would be understandable," Piper said. "Since the orb, especially, is such a big part of their history."

"Yeah, but it's an integral part of Yancey's history too."

Cole slid his arm around Bailey's waist, focusing back on her, on what was welling inside him to say. "Agnes would be proud you're carrying on the tradition. Looking for heirs, protecting the treasure, running the Post."

She smiled up at him. "Thanks."

He leaned in and whispered, "And one day you can pass the torch on to our children."

She straightened, her eyes widening.

It was time. "If you'll excuse us," he said, tugging Bailey away before any of his siblings could protest.

He pulled her into the kitchen and shut the door behind them.

"Our children?" she said, sinking against the counter.

He pulled her back into his arms, loath to ever let her go. "I was thinking at least three."

"Oh, you were, were you?" A smile danced across her lips. "Don't you think that's jumping the gun just a little bit?"

He nuzzled her nose with his. "That depends."

"Oh, really?" She giggled. "On what?"

He slipped the ring from his pocket. "On your answer to my question."

Her eyes lit with delight.

Acknowledgments

Jesus—Everything I am and have is from You and because of You. Thank You for saving me and loving me—in spite of me. May everything I do glorify You.

Ty and Kay—My beautiful girls. God couldn't have blessed me with two more amazing daughters. Thank you for putting up with all my writing quirks. For plotting with me even when it takes bizarre and hilarious tangents. For making dinner so I could write. For ignoring all the clutter and weathering the post-book cleaning sprees. Most of all, thank you for being you. I love you both beyond measure.

Dee Henderson—You are an amazing writer and an equally amazing person. Thank you for taking me under your wing and for shepherding me not only in the writing craft, but in the writing life. I will be eternally grateful for your encouragement, patience, guidance, and friendship.

Dave Long—Thank you for not running the other way when I pounced on you after your Spotlight session, for championing *Submerged*, and for making my publishing dreams come true.

Karen Schurrer—I love your meticulous attention to detail, your enthusiasm for stories, and your generous heart. I am a better writer for it. It is an absolute joy to work with you.

Chip MacGregor—Thank you for your knowledge, insight, encouragement, and support. Thank you for always checking in and for only being a phone call away. You have an amazing gift, and I am so thankful you decided to share it with me.

Deborah Larsen and Noelle Buss—For your creativity and joyful enthusiasm. Thank you for guiding me through the marketing and publicity process, and for answering my numerous questions with joy and patience.

The entire Bethany House team—I am so grateful to have the privilege of working with you all. I have never met a more loving and talented group. I am so blessed to be part of the Bethany House family.

Jimmy—For all you do. If I listed everything, the pages of this book could not hold it all. I am so very thankful and appreciative of your help, kindness, Christian example, and for being the best Pop-Pop my girls could ever have.

Sis—For your love and support all these years. And for understanding my wacky game clues (aka sister speak). I love you.

My family—Dad, Grammie, Beanie, Captain Awesome, Doug, and Scott: Thank you for always believing you would be holding this book in your hand one day. Thank you for your constant support and love.

Lisa—You are the best, best friend a girl could ask for.

Donna—You are such a dear and treasured friend.

Maria—Thank you for my sanity checks (aka coffee hour . . .

Okay, who am I kidding—hours). I have the most fun with you—wooden Indians included. God certainly knew what He was doing when He brought us together, and I'm sure He has been chuckling ever since.

MAD Mommas—For making Monday mornings so much fun!

Shirlee McCoy—For always reading anything I send you even when your schedule is crazy. Thank you for your support and wonderful sense of humor.

Diane Wylie—For reading my manuscripts and being my conference buddy.

Gayle Roper and Gina Holmes—For your amazing critiques of the opening chapter of *Submerged*. Your insight and encouragement helped shape the opening pages into a story that grabbed an editor's eye. I am so appreciative.

The wonderful ladies at Joppa Library—Donna, Rose, Bobbie, and Margie. Thank you for fueling my book addiction and for supporting me throughout my writing journey. I am so glad I get to celebrate this with you.

A special thank you to Mike Parker, with SPE Dive School, and Matt Skogebo, of Annapolis Scuba Center, for answering my dive questions and sharing their expertise. You both were a big help. Any dive errors are mine alone.

Dinah—For your guidance, support, and belief when I needed it most. I thank God upon my every remembrance of you.

Last, but certainly not least, Kelli Standish—Thank you for your enthusiasm—for me, my writing, my gorgeous Web site, and for life. It is a joy to know and partner with you.

DANI PETTREY is a wife, home-schooling mom, and author. She feels blessed to write inspirational romantic suspense because it incorporates so many things she loves—the thrill of adventure, nail-biting suspense, the deepening of her characters' faith, and plenty of romance. She and her husband reside in Maryland with their two teenage daughters. To learn more about her, visit *www.danipettrey.com*.

If you enjoyed *Submerged,* you may also like...

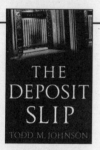